Chapter One

I ain't a killer, but don't push me.

The words of Tupac Shakur pounded from the stereo of the 1999 Chevrolet. The car's system wasn't all that, just the regular factory Delco that came with the car, but at least it had a CD player.

Mr. Blue sat in the back seat and stared down the street at the objective. He always took this time to focus on the task at hand, to see the entire job unfold, executed to perfection in his mind. There would be no mistakes, no hesitation, and no slip-ups. But there never were, so why should today be any different?

Mr. Green and Mr. White sat in the front seat. Mr. Green nodded his head to the beat of the music while Mr. White tapped nervously on the steering wheel. Each was dressed in black—floor length trench coats over black jumpsuits, gloves, and wool hats. All sat in complete silence, mentally preparing for what they were about to do.

"Time check," Mr. Blue said as he looked at his watch.

"Ten-forty," Mr. White replied as both she and Mr. Green checked their watches.

"Ten-forty, check," Mr. Green said. "They're late." He slumped down in his seat and nodded his head to the beat as Tupac continued to put it down. He hated waiting and was becoming restless.

"Never mind that, Mr. Green. Weapons check," Mr. Blue said, trying to keep them focused and on task. He checked the 12-gauge pump shotgun in his lap and then the two 9 millimeter pistols that were holstered under his coat. Mr. White and Mr. Green checked their nines and verified that they each had six extra clips.

"We're ready! These muthafuckas just need to get here," Mr. Green spit out as he placed one of his weapons back in its holster.

"Patience, Mr. Green," Mr. White said. "You'll get to bust that baby soon enough."

"Patience is your thing, Mr. White. You know what an adrenaline junky I am," Mr. Green said, brandishing the other nine before returning it to its holster.

"Maintain operational silence," Mr. Blue said.

At that moment the target vehicle turned onto the street. "Mr. Blue," Mr. White said, "late model Lincoln Continental limousine approaching on your nine."

"Acknowledged," Mr. Blue replied as he put on his headset and turned on the monitor.

"About time. Here we go," Mr. Green said, smiling as he and Mr. White put on their headsets.

"Sound check," Mr. Blue barked. "Mr. White?"

"Check one, check two."

"Acknowledged. Mr. Green?"

"Sound check, one, two."

"Acknowledged," Mr. Blue said as the Lincoln pulled up in front of Victoria jewelry store. The driver got out and opened the rear passenger door on his side. "Mr. Green."

With that, Mr. Green exited the Chevy and walked quickly down the street toward the store. One very large black male exited the Lincoln and looked around before he walked around to the other side of the limo. While the driver approached the door of the shop, the black male opened the rear door on the car's passenger side.

MOB

A street saga by

roy glenn

Urban Books
6 Vanderbilt Parkway
Dix Hills, NY 11746

ISBN 09743636-0-X

First printing December 2003

10 9 8 7 6 5 4 3 2 1

Distributed by Kensington Publishing
850 Third Ave
New York, NY 10022
For store orders call 1 (800) 221- 2647 ext. 527

Printed in Canada

Jacket design: ***www.mariondesigns.com***

MOB

"Mr. White," Mr. Blue said.

Mr. White started up the Chevy and maneuvered into position directly in front of the Lincoln. Mr. Blue and Mr. White exited the vehicle. The big man had opened the back door and was holding it open while his employer got out. He was a mousy little man in an expensive suit, clutching close to his chest the briefcase that was handcuffed to his waist.

Mr. Blue and Mr. White fell in behind them and pulled down their masks as they approached the door of the jewelry store.

Mr. Green had followed the driver into the store and pulled down his mask. He immediately removed a can of black paint from his pocket and sprayed the security camera. He stepped inside and pressed the barrel of his gun into the security guard's back. The guard started to reach for his .45. "Don't do it," Mr. Green whispered in his ear. "You don't make enough money to die for somebody else's shit." Realizing that an excellent point had been made, the security guard moved his hand away from his gun as Mr. Green pulled out his other gun and stood ready.

As big boy and his boss entered the store, Mr. Blue and Mr. White entered behind them. Mr. White locked the door and pulled down the shades. Mr. Blue put his foot in big boy's back and kicked him to the floor.

"Everybody down!" Mr. Blue yelled, standing with arms spread eagle and a gun in each hand. The customers and the store employees looked at the three masked bandits and began to scream as they did as they were told and lowered themselves to the floor.

Mr. Green took the gun from the security guard and quickly removed the shells from the clip. Then he went to each of the three remaining security cameras and applied black spray paint to the lenses. With that task complete, he went into the back office and disabled the display case sensors, so when the glass was shattered no alarm would be activated.

Mr. Blue put his foot on big boy's neck. "Mr. White," he said into the mike.

Mr. White moved quickly to disarm and handcuff the big man. With the cameras, big boy and security disabled, Mr. Blue holstered one weapon and pulled out a stopwatch. "Two minutes."

Mr. White and Mr. Green immediately took out large cloth bags. Mr. White took out a small but sturdy set of bolt cutters and cut the handcuff chain, freeing the briefcase from the mousy little man. She opened the case and examined the contents. As expected, the case contained unmounted and uncut diamonds. Mr. White put the briefcase in her bag.

Mr. Green moved to the first targeted case, which was filled with gold and diamond-studded bracelets. Mr. Blue had briefed them thoroughly on which pieces they were interested in obtaining. With the butt of his gun, Mr. Green broke the glass. He picked up the designated pieces and placed them in the bag before moving on to the next case.

"Ninety seconds," Mr. Blue said into the mike.

Mr. White moved to the necklace case. Once the glass was broken, she to removed the designated pieces and put them in her bag. The watches were next.

"One minute," Mr. Blue announced.

Mr. White broke the display glass and quickly removed Rolexes and other expensive watches then placed them in the bag.

MOB

Mr. Green lit a cigar and moved to the display case that contained diamond rings. This case was different from the rest. Unlike the other alarm sensors, which were triggered by the sound of glass shattering, this case was armed with sensor beams that were invisible to the naked eye. If the beams were broken in any way, they would set off an alarm. Entering a code, which they did not have, was the only way to disable this device.

Mr. Green removed a glasscutter and a suction cup from his pocket. He placed the suction cup on the glass and with the glasscutter, made four even cuts. He carefully lifted the glass from the case and placed it on the floor at his feet.

"Thirty seconds."

Mr. Green blew smoke from the cigar into the display case. Once in contact with the beams, the smoke made them visible and minimized the risk. Cautiously, Mr. Green reached in and began to remove the designated rings, dropping them in the bag. Out the corner of his eye, Mr. Green could see the store manager reaching for something. "Movement, Mr. Blue. On my three."

Mr. Blue moved toward the manager and pointed a gun at his head. "I don't want to kill you and you don't want to die." The manager stopped moving and Mr. Blue returned to his position.

With his attention diverted, Mr. Green accidentally allowed his hand to come in contact with one of the beams and set off the alarm. The manager reached for a gun; Mr. Green immediately pulled his gun and fired one shot in the direction of the manager. He stepped to the manager, kicked the gun from his hand then began kicking him in the head.

"Time," Mr. Blue said as he put away the stopwatch. "Mr. White, your assistance."

While Mr. White moved toward Mr. Green, Mr. Blue removed the pump from under his coat. Mr. White grabbed Mr. Green. "We don't have time for that, Mr. Green. Stay focused and on task," Mr. White said before moving back over to where Mr. Blue was standing.

Mr. White placed the bag she had filled with watches and necklaces at the feet of Mr. Blue. Then Mr. White made her way out of the store. She got in the car, took off the coat, and moved the Chevy into position for the three to make their escape.

With the alarm blaring, Mr. Green returned to the case and removed the remaining pieces, placing them in his bag. Mr. Green stepped to Mr. Blue and placed the bag at his feet.

Mr. Blue passed the pump to Mr. Green. With Mr. Green now covering the room, Mr. Blue dropped to one knee. He opened the briefcase and emptied its contents into one of the bags, then placed both bags into one and secured it to his waist. "Mr. White, report?"

"As expected, one security vehicle approaching from the north with two rental cops inside. Estimated time to police intervention, ninety-six seconds," Mr. White returned.

Mr. Blue looked at Mr. Green and shook his head. Knowing that his error caused their current condition, Mr. Green mouthed the words *my bad*.

"Acknowledged, Mr. White. Assume defensive position one and stand by."

"Acknowledged and in position, Mr. Blue," Mr. White said.

Mr. Blue turned to his partner. “Don’t sweat it, Mr. Green. Shit happens. Let’s just get the fuck out of here.”

As Mr. Blue and Mr. Green exited the jewelry store, the rental cops got out of their vehicle. They cautiously approached the two masked men. The two rental cops raised and pointed their weapons. “Freeze!” one yelled.

“Drop your weapons!” screamed the other.

“Mr. Green, repel with zero causalities,” Mr. Blue said as he continued toward the Chevy.

“Acknowledged.” Mr. Green raised the pump and fired several shots in the direction of the rental cops. He fired over their heads and they took cover behind some cars. This allowed Mr. Blue to get to the Chevy. Mr. Blue removed the bag from around his waist and handed it to Mr. White.

“Estimated time to police intervention, Mr. White?”

“They should be here by now,” Mr. White replied.

Mr. Blue took out both of his 9 millimeters and began firing at the rental cops, who were still pinned down behind the cars. This allowed Mr. Green to make it safely into the Chevy. Mr. Blue heard the sound of police sirens approaching. He got in the Chevy. “Escape pattern five, Mr. White.”

“Acknowledged.” Mr. White dropped the Chevy into drive and sped off down Canal Street then headed northbound on Baxter Street. Two police cars were now in pursuit.

Mr. White drove the Chevy up Baxter Street and made a hard left against oncoming traffic. They were headed westbound on Grand Street with the police car maintaining its pursuit. Mr. White made a sharp right onto Lafayette Street and proceeded northbound. With the police closing in on their vehicle, Mr. Green open the sunroof and came up firing several rounds from the pump. The police car dropped back as Mr. White made a left on Bleeker Street and another left onto Broadway. With the police momentarily out of sight, Mr. White stopped the car at the Broadway-Lafayette Street train station.

Mr. Blue and Mr. Green exited the Chevy and headed down the stairs into the subway. Mr. White took off again and turned into a parking garage. She quickly made her way to the top level and parked the car near the steps. Mr. White got out and ran to the stairwell and down the steps to the next level just as the police arrived at the Chevy.

She took her time walking to the escape car, a silver 2004 Lexus sedan. She got in the car and started it up. "Mr. Blue."

"Go ahead with your traffic, Mr. White," Mr. Blue yelled over the roar of the train.

"Exiting parking structure now. Proceeding to pick-up point."

"Acknowledged, Mr. White. Drive safely," Mr. Blue said.

Mr. White turned on the CD player in the car. Once again, Tupac's music filled the car. *Outlaw, Outlaw, Outlaw, the game ain't the same. Outlaw, Outlaw, Outlaw, dear God, I wonder can you save me?*

Chapter Two

Mr. Blue, whose real name was Travis Burns, and Mr. Green, a.k.a. Ronnie Grier, stood on the corner of 34th Street and 8th Avenue and waited for Mr. White, whose name was Jacquelyn Washington, to arrive. While they were on the train, they went in between the cars and took off their coats and jumpsuits and were now dressed in business suits and ties, but they still wore their gloves.

Travis looked at his watch and wondered what was taking Jackie so long.

"Where is she? She should be here by now," Ronnie said.

"It's almost lunchtime. She's probably just stuck in traffic. Don't worry, Ronnie. She'll be here soon," Travis said, looking at Ronnie and recalling the day's events. This was the closest they had ever come to getting caught. They'd had some issues before, had to do a little shooting, but the cops had never been close enough to chase them.

This was never the life Travis had intended for himself. He had gone to college and graduated with a degree in computer science, a field that promised plenty of opportunity. Ronnie had earned a dual degree in finance and economics, but now look at them. Now Travis was standing on the corner of 34th and 8th with a briefcase full of stolen jewelry, wondering what went wrong with his life.

It wasn't supposed to turn out this way. Is this what his years of college had prepared him for? Once upon a time they had been three eager college students, ready to go out and conquer the world, armed with their degrees.

MOB

They thought they were so prepared; they had even created their own list of rules to live by to aid in their success.

It all began one night when they were fucked up, smokin' bomb-ass weed and drinking Hennessey, listening to 2Pac. While listening to "Blasphemy" from *Makaveli, The Don Killuminati: The 7 Day Theory*, the trio heard 2Pac rapping about the rules his father taught him.

"M.O.B., money over bitches," Travis said. "That's some deep shit."

"That's some true shit," Jackie added quickly.

"I wonder what the other rules are? He only told us two," Ronnie said.

"I guess we'll never know," Travis said as he hit the blunt and chuffed.

"Why not?" Ronnie asked.

" 'Cause Tupac is dead, asshole," Jackie stated flatly and laughed.

"No, he ain't," Ronnie said and stood up.

"Yes, he is, Ronnie. I saw the autopsy pictures," Travis threw in.

"That don't mean nothing. Pictures can be doctored. My cousin edits film for the networks and he tells me all the time about the wild shit they have him do to put whatever type of spin they want on those images. If they can do it with film, they can do it with stills," Ronnie argued. He hit the blunt. "If he's dead, why wasn't there no funeral?" He too started chuffing.

" 'Cause his momma had him cremated," Jackie explained, taking the blunt from a still chuffing Ronnie.

"Yeah, I know. That's my whole fuckin' point. Pac never said anything about crematin' his ass. He said bury him a G. He said bury him with ammunition, weed and shells. Y'all niggas know that shit just like I do. Pac ain't dead," Ronnie stated again.

As the CD played, the debate raged on for almost half an hour before Travis said, "Look, whether he's dead or not, those are still some words we need to live by."

"Why? We ain't no thug niggas," Jackie said. "We're college students listening to Mr. Makaveli puttin' it down thug style."

"True that. I was just thinking about puttin' y'all out so I can study for an economics test," Ronnie said.

"Yeah, yeah, I know that," Travis said. "But listen to what Pac's sayin'. You can't tell me some of that shit don't apply to us."

"He damn sure right about that, Jackie," Ronnie agreed.

"Rule one: Get your cash on, M.O.B. Money over bitches," Travis stated with passion. "Ain't no truer shit than that."

Both Travis and Ronnie turned to Jackie.

"As long as we can all agree the term 'bitches' don't necessarily apply to women only," Jackie said. " 'Cause you know sometimes you niggas can be bitches too."

"Agreed," both Travis and Ronnie said.

"What about rule two, Tee?" Jackie asked, referring to Tupac's second rule in "Blasphemy". "You tryin' to say you need to watch us? Like you don't trust us?"

"No, that's not what I'm sayin'. You two are like blood to me. I know none of us will ever betray the other. What I'm sayin' is that you gotta watch your homies, because everybody you roll with that you may think is your friend, ain't."

"True that," Ronnie said as he poured himself another glass of Henny. "Everybody you think is cool, ain't." He passed the bottle to Travis. "But we still eight rules short."

Travis poured himself a drink and filled Jackie's glass. "So, we'll make up our own rules." He got up and walked over to Ronnie's desk to get a piece of paper. He returned to his spot and began to write. "All right, we got rules one and two. What else? Remember, these are our rules. Shit that applies to us and what we're tryin' to do. It ain't gotta be that outlaw immortal, thugged-out shit."

With Tupac's lyrics as their inspiration, they created a list to fit the bright futures they believed they would have.

"Get off your ass if you plan to be rich definitely needs to be on the list," Jackie said, and they all agreed. Travis wrote it down.

"I got one," Ronnie said as he got up and changed the CD. He put in *Thug Life*. "Bury Me a G" jumped off.

"Stay smart," Ronnie suggested, " 'cause it's all about survival."

"That got to be one. And definitely keep your mind on your money," Travis said.

"So, what we got?" He began to read from the list he was writing. "Rule one: Get your cash on, M.O.B. Rule two: Keep your enemies close. Rule three: Get off your ass if you plan to be rich. Rule four: Stay smart. And rule five is keep your mind on your money," Travis said, reading from the list.

"Come on now, we need five more," Jackie said.

"What about give back what you earn?" Travis offered.

"No doubt," Ronnie agreed. "We had this chance to raise ourselves up. It's only fair that we give somebody else a chance."

"So, what you talkin about doin', Travis?" Jackie asked. "You talkin' about startin' a foundation or something like that?"

"I don't know. There's a lot of things we can do to give something back. You know we can do volunteer work or give to United Negro College Fund or whatever. But I think it's important that we give something back, you know what I'm sayin'?"

"Chill out, Travis. We know what you sayin'." Jackie laughed.

"I got one," Ronnie announced, once again inspired by the music.

"What's that?" Jackie asked.

"Don't fuck with trick niggas."

"That's good," Travis said.

"I got one," Jackie offered. "Snitches get dealt with."

"Right. 'Cause y'all know we gonna meet up with some of them, even if we are headed for corporate America," Travis said as he continued to write.

Jackie stood and walked over to the window. "I don't want y'all to take this the wrong way, but I love you two. I mean, I love y'all like y'all were my blood. Shit, I love y'all more than I do them two lazy muthafuckas that call themselves my brothers. They only know me when they think I got money. I love you two. Y'all my family. So I got another one." Jackie turned around and raised her glass. "Let no one come between us."

Travis and Ronnie both stood up and joined Jackie at the window. Ronnie poured everybody another glass full of Hennessey. They all raised their glasses and repeated the words together. "Let no one come between us." They turned up their glasses and they came down empty.

Ronnie poured himself another. "That's word, for real. I would die for you niggas," he said and passed the bottle to Jackie.

"That's how it is for me, too," Jackie said as she drained her glass. She passed the bottle to Travis.

Travis poured and quickly emptied his glass. "Shit, y'all can die if you want to. I plan on livin' forever." They all laughed.

"So, that's only nine. Come on now, we need one more rule to make ten," Jackie said.

"I know what number ten should be," Travis said.

"What's that?" Ronnie asked as he filled each of their glasses again.

"Even though it isn't exactly a rule, number ten should be bless me please, Father."

Chapter Three

Ronnie paced back and forth, trying to contain his thoughts. He took a deep breath and continued to pace until he could no longer hold it. "Travis, look man, I'm sorry. I fucked up. I let myself get distracted and tripped the alarm. I got careless."

"Don't sweat it, Ronnie. We got everything we came for. We didn't get caught and we didn't have to kill anybody. Besides, it's not your fault; it's mine. I should have known that the store manager would have a gun somewhere. I should have anticipated that contingency and planned for it."

"Come on, Travis, you're good, but there is no way you could have know that he had a gun and would be stupid enough to go for it."

"Maybe, but I should have. It was logical for him to have one. Maybe we're running on too tight a timeline. I don't know. It would have only taken what, another thirty seconds to check and make sure he wasn't armed?"

"Now you're second-guessing yourself. You had the job planned down to the second, Travis. Another thirty seconds could have meant the difference between us standing here kickin' it with that briefcase full of jewels in your hand or some cop telling you to relax your hand so he can get a good fingerprint."

"I know, but still . . ."

"But still my ass, Travis. You said it yourself; timelines are tight for a reason. If we don't have tight timelines, we get relaxed. Get sloppy, get careless and get caught."

"Did I say that?"

"Yes, you did. You said it when I complained about the timelines being too tight. Now I can really see why they're like that. You had the whole thing planned out to the very last detail. When they'd get there, how many cameras. You knew what kind of security and what devices we'd run up on and how to disable them. You knew what to take and how long it would take to get it all," Ronnie said as Jackie pulled up in the car. "It wasn't your planning. It was my execution that got us fucked up today."

Travis was listening but he wasn't hearing what Ronnie was trying to say. As far as he was concerned, it was his fault. He should have known that the manager would have a gun somewhere in the store. It was his job to know that. That mistake could have gotten them killed or caught. He knew the timelines were too tight. He planned it that way. Tight timelines equal tight execution.

"Sorry I'm late, y'all. I got caught up in lunchtime traffic. And you did say to drive safely," Jackie said as Travis and Ronnie got in the car.

"See, Travis. You even knew Jackie was caught in traffic. Ain't nothing wrong with your planning skills, Spock. I just fucked up, that's all."

"What's he talking about?" Jackie asked.

"I told him it was my fault that things went down the way they did. I should have known that the manager had a gun somewhere. We should have taken the time to make sure that he didn't. He thinks it's his fault."

"No, Travis, you're wrong about this one. It is most definitely his fault. What the fuck were you thinkin', Ronnie?" Jackie asked angrily.

"I'm sorry, Jackie. Damn," Ronnie pleaded.

"Sorry don't get it done. Not this time. It wasn't the fuckin' timeline. That shit was tight and on time. It was them extra fifteen seconds I had to spend gettin' you off that man's ass that fucked shit up. Kick the fuckin' gun out of his hand and get the fuck back to work. But no, mister fuckin' adrenaline has to have a kick fit," Jackie argued. "It was those fifteen seconds that allowed rental cops to get there and in position and then allowed the cops to get close enough to actually chase us."

"Enough already," Travis shouted.

"No, Travis, Jackie is right. Those are the fifteen seconds that put us all in jeopardy. It won't happen again."

"Good," Jackie said. " 'Cause if it does, I'll shoot you myself."

Everybody laughed.

While Jackie drove back to the Bronx and argued with Ronnie, Travis closed his eyes and leaned his head back. He thought about how they went from college students to robbing crew.

They had known each other since the third grade at PS 87 in the Bronx and had been friends, the best of friends, ever since. They were inseparable; they did everything together. They went to their first party together. They smoked their first joint together. When it came time to fight, it wasn't one, it was all three that had to be dealt with. And when it came time for Travis and Ronnie to satisfy their curiosity about sex, there was never any question in any of their minds about how it was going to happen. Ronnie made a big deal about going first, but Travis believed that Jackie had saved the best for last. And when it was all said and done, Jackie, who had already explored her sexuality prior to that day, came away knowing that her closest friend would be the last man she would ever have sex with.

Above all else, they were good students who looked forward to attending good colleges and getting good jobs after graduation. And it worked out just that way, at least for a while.

Travis was the leader and always called the shots. Even as a young boy, Travis was very logical and disciplined, but he loved to have fun. After high school graduation, Travis attended the University of Connecticut and studied computer science. He was a natural born programmer. It was the way he thought: *if, then, else*. If this happens, then do this, or else do this.

Jackie was always interested in science; she attended Rutgers University and took up chemistry. Ronnie Grier was the wild one, always high energy. As for Ronnie, he loved New York too much to leave the city. He went to Columbia University and concentrated on finance.

After graduating from college, Travis quickly got a job as an entry-level programmer at Software Solutions in New Jersey. Jackie also got a good job after graduation. She began working as a chemist at Frontier Pharmaceuticals. As for Ronnie, he graduated at the top of his class with dual degrees in finance and economics. Wall Street was his next stop.

The remainder of the Nineties was great. Money flowed and their individual careers flourished. This afforded each the opportunity to explore and indulge their passions for gambling, liquor, weed, and the pleasures of women. However, the new millennium brought changes for all Americans, especially those Americans of color.

MOB

Travis was the first to feel it. Y2K had been a boom for those in the technology field, and most especially programmers. Once Y2K came and went without any major incidents, the technology bubble burst. Although his work was superb, Travis was one of the first programmers at his company to be laid off. "Not a problem," Travis told Jackie and Ronnie. "I'll have a better job by the end of the week." But that wasn't happening. The economy had started its historic downturn.

Ronnie had been working as a trader on Wall Street. As the economy continued its slide, so did Ronnie's career as a trader. His pink slip was next. His firm dropped the news on him late one Friday afternoon. He wasn't all that surprised. He had watched week after week as colleagues lost their jobs. It became known as the Friday afternoon death march.

On Friday nights, Ronnie always met Travis and Jackie at Cynt's, a private gambling house with strippers. The place was run by Mike Black's organization. By the time Ronnie arrived at Cynt's, he had already been drinking with the other fired trader and came in cursing. "God-damn muthafuckas fired me today!" he told Travis and Jackie.

Travis had been out of work for two months by this time and was surviving on unemployment checks. "What! You bullshittin', right?" Travis asked, but he could tell by the look on Ronnie's face that he wasn't. "Jackie got fired today too."

"Get the fuck outta here. You the best fuckin' chemist they got." Ronnie had believed Jackie's job with Frontier Pharmaceuticals was secure. "Everybody out there knows that shit. Muthafuckin' pharmaceutical industry doin' fantastic. Last quarter's numbers were phenomenal. Shit, all them fuckas poppin' pills 'cause they got fired or 'cause they worried about gettin' fired, shouldn't be no fuckin' layoffs in pharmaceuticals."

"I didn't get laid off, Ron. I got fired for insubordination," Jackie said quietly.

"You? Got fired for insubordination? What'd you do, tell the president of the company that you had sex with his wife at the last Christmas party?" Ronnie laughed.

"No, Ronnie, I'm not stupid enough to tell him nothing like that. My supervisor, a bitch made busta named Jake Rollins, fired me 'cause I refused to work on some project he had goin' on."

"Shit, Jackie. You were supposed to get fired for that. That is insubordination."

"Yeah, I know, but he wanted me to work on my own time. Then he lied about it."

"That's fucked up."

"For sure."

As the months dragged on, the New York economy went from bad to worse, and then September 11 changed the world. But through it all, they stayed true to one another and tried to help each other get through these hard times. They still met at Cynt's every Friday, but one particular week they agreed that this would be their last Friday, as it was something they could no longer fit in any of their budgets.

Since this was to be their last night, they decided to go out in high style. Their glasses were never empty, and there were never less than two women dancing at their table—that is, until Travis sent them away.

"Hey!" Jackie said. "What you send her away for?" she said of the dancer who was making her cheeks clap while standing on her hands. "I was just about to make a move on her."

"Shit, save them two bills, Jackie. You know you got better things to do with that money," Travis said. "It ain't like she was gonna fuck you for free."

"Now, Travis, you know I got half these bitches in here linin' up to suck this pussy. I don't have to pay any of them." Jackie laughed. She was a very attractive woman and had no problem getting anyone she wanted.

She liked hangin' out at Cynt's with Travis and Ronnie. She liked watching the women dance, but her vice was gambling. She loved to play poker. "Payin' for pussy is Ronnie's thing," she said playfully.

"Watch that shit, Jackie. Girlie or not, you can still get your fine ass kicked," Ronnie said and finished his drink.

"I guess you forgot what happened the last time you tried that. I was the one who kicked your ass."

"Give me a fuckin' break, Jackie. We were nine and I slipped on some ice. That's how you got me. I also remember Travis grabbin' and holdin' me when I got up, and you running away."

"But I ran away after I kicked your ass, and I ran home laughing all the way."

"Anyway," Travis said. "I got something to say."

"What's that?" Ronnie asked. "Better be important enough to send away the women."

"It is. I was just thinkin' that we need to find another way to make some money. Ain't no jobs out there and ain't none comin'."

"What you got in mind? Startin' a business? That takes money too," Jackie said.

"Yeah, I'm talkin' about goin' into business for ourselves, but just not the type of business you're thinkin' about. Look around this room. There's plenty of money up in here. Muthafuckas in here spendin' mad cash like it's goin' out of style tomorrow morning. Ain't no recession in here."

"Yeah, Tee, but these muthafuckas are ballers and gangsters. That's why they got paper. They out there takin' theirs," Jackie said as she finished her drink. "My glass is empty. Can I at least get a waitress over here?" she asked and flagged one down.

"So, what you got in mind, Tee?" Ronnie asked.

"What's rule number three?"

"Nigga, get off your ass if you plan to be rich," both Jackie and Ronnie said in unison.

"That's right. We've been sittin' on our asses waitin' for shit to get better. That shit ain't happening. We got to go out and take ours," Travis said.

"So, I say again," Ronnie questioned, "what you got in mind, Tee? You talkin' about us rollin'?"

"Hell no! You know everybody and his pops tryin' to sling rocks."

"Then what you talkin about?" Jackie asked.

"Let's get outta here," Travis said as he stood up. Jackie and Ronnie got up and followed Travis toward the door.

"Yo, Tee, there go your boy Freeze," Ronnie said.

"Where?"

"Over there, at that table in the corner."

"I need to holla at him real quick. I'll meet y'all outside." Travis stepped toward Freeze. "What's up, Freeze?"

"What's up, Travis?"

Freeze had been a captain in Mike Black's organization for years. But with Black gone to the Bahamas and Bobby Ray being semi-retired, Freeze ran the day-to-day operations. He had known Freeze since junior high school, when Travis used to do Freeze's homework for him. Freeze liked Travis and respected him for what he had accomplished.

"I need to holla at you for a second."

"Have a seat," Freeze instructed. Travis sat down. "So, what's up?"

"I need to get some guns."

Freeze stared at him. He was little disappointed to know that Travis didn't make it legit. But at the same time, Freeze saw a valuable opportunity in having somebody like Travis on the team. "What you lookin' for and how many?"

"Six. Nine millers."

"I can do that," Freeze said. "Clean, no serial number."

"How much?

"What you need them for?"

"How much?" Travis laughed and asked again.

"Look, Travis, I can get you the guns you need, any kind you need and as many as you want. That's not a problem. I know you got your people waitin' for you, but answer my question and then listen to what I got to say."

"I've been lookin' at a little spot I wanna hit."

"Thought so. Now listen. Here's the deal. I give you the guns and whatever else you need, you give me a cut of the job." Travis sat back and didn't answer. "I know what you're thinkin'. Why don't I just buy the guns myself and keep all the money?" Freeze said with a smile.

"The thought had occurred to me."

" 'Cause if you do it my way, you work for me. You have my protection, and the protection and services of this entire organization. If you need something, you come to me. You have a problem, you come to me. You get caught, you call me. You keep your mouth shut and I take care of you. You tell me what you're gonna hit, I tell you first if it's gonna be more of a problem than it's worth, if you dig what I mean. Then, if it's worth your time . . ."

Travis thought about what Freeze was saying. It sounded appealing, but he wasn't sure it was something he wanted to get involved in. He had known Freeze for years and knew how he rolled.

Travis remembered seeing Freeze and Mike Black one night when they were involved in a running gunfight through the streets. They had shot one man on the run; the other had run out of bullets. Black ran him down and pistol-whipped him while a crowd formed. A woman ran up on them and tried to shoot Black in the back. She missed, though, and hit him in the arm. Before she could get off another shot, Freeze shot her. Black yelled, "That bitch shot me! Hey, muthafucka, your bitch shot me!" Black made the beaten man get on his knees and shot him once in the head.

"I don't know, Freeze," Travis said quietly.

"I don't make this offer to just anybody, but I know you. You a smart, schemin'-ass nigga. Always was. I know you got this job, whatever it is, planned out to the very last detail. And I know you plannin' on hittin' someplace that's gonna be worthwhile for you. If you wasn't that type o' muthafucka, I wouldn't fuck with you."

"How much you want?"

"Ten percent. But don't answer me now. Think about it. Talk it over. I know you ain't talkin' bout rollin' up in nowhere by yourself. I know they down with you. Six hands, six nines."

That was two years ago, and since that time, Travis planned and the trio executed four robberies each year. The days and times would vary depending on the particular job. They robbed banks, grocery stores, jewelry stores, and anything else that they could hit quick and come away with a large return for their investment of time. They were organized, prepared, and over all else, disciplined.

They created names for themselves so they would never make the mistake of calling their real names during a job. Travis, whose last name was Burns, became Mr. Blue. Ronnie Grier became known as Mr. Green. There was a lot of discussion about whether Jackie should be Miss White, Ms. White, or Mr. White, but it was Jackie who had the final say. "I think it's more important for us to be uniform and consistent than politically correct. And besides, *Miss* White sound too soft for a robber, and *Ms.* sound lame." So, despite the fact that she was a woman with a model's good looks, Jackie Washington became Mr. White.

Jackie pulled the Lexus up in front of the home of Murray Sewell, a fence that Freeze had put Travis onto. Freeze had done business with Sewell for years. He was a dirty, low-down, cutthroat, back-stabbin' muthafucka, but he paid, and he paid well.

When they arrived, Murray was standing outside the house talking with another man. Once the other man looked up and saw Travis coming toward the house, he dropped his head, turned and walked away quickly.

Murray looked at Travis and frowned, but just as quickly, he posted a big, shit-eating grin and raised his arms as if Travis were his best friend.

"Travis, good to see you. Come inside. Best you're not seen. You know how the old ladies like to talk in this neighborhood."

Travis and Ronnie walked in the house past Murray. When Jackie entered the house, she handed Murray the keys to the Lexus. "What year?" Murray asked as he looked at the car parked in front of his house.

"Two thousand four," Jackie replied.

"And the keys? Where did these come from, may I ask?"

"Key box. Under the car, beneath the driver's side door," Jackie advised.

"Very obvious, but good for you for thinking to look there," Murray said as he walked out to the car and took a look at it. He unlocked the car and got in, started the engine and checked the mileage, then drove the car in back of his house to park it in the garage.

Once he came in the house, he picked up the phone. When the party answered, Murray spoke about the Lexus and agreed on a price. "Eight thousand, minus my fee?" Travis nodded his head.

Murray hung up the phone and turned his attention to the bag that Travis was carrying. "So, Travis, what else have you got for me?"

"I have the items we discussed," Travis said. He handed the bag to Murray.

"Come into the dining room, Travis," Murray made a point of saying. "You two sit. Make yourself comfortable. We won't be long." Murray waved his hand at Ronnie and

Jackie. "What am I saying? You know we'll be a long time, so sit."

Ronnie and Jackie looked at each other. Travis nodded his head to let them know that everything was cool. Jackie grabbed the remote and plopped down on the couch. Ronnie shook his head slowly.

"Can I get you anything?" Murray asked before he disappeared into the dining room, followed closely by Travis.

"Just our money," Ronnie said as he sat down in a chair.

As Travis followed him into the dining room, Murray whispered, "Sorry it has to be this way, Travis. Things will go smoother this way. You'll see. It's not so much Jacquelyn, but that Ronald . . . Whew, he can be such a hothead."

"I understand, Murray. Let's just do this."

Murray sat down at the table and proceeded with his work. He meticulously looked over each piece while Travis watched in silence. Every now and then, Murray would make a sound or say, "Hmm." After about an hour, Murray put down his eyepiece. He looked at Travis. "Very good work, Travis. Very impressive indeed."

"How much, Murray?"

"A hundred and ten is the best I can do."

"Including the car?" Travis asked, not believing what he was hearing.

Murray nodded his head and shrugged his shoulders. "Including the car, that's the best I can do."

"What the fuck you mean that's the best you can do?"

"Just what I said, Travis. One-ten is the best I can do for you for what you got here."

"Give me a fuckin' break, Murray. I know you can do better than that. Come on now, we talked about this."

"Travis, I know what we talked about. But things are different now," Murray said softly.

"Murray, be fair with me. The diamonds are worth a hundred grand on their own. Eight grand for the Lex. So, what you're tellin' me is that you're only givin' me two grand for the rest of this shit?"

"Travis, I'm sorry, but that's the best I can do. The word is already on the street. Gun play inside the store. Gun play outside the store with the police. Car chases through the street with the police. Travis, please understand. The stuff from the store is so hot now that it's gonna be very difficult to get rid of," Murray said.

"Get the fuck outta here!" Travis yelled loud enough to get the attention of Jackie and Ronnie.

"Please, Travis, lower your voice. There's no need for shouting," Murray said as Jackie and Ronnie came into the room.

"That's bullshit, Murray, and you know it!" Travis yelled as he raised up from his seat.

"What's up, Tee?" Jackie asked.

"This muthafucka only wanna give us two grand for the stuff we got from inside the store," Travis said, moving closer to Murray.

"What!" Ronnie screamed. "This muthafucka think he gonna rob us like that?"

"Like I was explaining to Travis, with the gun play and the involvement of the police, Ronald, it's going to be very hard to move the items from the store. No one locally is going to want to touch them. I'm probably going to have to go outside the country to move these items."

"Now you see what them fifteen seconds is gonna cost us, mister adrenaline?" Jackie shook her head.

Travis observed what was happening and smiled with satisfaction. He took a step back and let things develop.

"Shut up, Jackie. This ain't even about them fifteen seconds. That's a whole other matter. This is about this bitch here thinkin' he gonna rob us," Ronnie said and pulled out his gun.

Murray jumped out of his chair and backed his way into a corner. "Calm down, Ronald. Please. The stuff is too hot right now. Really, that's the best I can do. You know I'll make it up to you on the next job."

"Next job my ass, muthafucka." Ronnie followed Murray into the corner and put the gun to his head. "You better come correct on this job right here, right now, or you gonna die wishin' you had."

"Travis, please!" Murray screamed as he dropped to his knees.

Travis smiled and laughed to himself. He didn't think Ronnie would really kill Murray, but there was no point carrying it any further than it had gone. He and Jackie stepped up behind Ronnie from either side. Jackie grabbed Ronnie around the shoulders while Travis put his hand gently on the barrel of his gun. "Don't kill him, Ronnie. Just give me the gun and it will all work out," Travis said calmly. Ronnie slowly moved the barrel away from Murray's head and handed it to Travis. "Thank you." Travis helped Murray get up from the floor and walked him back to the table. He handed the gun back to Ronnie and pulled out his own. "Sit down, Murray."

Murray removed a handkerchief from his pocket and wiped the sweat from his brow. Maybe Travis knew Ronnie wouldn't kill him, but Murray thought he was going to die. He sat down at the table and looked at the gun that was now in Travis's hand. He looked around the room. Jackie had let Ronnie go and now she also had her gun in hand. Murray turned quickly to Travis. "One-two-five, Travis. Please. I'm cutting my own throat here."

"One-two-five is good, Murray." Travis smiled and put away his gun. "In small bills, if you don't mind."

With money in hand, they left Murray's and drove off. Travis sat quietly in the back seat, counting the money and listening to Jackie and Ronnie argue. Once again, he was lost in his thoughts. Although he didn't believe that Ronnie was really going to kill Murray, the possibility did exist. Ronnie was becoming more and more unpredictable every day. He and Jackie had always had their disagreements, but they were occurring much more frequently. And this day's events only proved to be another point of contention between the two.

Maybe it's time to quit.

The words rolled around in his mind, over and over again. Maybe it was time to find a way to make it out of the game. They had been doing this thing for the last two years. They had made plenty of money during that time.

Travis reached forward and handed Ronnie his cut of the day's job. "Here you go, Ronnie." He handed a stack to Jackie. "That's for you, Jackie."

"I think I should get a bonus for drivin' us out of Ronnie's mess," Jackie said with a laugh.

"Ronnie," Travis said, "I think Jackie has a point." Travis counted off two thousand dollars and handed it to Jackie. "That's two grand. Thanks for gettin' us out of there."

"Shit. All right," Ronnie said reluctantly. "Here. Thanks."

"I was only kiddin' y'all, but thanks," Jackie said and continued laughing.

The $37,500 that they had each earned that day was about average for the jobs they did. In that time, Travis had built himself a nice house in Connecticut, bought a timeshare in Freeport and had $75,000 in an account in the Cayman Islands. *That's not enough to retire on. A half million or so is what I need to have before I even consider retiring. Just a few more jobs with no mistakes and I'll be set. But maybe it's time to quit.*

"Where to now, Travis?"

"To Cuisine. I might as well give Freeze his taste now and get it over with."

Chapter Four

With Mike Black out of the business and Bobby Ray being semi-retired, Freeze now had complete control of the New York operation. Black put Freeze in charge of Cuisine, a small supper club that offered fine dining, an intimate atmosphere, and a small dance floor. It featured Que, a jazz combo with a female vocalist. Until Freeze took over, that is. With Freeze running the supper club, what was an intimate atmosphere had begun to change when he began conducting business there. More and more of Freeze's "business associates" began to frequent the establishment to pay him. They would hang out, have some drinks maybe, but not much else.

Travis entered Cuisine along with Jackie and Ronnie. Usually he went there alone, since he knew that Freeze didn't like the way Ronnie carried it, and was frustrated by Jackie, who didn't have any interest in giving him any. This time, however, he wanted to get it over with. Besides, Freeze needed to be made aware of the issues they had encountered just in case it became a problem.

"Can I help you?" the hostess asked.

"I'm here to see Freeze," Travis said and smiled at her. She picked up three menus and they followed her.

"I'll let Freeze know you're here," she said as she led them to a table.

"Wait a second. Don't be in such a rush. Don't you remember me? Travis? We talked about a month ago," he said as she seated them. "Your name is Diane, right?"

"That's right, it is. And I do remember you," Diane replied and cut her eyes.

"So, what's up?"

"Nothing," Diane said coldly as she walked away.

"Damn, it's like that?" Travis asked, but Diane simply kept going without a word.

"She just cold dissed you, Tee," Jackie said.

"Whatever, Jackie. I've been dissed by finer women than her and in better places than this. She's not the first woman to dis me, and she damn sure won't be the last," Travis said as the waitress arrived.

"Can I get you something from the bar?"

"Hennessey straight up all around," Ronnie ordered. She disappeared to get their drinks. "So, this is the house that Vicious Black built? It really is a nice spot, Travis. Nothing like what I thought it would be."

"Yeah, but it's changed a lot since Black's been gone."

The changes in clientele and atmosphere brought with them a significant decline the club's revenue. This fact did not go unnoticed by Wanda Moore, the organization's lawyer and business manager. She handled the money, making smart investments, and made the members of the organization a ton of money over the years.

Wanda entered Cuisine and looked around at the half-empty club. She shook her head and went off in search of Freeze. As Wanda walked by, she stopped and looked in Travis's direction. Travis waved to her, but Wanda just rolled her eyes and continued her search.

"Who is that fine-ass muthafucka there, Travis?" Ronnie asked.

"If you fuck up on a job again, you'll be spending a lot of time with her," Travis advised.

"What you talkin' about?"

"That's Wanda Moore." Ronnie and Jackie both looked at Travis with questioning eyes. "She our lawyer."

"Oh," they both said as they watched Wanda walk away.

Wanda made her way around the club and found Freeze seated at a table in the back. She should have known where to find him. Freeze always sat in the back of anyplace he went, and always with a clear view every door. That way he could see who was coming in and would have time to respond if it became necessary to do so.

"Yo, what's up, Wanda? Have a seat."

"Stand up, Freeze," Wanda commanded. Freeze took a deep breath and complied with her request. "Look around this place. Do you see anything wrong with this picture?"

"It's a little empty. But it'll pick up later in the evening."

"I've been looking at the numbers for the last few months. Revenue has been steadily going down since you took over."

"It has?" Freeze asked. "I hadn't noticed that."

"Well, you need to start payin' attention to what's goin' on in here," Wanda demanded.

"All right, Wanda. I got it. But like I said, it picks up later in the evening."

"What do you mean later in the evening?"

"I mean later. You know, a time that comes after now."

"I don't think you're understanding me, Freeze. This is a supper club, not some after hours spot. There are supposed to be people in here having dinner. And what are all these thugs doin' up in here?"

"They're just some of my peeps come to hang for a minute, that's all."

"This is not that type of place, Freeze. This is not the Late Night; this is not a thug hangout. We are marketing to a different, more upscale clientele here, Freeze, not to the people you do business with. And who the hell is that no-singin' bitch you got on stage?"

"That's—" Freeze started to say, but Wanda cut him off.

"I don't give a fuck who she is. Fire her no-singin' ass tonight. The next time I come in here I better see Que back up on stage and Angela Gray up there singin' her ass off. And you need to tell all your thug buddies that they can't come up in here without a suit," Wanda said and paused.

"Freeze, you're doing a great job running the organization, but I think Black made a big mistake leaving you in charge of this place. But this is where he wants you, so that's that. Just try to understand this is Black's baby. He worked very hard to make something of this place. He left you to run it for him. Not me, not Bobby; he left it to you to run for him, Freeze. So please, don't disappoint him. He and I both expect you not to run it into the ground. Am I getting through to you?"

"Yeah, Wanda, damn. I understand what you're sayin'," Freeze said quietly. He didn't like being punked like that by anybody, not even Wanda. But he knew she was right, so he didn't push it.

"And isn't that your buddy, the high-tech wannabe robber?"

"Yeah, what about him? He got a suit on, don't he?"

"That's not the point. What's he doing in here, Freeze?"

"He came to give me my taste of the job he ran today."

"Freeze, you can't do business in here or Impressions or any other legitimate business we got. Meet them anywhere but here," Wanda said as she started to walk away. "And Freeze, you need to start wearing a suit when you're here."

"Yes, Wanda."

Wanda stopped and turned around. She walked back toward Freeze. "I heard that Nick was back in the city. Have you seen him?"

"No, why?"

"Just wondering why he hasn't been around to see anybody," Wanda answered.

"You know as well as I do, maybe even better than I do why Nick ain't been around, Wanda," Freeze said and sat back down at his table. "Don't play dumb. You know Nick ain't been around 'cause of that shit with him and Bobby."

"Well, if you see or talk to him, tell him to call me," Wanda requested.

As Freeze watched Wanda walk away he mumbled, "Yeah, right. I'm sure Nick is just dyin' to talk to your shit-talkin' ass." Diane came toward his table.

"Excuse me, Freeze. Travis is here to see you. Do you want me to show him to the office?"

"No, that's all right, Diane. I'll go over there and talk to him." Freeze paused for a second. "One more thing, Diane. Start enforcing the old dress code. I'll make sure you have security up there to back you up."

"You're the boss," Diane said and walked away.

No, the boss just left.

Freeze got up and walked toward the table where Travis was sitting. "What's up, y'all?" he said as he took a seat.

"What's up, Freeze?" Travis reached in his coat for the envelope containing the money he had for Freeze.

"No," Freeze said quickly in anticipation of what Travis was about to do. "Meet me at Cynt's in two hours. We'll talk there. And from now on, when you need to see me, page me and I'll tell you when and where to meet me. Understood?" Freeze said and moved on to the next table.

"What's up with that?" Ronnie asked.

"How should I know?" Travis replied. "We'll just meet him at Cynt's in two hours. I'm sure you two won't mind, since that's probably where y'all were goin' anyway. Spend some of that money. I know it's burnin' a hole your pockets," he said as he got up and started for the door.

"Shit, like that wasn't where you were goin'," Jackie said as she followed Travis and Ronnie to the door.

Four hours later, Freeze still hadn't arrived at Cynt's, and it really didn't seem to matter. Cynt's was the kind of place where you went to escape. Cynt's was the kind of place where you went to indulge all of your passions, no matter what they were. You could be or do anything you wanted, as long as it didn't hurt or bother anybody. Liquor, gambling, and of course, you could experience the pleasures of the women in the house. Cynt's was a place where fantasies did come true.

Travis sat at a table in the corner of the room where Freeze always sat when he was at Cynt's. While he waited for Freeze to arrive, a dancer who called herself Mystique was entertaining Travis. She was a tall woman with beautiful, dark eyes and deep caramel skin. Travis had never noticed her on any of his other visits to Cynt's, although she'd been there every time. He sat, watching her dance, and losing himself in the seductive movements of her hips.

Maybe it's time to quit.

He couldn't escape the thought that their run was over and it was time to get out. Mistakes on the job, Murray holding out on the money, and now Freeze wanting to talk. No matter how he turned it, it still came up the same way. Travis was sure of what the flaws were in his plan. First off, he confirmed what he already knew: he never created a contingency plan if anything went wrong in the store. It wasn't the tight timeline, it was his failure to plan for the manager having a weapon, and his lack of contingency planning once the alarm was triggered.

There was one other factor that Travis had to consider. Had he given Ronnie too many crucial responsibilities in the execution of the job? Jackie had only one primary responsibility, secure the objective, whereas Ronnie had several tasks to complete that were vital to the successful execution of the job. Ronnie had to disable the security cameras, disarm and immobilize the security guard, and disable the security system. And after all that, Ronnie still had to cut and remove the glass and remove the pieces without triggering the alarm.

Why did he assign Ronnie all the vital responsibilities? Was he putting too much on Ronnie? Knowing Ronnie's personality, was it more than he could handle? Maybe it was only because Jackie was a better getaway driver. Or maybe he didn't think Jackie could handle the responsibilities. He wondered if he should create contingency plans that allowed for Ronnie's adrenaline junky personality.

Ronnie was right about one thing: Travis was beginning to second-guess himself. That wasn't good.

Maybe it's time to quit.

"Yo, Travis!" Jackie yelled, snapping Travis out of the trance that his thoughts and Mystique had placed him in.

"What?"

"Where this nigga at?" Jackie inquired. "We been around here all this time and Freeze still ain't showed."

"So, you in a hurry or something?"

"No."

"If you got something to do, then bounce and go handle it. But it's all good here in this little corner of the world," Travis said to Jackie without taking his eyes off Mystique as she continued to move her body.

Jackie looked at Mystique, who cast her spell upon her as well. "Yeah, I see," she said slowly. "But check this out. Me and Ronnie were talkin' about havin' a little set this weekend. You know, throw some meat in the grill, invite some ladies over. We'll be sure to invite this lovely lady here if you want. You down?"

"Yeah, yeah, whatever. I'm for all that."

"Good," Jackie said as she got up to go to the bar. "It's your turn, so the party's at your house. Cool?"

"Like I said, whatever," Travis said and lost himself in Mystique once again.

It wasn't too long after that when Freeze appeared before him. "Mind if I join you?" Freeze asked as he took a seat next to Travis.

"This is your spot. I was just keepin' it warm until you got here," Travis answered.

"Yo, Mystique. Why don't you give us a minute?"

"No problem, Freeze," Mystique said as she picked up her clothes and disappeared into the crowd.

"You got something for me?" Freeze asked, holding out his hand.

Travis handed Freeze the envelope. "It's only twelve-five. Murray nutted up on me."

"Why?"

"That's what I need to talk to you about. During the job, Ronnie accidentally tripped an alarm and we had to deal with a couple of rental cops."

"Any police action?"

"Yeah, that too. They followed us away from the scene, but Jackie lost them. Anyway, Murray heard about the gun play and the police involvement and told me that the stuff from inside the store would be harder to get rid of because of that."

"Did he come correct on the diamonds?"

"All that was cool. And I was able to get a little more from him on the store items."

"Murray's a slippery fuck, but he's right. Nobody in town is gonna want to fuck with the shit from the store."

"That's what he said. Said he'd have to sell them outside the country. But I wanted you to know about the police involvement just in case anything came of it."

"I'll let my people know what's up. But you, Travis, you need to start keepin' a tighter reign over that wild-ass nigga Ronnie. He gonna get y'all killed one day."

"I can handle Ronnie, Freeze. You don't have to worry about him," Travis insisted, even though he had the same thought. "I got him."

"Make damn sure that you do, 'cause if one of his wild man stunts puts this organization or me in jeopardy, I'll kill him myself. Believe that.

"Now, what I just said, it ain't got nothing to do with you. I got nothing but respect for you. You're a smart man and you're runnin' a tight operation, but that nigga is dead weight on the ship."

"I hear what you're sayin', Freeze. But me and Ronnie go too far back for me to cut him loose. Not over no little shit like this."

"I appreciate you being loyal to the muthafucka. Loyalty is important, especially in this game. We value loyalty above all else. Just make sure you got him in check or I'll do it for you. That's all I'm sayin'. But like I said, understand that it won't have anything to do with you. It's just business."

"I understand," Travis said and looked over at the table where Ronnie was sitting. He watched as Ronnie got up and followed one of the dancers away from the table. Travis lost sight of him in the crowd.

"But for now, relax. Enjoy all of the pleasures that the house got to offer." With that, Freeze raised his hand and snapped his finger. Not only did Mystique return to the table, three other dancers also responded to Freeze's motion.

"Do four women always come when you call?" Travis asked and Freeze laughed.

"Travis, when I snap my finger, every woman in the house who ain't dancin' is coming 'cause they know somebody, if not all of them, are about to get paid." Freeze turned to the dancers. "Ladies, take care of my friend here. I mean take real good care of him," Freeze said as he stood up. He noticed that Bobby Ray had come into the club. "If there's anything you need, Travis, anything at all, you let me know. I need to go holler at Bobby for a minute," he said and walked away.

After Freeze disappeared into the crowd, the dancers converged around Travis. Mystique looked at the other three dancers and shook her head. She started to walk away when Travis grabbed her hand. "Where you going?"

"I don't compete. I'm a private dancer. But I know they gotta do what Freeze says. So, enjoy yourself. I'll be back when I have your undivided attention."

The other three dancers continued to do their thing while Travis watched Mystique walk away. She had definitely gotten his attention.

Jackie quickly joined Travis. "You can't have a show like this without me."

Travis pointed at one of the dancers and motioned for her to dance for Jackie. She smiled seductively at Jackie and complied immediately. Jackie leaned toward Travis. "You handle your business with Freeze?"

"Yeah."

"What did he want to talk to you about?"

Travis looked at Jackie for a long moment before answering. "Loyalty."

"Loyalty? What the fuck is that supposed to mean?"

"Nothing major, Jackie. He was just stressin' that loyalty is important to us in what we're doin', that's all."

"True, but that ain't something he gotta stress to us. Nobody more loyal to each other than the three of us."

Travis looked at Jackie and wondered whether he should tell her what Freeze said about killing Ronnie. He also thought about whether he could actually stand by and let Freeze kill one of his two closest friends and not do anything about it just because it was business. He didn't know, and he didn't want to think about it. He would just have to keep Ronnie in check.

"Where's Ronnie?" he asked.

"He's either upstairs gettin' his freak on or downstairs losin' all his money," Jackie advised.

"I'm surprised to see you up here for this long. You ain't been downstairs all night."

"I got too much cash money on me right now for me to go down there," Jackie admitted.

"You afraid you could lose it all?"

"Not all of it. I hope I'm not that far gone to go out like that. But trust me; it's better this way."

"Count off what you're willing to lose and give me the rest. I'm gettin' ready to go."

Jackie counted off ten thousand dollars and looked at Travis, then at the money in her hand. Travis knew her gambling was getting worse. Jackie handed the rest of her money to Travis.

"Who's that Freeze is going to talk to?" Jackie asked.

"That's Bobby Ray."

"You know him?"

"I wouldn't say I know him. I met him once."

"What about Vicious Black? You ever met him?" Jackie asked excitedly.

"Nope. I seen him once, but I never met him."

"What's he like?"

"I don't know. Like I said, I only saw him that one time. But I will tell you this: he don't look like the kinda nigga you wanna fuck with," Travis said as he got up from the table. "Look, Jackie, I'm out. I think I'll just drive for a while. I need to clear my head."

"Where you goin', to your house in Connecticut?"

"Yeah, that's a good idea. I'll be back on Saturday. You just make sure that Mystique is there."

"Done. I'll see you when you get back."

* * *

Freeze walked up to Bobby, who was standing at the bar talking to Sammy. "What's up, Bobby? What brings you out tonight? I know Black ain't in town, is he?"

"No, Mike ain't in town. I just wanted to check on how things are going. I been to all the other houses tonight."

"And?" Freeze asked with a bit of a bite. That was the second time that night somebody had been checking on how he was running things in Mike Black's absence, and he didn't like it.

"Everything is running just the way it could be," Bobby said with a smile. "Yeah, Wanda called me."

"What she say?"

"That maybe I needed to be more active in the business. She said that you were runnin' Cuisine into the ground. Is she right?"

"She made her point and I moved to correct the situation," Freeze replied.

"That's good enough for me. Look, Freeze I ain't got no problem with the way you do your thing. I think you've been good for business. But you know how Wanda is, right?"

"Right."

"So, until you hear me or Mike say, 'Freeze, you're fuckin' up,' just do you," Bobby said. He held up the glass in his hand and Sammy quickly refilled it.

"Did you know Nick was back in the city?" Freeze asked.

"Yeah, Mike mentioned that to me."

"Don't you think it's time to lay that Camille shit to rest?"

Bobby stared at Freeze for a second or two. He didn't spend a lot of time thinking about it and he never liked being reminded of it. "Don't you think you should stay out my business?" Bobby asked as one of the dancers walked by him and Freeze.

"Hey, Freeze," she said as she passed and touched his face. She was dressed in a black cat suit with a small tail and mask to match. She was about five foot three and at best she weighed 110 pounds.

Bobby watched her as she approached somebody at the bar and started talking. "Who is that?"

"That's Cat. She just started workin' here a couple of weeks ago. Cynt says words can't describe the way she dances. Said it's something you just have to experience."

"I'd be interested to see," Bobby said.

"I can arrange that," Freeze said. "Yo, Cat!"

Cat excused herself from the person she was talking to and stepped toward Freeze. "What's up, Freeze?"

"Cat, I want you to meet somebody. This is—"

"Bobby Ray," Cat said as she stepped closer to Bobby. "I've been wanting to meet you for a long time."

"Really? And why is that?" Bobby asked.

"Because powerful men turn me on," Cat said and grabbed his hand.

Freeze laughed as he watched Cat lead Bobby upstairs to the private rooms. "That's how the trouble always begins."

Chapter Five

On Saturday afternoon, Travis returned to his house after a couple of very restful days in Connecticut. The time alone did for him exactly what he wanted it to do. It gave him time to think and clear his head. There were no phones in the house, and he turned off his cell phone so he wouldn't be disturbed.

Travis spent most of the first day in bed, either sleeping or listening to the CD that he'd been looking for, for months: *The Complete Bitches Brew Sessions* box set by Miles Davis. He thought a lot about getting out of the robbing game, but no matter how he sliced it, Travis always came to the same conclusion. He didn't have enough money to retire.

He spent most of his time thinking about Ronnie. The words Freeze spoke to him rolled over and over in his mind. *'Cause if one of his wild man stunts puts this organization or me in jeopardy, I'll kill him myself. Believe that.*

Travis had no doubt that Freeze would kill Ronnie, but he also knew he couldn't knowingly let that happen and do nothing to prevent it. He would have to kill Freeze if he did it, even if it meant his life. 'Cause killing Freeze, or even trying to for that matter, would be a death sentence.

Travis didn't even know if he could kill somebody. Shooting your gun in somebody's direction is a long way from standing in a man's face and pulling the trigger. Especially Freeze. He had known Freeze for a lot of years; not as long as he'd known Ronnie, but they still went back some years. What he did know was that he had to do whatever it took not to let things come to that.

Once he went through the mail that had collected during his stay in Connecticut, he checked his voice messages. His mother had called to thank him for the three thousand dollars he had deposited in her account. Not wanting to arouse the suspicions of his mother or that of the IRS, Travis never deposited too much money into her account at one time. He put just enough to be sure she was taken care of.

After his father died in his sleep six years ago, Travis decided that the Bronx was no longer a place where he wanted his mother to live. “Especially now that Daddy’s gone. I would just feel a lot better if you lived someplace else. Someplace safer.” So, after two more years of singing that same old song, Travis finally moved his mother out of the city. While he still had a conventional job, he made a decent down payment on a house in Fort Myers, Florida. She was near an old friend and some relatives who she’d lost touch with, so she was very happy there.

There were a few calls from women who no longer held his interest and wanted to know why he’d stopped calling. *Why don’t you call me anymore?* This was frequently the question they asked.

Ronnie called to see if the party was still on. “Better be, ’cause we’ll be there around eight, and we got with your girl Mystique, and she says she’ll be there. Yo, what kind of name is Mystique any damn way?”

Travis had given some thought to Mystique during his hiatus. She was a beautiful woman, to be sure, and he liked the way she moved. He would be very interested to see if her seductive dancing translated into seduction in the bed. But he was getting tried of messing around with dancers and the other type of women who were in or hung around the game. There was definitely no future in fuckin' around with them. But then again, until these last couple of days, he'd never thought about the future in those terms.

After he cleaned up the house enough to receive company, Travis left the house and headed for the store to pick up a few things. First he went to the liquor store and picked up a case of beer, a couple of bottles of Hennessey, a bottle of Alizé, and two bottles of Moet. Then he headed for the grocery store.

Travis wandered casually through the store and picked up the things he wanted. He threw some steaks, T-bones and Porterhouses, in the cart, then he proceeded to the seafood counter. He wanted to get ten pounds of fresh shrimp. He loved shrimp and was determined to make sure he didn't run out like they did the last time. Maybe he'd get some scallops as well.

Travis waited patiently with the crowd of people gathered around the counter for his number to come up. Each time the number on the NOW SERVING sign changed, he'd look at his number and think, *Damn, how long is this going to take?* Finally, his number appeared on the screen and he stepped up.

"Can I help you, sir?"

"Yeah, let me have ten pounds of your tiger shrimp and two pounds of—Ouch!" Travis yelled as someone ran a shopping cart into the back of his ankle.

"Oh, I am so sorry. I wasn't looking where I was going," the woman said.

"Well, maybe you should look," Travis started to say angrily until he turned and saw her. She stood before him looking so innocent and very apologetic with a box of cereal in her hand. "That's all right," Travis said with a brand new attitude. "I shouldn't have been in your way." All he could think was, *My God, she is so beautiful.*

"Say, you want ten pounds of your tiger shrimp and two pounds of what, sir?" the counter attendant said to snap Travis back to reality.

Travis turned to face the attendant. "That was two pounds of scallops, please," Travis said quickly and turned back to the woman, but she was gone. He left the seafood counter and walked across the back of the store, looking down each aisle as he passed. "Where did she go so quick?"

Travis returned to the seafood counter to pick up his order and headed toward the front of the store. All the while he kept looking for her. *Damn, Travis, the least you should have done was ask her name.*

He searched up one aisle and down the next, but she was nowhere to be found. He finally gave up and went to the cashier. Travis paid for his items and headed out of the store to his car, still looking. He couldn't get the picture of her out of his mind.

She was the prettiest woman he'd ever seen. She stood about five feet seven inches tall, about 150 pounds, he guessed. She was dressed very conservatively in a blue pants suit and modest two-inch heels. And she had pretty feet; he loved a woman with pretty feet. Her skin was the color of coffee once the cream was added. Her hair was jet black and pulled back in a ponytail. She had very pretty eyes, even though she hid them behind small-framed glasses that sat on the end of her nose. The sound of her voice floated around in his mind as he drove home.

Oh, I am so sorry. I wasn't looking where I was going.

Travis was hooked and he knew it. Only problem was, he didn't know her name; he didn't know where or how to find her; he didn't know anything about her. He just had a picture of her that he couldn't get out of his mind, and the sound of her voice rang continuously in his ears. He stopped at a red light and closed his eyes. Like a movie playing in his mind, he saw her standing there with that box of Special K in her hand. *Oh, I am so sorry. I wasn't looking where I was going.* The sound of horns honking behind him quickly brought Travis back and he drove on.

When Travis got back to his house, Jackie and Ronnie were not only there, they were inside the house waiting for him. That was cool, since they all had a key to each other's houses.

He entered to find Ronnie in the dining room, seated at the table with an ounce of weed and four boxes of Phillies in front of him. "What's up, Ronnie?" he asked.

"Yo! I was startin' to wonder if you were comin' back in time for tonight's set."

"Been back for a couple of hours," Travis said as he put the beer in the cooler. "Just ran to the store to pick up some meat to throw on the grill. Where's Jackie?"

"You know grill master Jay is outside firing up the grill."

"Good. I wanted to talk to you alone," Travis said. He had wondered how he was going to approach the subject with Ronnie. He didn't want to come right out and say, "If you keep fuckin' up, Freeze is going to kill you." All that would do is make Ronnie want to confront Freeze, and that definitely wasn't the way. Travis would have to find a less dramatic way to go about it.

"What's up?" Ronnie asked as he continued to roll blunts.

Travis sat down at the table across from Ronnie and looked at his friend. "I've been doing a lot of thinking these last couple of days. Thinking about the how things went down in the jewelry store."

"I kinda figured that was what this was all about, and before you say anything, I want you to know that I'm sorry. I lost my head and that will never happen again. Jackie was right, those extra fifteen seconds I spent kickin' old boy in the face was the difference between us walking away with no problems and us havin' to shoot it out with the rent-a-cops and gettin' chased by the cops."

"Not only that, it cost us big with Murray," Travis added.

"Yeah, I know." Ronnie laughed. "Now I got to be on a budget. Couldn't get my after the job freak on the way I like to. Got to make this money last until the next job."

"I been thinkin' about that too."

"You got something planned out already?"

"No. I been thinkin' about gettin' out," Travis said.

"Hold up. You ain't thinkin about quittin' because I fucked up, are you?"

"It's not just that, Ron. It's a lot deeper than that. Maybe I'm slippin'. I should have had a contingency plan in place if anything went wrong while we were in the store. It wasn't the tight timeline, it was my failure to plan for the manager having a weapon and include that in the timeline."

"You ain't still blamin' yourself for that, are you? I'm tellin' you the shit was my fault, plain and simple."

"That and my lack of contingency planning once the alarm was triggered."

"That shit went without saying. Get the shit as quick as we can and get the fuck out of there. It don't get no clearer than that. We didn't need no contingency plan for that."

"Yes, Ronnie, we did. We need to have a plan in place to counter anything that could possibly happen."

"Okay, I can see where you're right about that. So, what's up, Travis? You in or out?"

"I'm still down. I don't have enough money to retire. All I'm sayin is that I thought about it, and we—and that definitely includes my planning—need to tighten up."

"Tighten up on what?" Jackie asked as she came in the house.

"Nothing, Jackie," Travis said quickly, and Ronnie gave him a look.

"What's up, Travis? I hope you got meat, 'cause the grill is hummin'."

"It's all in the kitchen waiting for you, Jackie," Travis said.

"Travis talkin' about quittin', Jackie," Ronnie said with an attitude.

"What?"

"That we need to tighten up," Ronnie said, looking very seriously at Travis. It was obvious that he was angry and bitter about what he had just heard. "More to the point, I need to tighten up."

"No, both y'all niggas need to tighten up. Ronnie, you need to stop your bullshit and stick to the plan. No deviation, just do what the plan calls for," Jackie said. "Travis, you need to do a much better job at planning for contingencies. You got to have a plan, and a contingency plan for that plan. And then you need a contingency plan for that plan, just in case any one of us fucks it all up," she said as she began to season the steaks.

Ronnie and Travis sat across from one another at the dining room table and stared. Other than the sound that Jackie was making in the kitchen, silence and tension filled the room. Ronnie extended his hand. Travis reached out and grabbed it. "You know, it's funny, Travis. Jackie said exactly what you did, but I was mad at you for sayin' it. All you were tryin' to say is that we both need to tighten up, and I took it like you were just comin' down on me. I'm sorry, man. I don't know where my head was. Probably been smokin' too many blunts. But I got it in check, Travis."

"Good," Jackie yelled from the kitchen. "Glad y'all two got that settled."

Ronnie picked up one of the blunts he had rolled and lit it. He took a drag and handed it to Travis. "Let no man break up what we built," Ronnie said.

So now it was party time. They usually invited six women to the party. Three would be dancers, and the other three would be, for lack of a better word, regular women. The dancers were there to set the tone for the evening and get things started. They usually left around 11 o'clock to make it to the club in time to make money. The other women were invited to close out the evening.

This night was a little different. Since Travis had been out of town, he didn't invite anybody. He did tell Jackie to make sure Mystique was there, and Ronnie said in his message that she would be, but she was a no-show.

By the time 10 o'clock rolled around, the party had gone to another level. Everybody was having a good time; everybody but Travis, who try as he may, couldn't seem to get involved. And when he did, it wouldn't hold his attention for very long. No matter what he did, he kept thinking about the woman he met, or at least saw, at the store. He had made up his mind that somehow, some way he would find her.

By 11 o'clock, Ronnie had disappeared with two women and hadn't resurfaced. For her part, Jackie had a little dancing orgy going on in the living room with one of the dancers who called herself Cream. The woman she invited left earlier because the action was a bit much for her. Jackie said she understood the set was a little overwhelming, but still gave the woman a sample of what she was missing before she left.

Travis had settled onto the chaise lounge and was watching boxing when the doorbell rang. He wondered who was coming to his house unannounced and uninvited. He got up to answer it, since Jackie appeared to be in no position to do so. She did, however, lift her head. "You got that, Tee?"

"Yeah, Jackie, I got this. Go back to what you were doing," Travis replied as he made his way to the door. He looked out the peephole and couldn't tell who was there. Whoever it was knocked loudly on the door. Reluctantly, Travis opened the door.

"Hello, Travis." A female voice came from the shadows. As she stepped forward, Travis was surprised but not shocked to see that it was Mystique.

"Hello, Mystique. Come on in," Travis said.

Mystique stepped inside dressed in a black leather jumpsuit and black boots. "I see I'm not too late," she said, watching Cream wide-eyed and shaking as Jackie applied her skills.

"Not really. As far as I'm concerned, you're just in time. Make yourself comfortable."

"I've heard a lot about these parties of yours, Mr. Travis Burns. I was starting to wonder what you had to do to get an invite to one of these things."

"Well, it helps if I know you exist, which I didn't know about you until the other night," Travis said as he reclaimed his spot on the chaise and resumed watching the fight. Once Jackie and Cream acknowledged Mystique's presence, they too made a quick departure, leaving Travis alone with Mystique.

"Do you want me to dance for you, Travis?" Mystique asked as she took off her boots and pulled down the zipper of her jumpsuit.

"You can if you want to," Travis answered and glanced in her direction.

"You don't seem like you're in a very good mood. Maybe I should go."

"No!" Travis said quickly and much louder than he needed to. "Please, I want you to stay. I didn't mean to be rude." He smiled. "I know you want my undivided attention."

Mystique laughed too. "I did say that, didn't I?"

"Yes, you did. And I'm sorry if I seem a little distracted. I just have a lot on my mind. But believe me, that has nothing to do with you."

"Is it something that you can talk about?" Mystique asked and sat down on the chaise next to Travis.

"No, it's nothing I can talk about, but that doesn't mean that we can't just sit here for a while and talk about other things," Travis said.

"That would be nice," Mystique said. "Nobody ever wants to just talk to me. It's always dance, dance, dance."

So they talked. Every now and then a song would come on that Mystique liked and she would get up and dance for him. For the most part, she seemed content just to sit and talk. Mystique was beginning to like Travis, not as a client or someone she just danced for, but as a person. Travis was enjoying talking to her, too, but he had already made up his mind that there was no future in a relationship with a dancer. Still, he was always polite. Besides, Mystique was fine as hell, could dance her ass off, and she was a whole lot more intelligent than he thought she would be. Their conversation jumped from one subject to the other while the two shared drinks, blunts, and old stories. And they laughed; they laughed like little children playing in the park. Each was really starting to dig the other's vibe.

As midnight rolled around, the main event on boxing started. Mystique had danced her way completely out of her clothes. "I wanted to watch this fight, too," she announced.

"Why don't you sit down and watch it then?" Travis suggested. "But the leather on this chaise can get a little hot and sticky if you sit on it naked for a while," Travis said, and took off his shirt. He laid it out on the chaise and Mystique stretched out across it, easing her way close to Travis.

By round five of what was turning out to be a pretty dull fight, Mystique had snuggled up close to Travis and was running her fingers through the hair on his chest. By round seven of what was now definitely a very dull fight, Travis had put his arm around her and began to caress her back. Mystique started making circles around his nipples then quickly flicked her tongue at one. His body shook. Mystique inched closer to Travis and put her leg in between his legs. She ran that leg up and down, which made him harder with every stroke.

Halfway through round nine, Travis turned off the television. Mystique took off his pants and put a condom on him without using her hands. She got on top of him and rode him very slowly, grinding her hips and using her muscles until she could feel Travis begin to expand inside her, then she'd stop. Mystique did this again and again until Travis could no longer contain himself. He pushed her off of him and stood up. Mystique smiled; she knew she had his undivided attention now.

She turned her body away from Travis and crawled up on the chaise. "You're not afraid of me, are you, Travis?" she asked, looking over her shoulder.

Travis took a deep breath and looked at Mystique's wide hips and glistening bush. Then he laughed and said, "I ain't never scared."

He stepped up and grabbed Mystique by her hips and entered her slowly. She began to moan and squirm as she took in every inch. Once she had taken all of him inside her, she began winding hips. Travis let go of her hips and allowed Mystique to move her body freely. Every once in a while, Travis would grab and squeeze one of her cheeks as Mystique began to buck harder and harder. Travis leaned forward, grabbed Mystique by the shoulders, and began to pound furiously on that ass until her body started to tremble. "Oooooooooh!"

Mystique tried to move and change positions, but Travis wouldn't allow it. He slowed his roll and reached between her legs, fingering her clit with one hand and squeezing her breast with the other. He got into a long, rhythmic stroke, pulling almost completely out of her then slowly easing himself back inside. Each time he entered her fully, he smacked her ass. Not hard, but firm.

"Ooooh, Travis, I *like it like that,*" Mystique said as the steady motion gave her a chance to catch herself. She separated herself from Travis and rolled over on her back.

She lifted her legs and grabbed her ankles. "Come get this pussy, Travis."

With the weight of his body on his arms, Travis once again eased himself inside Mystique. He began the same slow and steady motion and Mystique wrapped her legs around his waist. Their bodies melted into a rhythm, with Mystique working her hips and inner muscles while licking his nipples. Now it was Travis whose body began to tremble, and Mystique who was pounding her hips furiously into him until they both reached a very loud and violent climax, then collapsed into each other's arms, laughing.

"Damn, that shit was good," they both had to agree.

Chapter Six

It had been exactly one week since Travis saw the woman at the grocery store, and he still couldn't get her out of his mind. Whenever he closed his eyes he would see her standing there just as she had been that day. Travis could still hear her voice echoing in his ears. *Oh, I am so sorry. I wasn't looking where I was going.*

In his dreams, however, his subconscious mind added more to their encounters. He dreamed about her almost every night since the first time he saw her. The dreams were always different, but the theme was always the same. Travis would try to get to her and something would prevent that from happening, then her image would fade just out of his reach.

One night, Travis dreamed that he was in a park and saw her walking alone down a path. It was a windy day and she was draped in white silk scarves that flowed freely in the wind. As he approached, a crowd of men began to form around her. They were thankful to be in her presence. They told her how beautiful she was and how much they would love to love her. Travis worked his way through the crowd with the hope of getting close to her, but the crowd was too thick and he couldn't reach her. He struggled against the crowd, but she got farther and farther away.

All at once, the crowd separated, leaving him with a clear path to her as she continued her walk. Travis started to walk faster then broke into a trot in an attempt to catch up with her. Suddenly, the seafood counter attendant, dressed like he was in a *Men In Black* movie, appeared from out of thin air. He held out his hand and Travis ran into it, falling to the ground.

"Oh, I am so sorry. I wasn't looking where I was going," the counter attendant said.

The woman stopped and laughed. "Well, maybe you should look where you're going," she said then continued her walk until her image faded.

Travis yelled out to her, "That's all right! I shouldn't have been in his way."

Another night, Travis dreamed that he was in Los Angeles at the Bonaventure Hotel. He had been there many times before; in fact, it was one of his favorite places. In his dream, he was sitting alone having a drink at the revolving Bona Vista Lounge, enjoying the view of the Los Angeles skyline, looking out at the Hollywood sign.

He saw the woman serving drinks. Travis got up to greet her. He walked up behind her and tapped her on the shoulder. She was startled by his sudden appearance and spilled the drinks from her tray all over him. Security guards appeared next to Travis and held him. This time it was Travis who uttered the line, "Oh, I am so sorry. I wasn't looking where I was going."

"No, I am so sorry. I wasn't looking where I was going," she said and tried to wipe him off, but before she could touch him, the security guards grabbed Travis and dragged him away as her image faded.

It was the dream that he'd had the night before that brought him to the edge. In this dream, he found himself on the beach outside his timeshare in Freeport, breathing ocean air, watching the palm trees bending in the wind. Travis was standing waist deep in clear blue water, looking back at the beach when he saw her walking by.

MOB

Once again, she was draped in white silk scarves that flowed freely in the wind. Travis called to her and she stopped and waved him on. While Travis made his way through the water, he watched her call for the cabana boy, who responded quickly to her motion. She raised two fingers and the cabana boy rushed off and returned with two beach chairs. Travis made it to shore just as she sat down in one of the chairs and crossed her legs. "Join me?" she asked, motioning for Travis to sit in the chair next to her.

It was at that moment Travis realized that she was now naked except for a pair of dark sunglasses. Travis sat in the chair and started to talk to her, but it was as if she could not hear him. He became very excited and started to yell. She turned to him slowly and said, "Shhh. I can hear you, Travis." With that, Travis became very calm, content to watch her glistening skin as beads of sweat formed all over her body.

"Tell me, what's your name?" Travis asked, but received no answer. He started to ask again when she turned to him slowly.

"Shhh," she said with a smile. "Just relax and enjoy me."

This seemed to satisfy him, but not for long. "Tell me, what's your name?" he asked again.

Once again she turned to him slowly. This time she leaned toward him. "Pleasure me, Travis," she whispered in his ear and spread her legs.

Travis stood up and stepped around to the front of her chair, then knelt down in the sand. He reached both hands forward and began to massage her thighs.

"Pleasure me, Travis. Please don't make me wait any longer. I'm here waiting for you. Pleasure me now."

Travis allowed his hands to move freely over her body. He very deliberately spread her lips with the thumb and forefinger of his left hand while making small circles around her clit with the tip of his right forefinger. All the time, he stared at her face. "You are so beautiful," Travis said again and again.

She reached out with both hands and grabbed his head. "Pleasure me, Travis," she said to him again while slowly lowering his head, raising her legs at the same time. Travis held onto her hips, slid his tongue inside her and sucked her moist lips gently. He felt her body quiver as he licked her clit with the tip of his tongue. Her clit grew harder, her thighs pressed together as her body convulsed uncontrollably.

When Travis opened his eyes from the dream, Mystique was lying next to him, gliding her hand up and down his ever-hardening erection. Mystique had become a regular feature at Travis's house over the last week. He could expect a call from her at least once a day, either before she went to work or after she got off. Their conversations were always very brief and to the point.

"Hello."

"It's me. Are you busy?" Mystique would ask.

"No," Travis would reply.

"I'm coming over," Mystique would then assert.

"Come on." And that was that.

Once he was fully erect, Mystique straddled and began to ride Travis. He stared into her eyes the entire time, but his mind was on the woman from the store. He believed his latest dream meant that he would be able to find her and get with her.

He looked up at Mystique and watched as she worked herself into a stuttering orgasm. You know, the type you have when your eyes roll back in your head. Travis had to laugh to himself thinking, *Here you are gettin' sucked and fucked daily by a beautiful woman, but you're fiendin' for some woman you've only seen once and never actually met. There is something seriously wrong with this picture. You could consider gettin' some help for yourself.*

Once Mystique left his house and was on her way to work, Travis set in motion his plan to find the woman who had so captivated his mind and taken over his dreams. Once he was dressed, Travis got his surveillance equipment and left the house. He got in his black '93 Thunderbird and drove back to the grocery store. His thinking was that if she lived or worked in the area, this would be the place where she shopped. And if that was indeed the case, he would simply have to wait; eventually she would show up.

The thought had occurred to him that maybe, just maybe, she was just passing through and stopped in to do some shopping. However, he figured that possibility to be slim. In the brief seconds that he spent with her, if you could actually call it that, he did take note that the cart she rammed into him appeared to be pretty full. The contents looked more like that of a person who was doing her regular shopping, as opposed to someone who was just passing through the area and picking up a few things.

He parked his car in an area of the lot where he would be able to see both entrances and exits to and from the store, as well as the entire parking lot. With the exception of using the bathroom and eating, Travis spent the entire day in his car watching the store. When he did need to use the bathroom, he went in the store and picked up something to eat at the same time. Before he left the store, Travis quickly checked every aisle. At the end of day one, he hadn't seen her.

Day two was no different from day one. Travis spent the day watching and waiting in vain. The pattern continued for the remainder of the week. He sat there all day and she didn't show.

When week two began, Travis took a whole new attitude. He began to pay attention to his surroundings. He took pictures of and made notes on all the people, employees and customers, who came and went on a regular basis. He noted the delivery days and times, who was the driver, and what he was delivering. He would take short drives around the neighborhood, checking streets and traffic flow.

Travis started spending more time inside the store, getting a feel for the layout. He even knew the armored truck schedule, and had developed a profile on the drivers. At first he told himself that all these things were just to keep him busy, to keep his mind sharp for the next job. How else does a planner sharpen his planning skills? He practices planning.

By the time Friday of week two had come and gone without the woman's return, Travis had just about given up on her. But if Travis was nothing else, he was persistent. He decided to give it one more week.

It was Saturday evening at 7:34 p.m. when his persistence paid off. A red 1999 Honda Civic pulled into the crowded lot and turned down the row of parking spaces where Travis had positioned himself. After two weeks of near misses, Travis wasn't the least bit excited when yet another woman who fit the profile drove by his position.

MOB

She parked her car almost directly in front of Travis and stepped out. He noticed she wore a black suit with a yellow blouse as she came around the car and walked right by Travis. As she passed, it appeared that she looked directly at him and said *pleasure me*. He knew he was trippin', but he gave her a ten-second count before getting out of his car and going in after her.

Travis entered the store, grabbed a shopping cart, and looked around. He spotted her in the produce aisle. He approached slowly, watching and waiting for what he considered the perfect opportunity to move on her. He began placing items in his shopping cart from whatever aisle she went down, to keep up appearances. In the last two weeks, he had bought enough stuff to last a month at his house, and had begun to give the stuff he'd bought to Jackie and Ronnie.

As she continued to shop, Travis kept her in sight, never allowing more than one aisle's distance between them. When she stopped at the magazine aisle, Travis made his move. He approached and posted up next to her as she flipped through the latest copy of *Essence*. Travis picked up a copy of *Black Enterprise* and began to flip pages as well. "Excuse me," Travis said. She turned to face him.

"Yes?"

All of a sudden, a cold chill ran through his body. Here he was, finally standing face to face with the woman he had been fiendin' for these last two weeks, and he couldn't think of anything to say. He briefly considered the direct approach: *Look, ever since you rammed your shopping cart into me two weeks ago, I've thought about nothing but you. Each time I close my eyes I see your face and I dream sweet dreams of you each night when I sleep. The sound of your voice echoes in my ears all the time. So please, tell me, what's your name?*

Instead, he said, "I thought that was you."

"I beg your pardon?" she said, looking very curiously at Travis.

"I guess you don't remember me. I was the one that you accidentally ran into with your shopping cart a couple weeks ago."

"Oh, was that you?" the woman asked, thinking that Travis was kind of cute. "I am so sorry. I guess I wasn't looking where I was going,"

"No, you were reading the label on a box of Special K," Travis said. He laughed as he pointed to the box of Special K she had in her cart.

"Yeah." She laughed too. "I always read the nutrition facts on everything that I buy."

"Nutrition facts?" Travis asked.

"You've never read the nutrition facts on the things you buy?"

"I'm ashamed to say it, but no, I don't," Travis said and dropped his eyes in mock shame. Inside, he was glowing.

"On the label of just about any kind of packaged food that you buy, there are nutrition facts," she said. "It gives you information that you need to know about the foods that you eat." She put her magazine back on the rack and reached into his shopping cart then stepped next to Travis. His heart began to pound.

She pointed to the nutrition facts on the package of frozen corn on the cob. "Look at the label on that package. It tells you that this corn has only ninety calories and that five of those calories came from fat. There's only one gram of total fat. It has no saturated fat or sodium.

Now look at that box of mac and cheese. Look at both packages and compare the two."

"Two hundred and sixty calories and four hundred if I use margarine and two-percent milk," Travis said.

"And who doesn't put margarine and milk in their mac and cheese?"

"Nobody."

"Now check out the amount of sodium it has, and compare it to the corn," she instructed.

Travis did as he was told. At this point, he would have hopped on one leg and barked like a dog if she said she wanted to see it. "The corn has no sodium, and wow! This mac and cheese has seven hundred twenty milligrams. That's a big difference."

"And it is so much more sodium than we black people, who are already prone to high blood pressure, need in our diets. So, we should really watch the amount of sodium in the foods we buy and the amount of salt we pour on it."

"But you know black people can't live without mac-n-cheese," Travis said playfully.

"True that, true that." She nodded in agreement and smiled. " 'Cause I love it too. But we shouldn't eat it all the time."

"Well, if that's the case, half of what we call soul food ain't all that healthy for us either."

"I know that's right, 'cause when I go to my aunt's house for Sunday dinner or on Thanksgiving and Christmas, there I am eating everything in sight, gettin' fat on my way back in the kitchen for a second plate. But I sure pay for it the next week."

"I don't know. You look pretty healthy to me."

"I try to eat right, you know, get a little exercise. You look like you're in pretty good shape," she said, peering in his cart. "Most of what you have is pretty healthy. Plenty of fresh fruit and vegetables."

"Thank you," Travis said, glad that he only picked up items in the aisles she went down. "By the way, my name is Travis. Travis Burns," he said and extended his hand.

"Me'shelle Lawrence," she said, accepting his hand.

"Well, Ms. Lawrence, it is truly a pleasure to make your acquaintance."

"The pleasure is mutual, Mr. Burns," Me'shelle said graciously.

"And thank you for the nutrition lesson."

"Not a problem. Everybody needs to be educated on some things sometimes. It's what I do."

"So, when you brutally attacked my ankle, what were you looking at?"

"The dietary fiber contents," Me'shelle said. "Always choose my cereal based on the amount of dietary fiber it has."

"Is that important?"

"Very," Me'shelle replied, thinking the reason why it was important was a little too much information for her to be giving for the purposes of this conversation.

"I'll have to watch that," Travis said. "And thank you again. Listen, would you like to go out with me some time?"

Me'shelle leaned back and looked Travis over. "I don't know if that would be a good idea."

"Why? Are you married?"

"No."

"Well then, I think it's the least you could do after you attacked my ankle," Travis said jokingly, but he was dead serious.

"Travis . . . that's your name, right? I usually don't go out with guys that try to pick me up in the grocery store. So, I guess that you'll just have to settle for a sincere apology."

"Well, if that's all I can have, then I will just have to be happy with that." Travis once again extended his hand. "It was truly a pleasure meeting and talking with you today, Ms. Lawrence. Hopefully we'll meet again some time. In fact, I'm sure of it," Travis said confidently.

Me'shelle accepted his hand and looked at him curiously. "Nice meeting you too." She was really starting to like Travis. *I wasn't expecting him to give up so easily,* she thought as she watched Travis walk down the aisle heading toward the checkout lanes.

For Travis, it was a totally successful first encounter. He came away knowing her name. *Me'shelle Lawrence.* The words seemed to float from her lips to his ears. He knew what kind of car she drove. He knew that she was health conscious, and he now knew that she was quite intelligent.

Travis paid for his items and headed for his car, knowing that he would see her again. He made a note of her license plate number and drove off.

Chapter Seven

On Sunday morning, Me'shelle got in her car and headed to her aunt Miranda's house in Queens for Sunday dinner. As she drove across the Whitestone Bridge, she glanced out her window at the water. She loved the water; it was so peaceful and allowed her to clear her mind and think. Of course, driving across a bridge may not be the best time to look at and enjoy the water, but it is what it is. Her dilemma that morning was her older brother, Bruce. How should she handle him, and what, if anything, could she do to get her niece, Brandy, out of that situation?

Like so many others, Bruce had lost his job. To make ends meet he began to sell cocaine for some character who called himself Chilly. Nothing major; he could flip a few grams, maybe an ounce here and there if he already had a buyer. But then he would step on it so hard that they didn't come back. You see, Bruce and his wife Natalie were big-time smokers, and having product around just made it worse because they would always smoke themselves in a hole—a hole that they continuously asked Me'shelle to dig them out of.

The night before, Bruce had come to her for help. It wasn't that they owed anybody money. That would come later. They had smoked all they had and needed money for more.

The calls began a little after 2:00 in the morning. She knew it was Bruce, and she knew what he wanted, so she didn't answer the phone. But the calls continued about every ten minutes until Me'shelle unplugged her phone at

3:00 in the morning. By the time she had drifted off to sleep, it was after 4:00. That sleep was interrupted by a loud banging at her door accompanied by, "Me'shelle!" Bruce yelled at the top of his lungs as he continued to bang on the door. "Open the door, Me'shelle! I know you're in there!"

Me'shelle jumped out of bed and ran to the door. She had to shut him up because the last time he pulled a stunt like this, her landlord, Mrs. B., told her if it happened again, lease or no lease, she was putting her out. She swung the door open, snatched Bruce by his shirt and dragged him into the apartment. "Are you crazy, Bruce? What are doin' knocking on my door like a crazy fool at four in the morning?"

"You wouldn't answer your phone."

"Did you ever think that I wasn't home or had company and didn't want to be bothered?"

"Nope. Since that blockhead Trent dropped you, you never go anywhere," Bruce said, looking around Me'shelle's apartment.

"He didn't drop me. We agreed that we should see other people," Me'shelle said, knowing Trent had dropped her.

"Whatever, Me'shelle. That's just some shit a muthafucka like him would say when he dropped your ass," Bruce cracked.

"Anyway, I still could've had a date."

"Who? You? Sister Mary-Me'shelle out on a date? I don't think so. You never go anywhere, you never do anything. You just sit here every night readin' them stupid self improvement books and gradin' them kids' papers."

"Books aren't stupid!" Me'shelle replied angrily. "Never mind. And stop looking around here for something to pawn. How much do you need?"

"Since you asked, I need two thousand dollars. But I know you ain't got it like that, so just give me fifty and I'm gone."

Me'shelle sucked her teeth, but she went to get her purse anyway. "You know what, Bruce? This is the last time. I can't keep supporting you and Natalie's habit. If Mommy and Daddy knew you turned out to be a crackhead and I was supportin' your habit, what would they say?"

"I don't know what *your* mother would say. And Pops wouldn'ta said nothin'. He woulda just sat in his chair and stared at the TV like he always did."

After that, she really didn't get back to sleep, and once the morning flooded her bedroom with sunshine there was no longer any point in trying. By the time Me'shelle got to the Liberty Avenue exit on the Van Wyck Expressway, she felt tired.

When she arrived at her aunt Miranda's house, it was like a burst of energy came over her. Me'shelle unlocked the door and wandered through the house hollering, "Good morning, Aunt Miranda! Aunt Miranda, where are you?"

"In the kitchen, Me'shelle," Miranda answered.

Me'shelle entered the kitchen and gave her aunt a hug and a kiss on the cheek.

"Mornin', Me'shelle. You look tired, baby. You gettin' enough rest? Anyway, you're just in time to help me pick and wash these greens so I can cook them for tomorrow. My arthritis is actin' up on me this morning. And I don't know what all that hollering was for. Where else would I be on Sunday morning?"

"I don't know, in bed or church maybe," Me'shelle answered as she rolled up her sleeves.

"When have you ever known me to be in bed past seven? I'm an early riser, and church, you know that's your Aunt Juanita's thing. She called me this morning like she does every Sunday, and invited me to go to church with her. And I told her no, just like I do every Sunday," Miranda said as she sat down at the kitchen table.

"You oughta go with her some time. Pastor usually preaches a sermon."

"Then you go with her."

"You know I used to before–" Me'shelle paused without finishing.

"You can say it. Before Trent started bringing that slut to church with him every Sunday. But you know that shouldn't stop you from goin'," Miranda said.

Me'shelle thought about all the things Bruce had said to her, not just about Trent, but about her parents. "Bruce came by at four in the morning."

"Oh Lord. That's why you look so tired. How much did he want this time?"

"Just fifty dollars this time," Me'shelle said with a look that let her aunt know there was something else.

"I've seen that face before. What did he say to you?"

"It's not what he said, 'cause what he said is the truth. It's the way he said it. I asked him what would Mommy and Daddy think if they knew he was a crackhead and I was supporting his habit."

"What did he say?"

"He said, 'I don't *know* what *your* mother would say.' Your mother. Like she wasn't his *mother* too."

"Come sit down, Me'shelle," Miranda said. Me'shelle stopped what she was doing and sat down at the table. "I can understand why your brother would feel like that. You both were very young when she died. He probably doesn't remember much about her."

"I know that, Aunt Miranda. I don't remember much about her either, but she's still his mother."

"You know, when my sister died in that car accident, me and your Aunt Juanita stepped in and tried to help Clay raise you children. We used to get both of you on the weekends. But your father stopped that."

"Why?"

"He thought we would turn Bruce into a sissy."

"What?"

"One weekend when we took y'all home, your brother was crying like a baby because you were playing dress up and we wouldn't let him play, mostly because we didn't have anything for him to dress up in."

"I remember that," Me'shelle said and smiled.

"After that, Clay wouldn't let Bruce come out here without him. So Bruce just sat there in front of that idiot box with your father."

"He said that too. He said Daddy wouldn't say anything about him being a crackhead. He'd just sit in his chair and stare at the TV like he always did," she said sadly.

"Your father wasn't always like that. Clay Lawrence was so full of life, and full of himself, for that matter. And he loved my baby sister Sabrina so much that when she died, a part of him died too.

"I remember when we were growing up in Columbia. Your mother loved Jackie Wilson. So your father put on a suit, came to our house, and put on a show in front of your mother's window," Miranda recalled.

"Daddy? Singing?"

"Singing and dancing. He started out singing "A Woman, A Lover, A Friend." Then he sang "Lonely Teardrops," broke into "Doggin' Around" and finished with "Baby Workout." By the time he was finished, half the neighborhood was out there watching your father perform."

"I can't believe that. You're talking about my father? Could he sing?"

"He could carry a tune, but he was no Jackie Wilson."

"I just can't see Daddy singing and dancing." Me'shelle laughed.

"Yeah, well, the man you grew up with ain't the same man I remember. Not the man your mother married. I hope you don't take this the wrong way, but I was happy for him when he died. I felt that only then could he be free from the life without Sabrina that made him so miserable. He told me once after you kids were grown that he wished he could go on and die so he could be with his Sabrina again."

"I never knew he felt that way," Me'shelle said sadly. "I knew he missed Mommy, but I never knew that he was just waiting for us to grow up so he could die," she said as the doorbell rang. "I'll get it, Aunt Miranda."

"I don't know why. It ain't nobody but Juanita. I don't know why she just doesn't use her key. Always wanna act like she's a guest," Miranda said, but Me'shelle went to open it anyway.

Me'shelle let her in. "Hi, Aunt Juanita."

MOB

"Good afternoon, Me'shelle. How are you today?" Juanita asked as she came into her sister's house.

"I'm fine. I'm a little tired, but other than that I'm fine." Me'shelle gave her aunt a hug and a kiss.

"Hey, Miranda," Juanita said as she went into the kitchen and sat down at the table next to her sister. "You both missed a good service this morning. Pastor Franks gave a fine sermon. My Lord, that man can preach."

"What was it about?" Me'shelle asked.

"Being honest and facing things about yourself, 'cause God knows who you are. You can't hide from him, so you might as well be honest."

"That's right," Me'shelle said. "Honest self-evaluation is a beautiful thing."

"Me'shelle, when are you goin' to stop gettin' your religion from those self help books and come back to church?" Juanita asked Me'shelle, but Miranda answered with a question.

"Was that big head Trent there with that slut?" she asked as she got up and began to put dinner on the table.

"Yes, he was there, and yes, she was with him."

"When him and the slut stop coming every Sunday, that's when she'll start going to that church again," Miranda answered and Me'shelle smiled.

"For the life of me, I don't understand why she has to show her cleavage for all the world to see," Juanita said, shaking her head. She got a knife out of the drawer and began to slice the ham.

Miranda stated the obvious answer. "Because she's a slut, that's why."

"It is a shame to see half the men in church falling all over themselves trying to find a reason to stand in front of her. And the older men are worst. Can't even look her in the eyes 'cause they're all down in that cleavage," Juanita said.

Me'shelle hugged both of her aunts. "You two are something else, but I love you both," she said and let out a deep yawn.

"What are you yawning for, Me'shelle? Did you have a date last night?" Juanita asked excitedly.

"No, her brother came by at four in the morning," Miranda said.

"You need to stop giving Bruce all of your money for him to smoke up," Juanita said.

"I know, Aunt Juanita, but he's my brother," Me'shelle said while she put the vegetables into bowls.

"He's my nephew, but I don't give him any money, and I don't allow him or Natalie to come in my house. I had to learn that the hard way, 'cause they will steal everything they think they can take to the pawn shop," Juanita preached while she carried a plate with the ham she had sliced, along with a plate of chicken, and put them on the dining room table. She came back in the kitchen still preaching. "I don't know why Miranda still lets him in here."

"I just don't let him out of my sight," Miranda said as she pulled the baked macaroni and cheese from the oven. "He's still family, but I ain't stupid. But hold up, wait a minute. Ain't you the one who always says that people like that need our prayers?"

"Yes, I am," Juanita said. "And I pray for Bruce and Natalie, and I especially pray for poor Brandy. She's the one that needs all of our help and prayers and understanding. Having two junkies for parents has to be hard on her. I only wish I could have gotten custody of her, but that Natalie's a smart one. She knew how to clean herself up and get her a job just long enough to have the judge let her stay with them."

"I wish you had too," Me'shelle said. "I try to spend as much time with her as I can, but I know it's not enough. She's fifteen now, going on twenty-two, and looking like it too. I think she's a little young to be hangin' out all night, but they let her do what she wants to. And did you know she started smoking cigarettes?"

"No, but I'm not surprised," Miranda said. "Next thing she'll be smokin that stuff with them and they'll have her out selling herself just like her mother so they can get high."

"You know, Aunt Miranda, it's just the three of us. Why do you cook enough food to feed an army? I have to go on a diet, starve myself and exercise so I won't get fat."

The doorbell rang and Juanita went to answer it. "Are you expecting somebody, Miranda?"

"No, not that I know of. Maybe Me'shelle talked up some guests for dinner," Miranda replied.

Juanita opened the door and there stood Bruce, Natalie, and Brandy. "What are you doing here?" Juanita asked, blocking the door.

"What? I ain't invited to Sunday dinner no more?" Bruce asked.

Miranda rushed to the door. "Of course you are. He is family, Juanita. Get out of the way and let them in."

"That's right, Aunt Juanita. We still a part of this family whether you like it or not," Bruce said as he walked by Juanita. Natalie followed him. Brandy just stood there looking at Juanita.

"Hi, Aunt Juanita. Can I come in?"

"Of course you can, child. Come give your aunt a hug. You look more and more like your grandmother, rest her soul, every day."

Miranda and Me'shelle came to welcome Brandy with hugs and kisses. "Yes, she does," Miranda said. "How are you doing, Brandy?"

"I'm doin' great, Aunt Miranda. What's up, Me'shelle?" Brandy hugged her aunt.

Bruce and Natalie didn't get the same reception. Their presence in the house was met with cold stares and a general feeling of tension. Juanita watched them closely while the rest of the food was set out on the table. She never took her eyes off of them while Me'shelle and Brandy brought out the silverware and set the table. Now that dinner was ready, they all gathered around the table and bowed their heads in prayer.

After dinner, Bruce stepped up to Me'shelle. "Can I talk to you for a minute?"

"Sure, Bruce. What do you want to talk about?"

"Let's talk outside." Once they were outside, Bruce said, "Me'shelle, I need two thousand dollars by Friday."

"No, Bruce. I told you last night I'm not gonna give you any more money. I can't keep doing this. And besides, where would I get two thousand dollars?"

"From them," Bruce said, pointing at the house. "Get it from your aunts. They'll give it to you with no questions asked. Tell them you need to get your car fixed or you're behind on your rent. It doesn't matter what you tell them. Please, Me'shelle, just get me the money."

"No, Bruce, I'm not gonna do that. I'll take you and Natalie to a treatment program to get yourselves together. Brandy can stay with me until you two got it together, but I won't ask *them for* any money so you can get high."

"You don't understand me, Me'shelle. They're *gonna* kill me if I don't have it by Friday. Please, Me'shelle, you're the only one I can come to."

"Bruce, if somebody's gonna kill you, the best thing for you to do is leave Brandy with me, and you and Natalie get out of town. I'll buy you two bus tickets to anywhere you want to go."

"Thanks for nothing, sis," Bruce said as he turned to go back in the house. Then he stopped and faced Me'shelle. "But how you gonna live with yourself when I'm dead?"

Chapter Eight

Travis lay in bed and concentrated all of his mental energy on the situation that he found himself in. There were things happening all around him that told Travis it was time to get out of this robbery game and focus his energy on more positive things. Foremost on his mind was the fact that Freeze had every intention of killing Ronnie if he fucked up one more time. Although Ronnie had promised to tighten up and stick to the plan, Travis knew Ronnie all too well. If some little thing happened that he hadn't planned for and it caused them to get caught, Freeze might take matters into his own hands.

No, getting out now before anything else happened was the only option that Travis saw available. However, there was still the issue of money. When he started out, he had set very specific financial goals that he wanted to accomplish. The plan was to have a half-million dollars in his numbered account in the Cayman Islands, his house in Connecticut and the timeshare in Freeport paid for, as well as his mother's house in Fort Myers.

He had never intended for this to become a way of life, but here he was two years later, still caught up in the game. He had been sidetracked from achieving his financial goals by giving into his passions. Travis liked to travel, so he'd been to Los Angeles, Vegas, Atlantic City, Miami, and the islands. He would fly to the islands at the drop of a dime. He also knew that hanging out with Ronnie and Jackie at Cynt's and places like that took a chunk of his money.

Travis glanced over at Mystique as he tried to focus on a solution. She was out like a light. The solution was simple: Make as much money as he could, as quickly as he could, with minimal risk. He had to become more disciplined about the way he spent his money. The words Jackie had spoken to Ronnie now had resonance for him. *You need to stop your bullshit and stick to the plan. No deviation, just do what the plan calls for.*

Travis glanced over at Mystique again. She was becoming an expensive habit too. It wasn't like she was charging a straight fee for her services, and her skills at providing those services were formidable, but she was getting very "needy." *Travis, I need this. Travis, I saw that. Travis, wouldn't that like look nice on me?* She was smoking up all the weed, and of course, he had to pay her to dance for him whenever he went to Cynt's. *She got to go too,* Travis thought, but her neediness and formidable skills aside, he was really starting to like Mystique. He had grown accustomed to having her around. *I don't care. She gotta go.*

And what about Me'shelle Lawrence? What was the deal with that? He saw the disappointed look on her face when he didn't press her for her phone number. Women like to be pursued, to be made to feel desirable, and he simply walked away like she was of no more importance to him than the next woman who passed his way. That definitely wasn't the case. All of her beauty and physical attributes aside, he found her to be quite thoughtful and intelligent. *How does she fit into your plan?*

There was no time to think about that now. Travis would make time to see her and establish some type of relationship with her when he solidified his financial position.

He picked up the phone and called Ronnie and Jackie, asking them to meet him at his house at 2:00 that afternoon. Then he woke Mystique and told her that when Ronnie and Jackie arrived, she would have to leave so they could talk business. "I understand," she said and headed for the shower. Although Travis never told Mystique what it was they did, and she never asked, she knew they were involved with Freeze. That was more than enough information for her.

When Ronnie and Jackie got to the house, Mystique politely excused herself and they proceeded to the business at hand. Travis started the conversation by talking about his desire to get out.

"When we got into this thing, I never planned on us still being at it two years later. I had a plan—we all did—a plan for what we were gonna do to set ourselves up so we could live comfortable for the rest of our lives. But all of us have gotten caught up in this lifestyle. Not that we've been flashy or no dumb shit like that, but we have been blowin' this cash."

With that said, he explained why he wanted to run a job so soon after the last one. "Last time we went out, we didn't come away with the amount of money that we expected to. Don't get me wrong, Ronnie. I'm not trying to call you out for the loss of money; I'm just stating a fact. What I've done is select a target that may present more of a risk than we're usually willing to take, but it will bring us the dollar amounts that we need to get done with this lifestyle."

Travis proceeded to lay out his *plan* to rob the armored truck *outside* the grocery store he'd been *surveying* while waiting to see Me'shelle. He had given some thought to the possibility that Me'shelle might be at the store during their robbery. He concluded that she was just there on Saturday night, so the possibility was slim.

"You want to rob a grocery store in the hood?" Jackie asked. "I don't know, Travis. I shop there."

"I do too, Travis. Isn't that more risk than we wanna take?" Ronnie asked.

"No. We're not going to rob the store or try to take the armored truck. This is basically a grab and run. Listen, at approximately 8:45 on Monday mornings, the armored truck arrives to pick up the cash from the weekend."

"How much money?" Ronnie asked.

"I don't know. But when the guy comes out he always has four bags full, two in each hand. So, his hands will be occupied. Police response time to the store is approximately three minutes.

"Now, this is going to be a two vehicle operation. Jackie, you'll be in the lead vehicle, and it will be abandoned at the conclusion of the operation. Ronnie and I will be in the second vehicle, and that one will be used for the escape. The armored truck will have two occupants—one driver and the bagman. I've developed a profile on them, and I don't believe they'll take any actions that would jeopardize their lives.

"The bagman enters the store and approximately twenty minutes later, he will emerge with the bags. The truck is equipped with a cellular radio system that the driver will use to call for assistance in the event of a robbery attempt. We have to disable this system first."

Travis opened the box that was sitting on the table and removed the device it contained. "This is a C-Guard Cellular Firewall. It's a cellular jamming device made by an Israeli-based company, but I picked it up from my tech guy for a grand. The device is relatively simple. It broadcasts a junk signal that floods the cellular frequency or sets up fake signals. Either way, the system loses its signal and is out of range. The device transmits low power radio signals, which cut off communications between cellular handsets and the cellular base station."

Travis placed a diagram of the front of the store on the table. "Jackie, approximately fifteen minutes prior to the armored truck's arrival, you will position the vehicle adjacent to the front of the store. When the armored truck arrives and the bagman has exited the vehicle, you will activate the device and set up a fake signal so it appears to the driver that his communications are still active.

"Ronnie and I will position the second vehicle adjacent to the front of the store with a direct angle to the back of the truck. When the bagman emerges from the store, Jackie will exit her vehicle and move into position to cover the driver to prevent him from exiting the truck. Ronnie and I will exit our vehicle and make a rapid approach to the rear of the truck to confront the bagman. Ronnie will assume a cover position where he will be able to cover both me and Jackie. When both driver and bagman are covered, I will disarm the bagman and relieve him of the objective.

"Once the objective has been secured, Jackie and I will move to the escape vehicle, and we will drive by and pick up Ronnie. The whole operation should take less than a minute."

Travis took out a map of the area surrounding the store and handed it to Jackie. "What's this for?" Jackie asked.

"It a map of the area," Travis replied and sat down next to Jackie.

"I know that. What you giving this to me for, is what I'm asking."

"I've decided to delegate parts of the operational control of all future jobs to the two of you. You may be able to see or better anticipate issues than I can. But all of the contingency planning that results from that delegation are subject to my review and approval, and I will integrate them into the larger plan."

"I think that's a good idea, Travis," Ronnie said. "What part of the job am I responsible for?"

"You primary responsibility is the safety of the participants. From your cover position, you are in the best place to see and anticipate issues that arise during the operation, like customers attempting to enter and exit the store, police involvement, stuff like that."

"What do you mean by police involvement? The way I see it, the way you got the job planned, the driver won't be able to call for assistance. Even if somebody calls the cops during the job, we should still have enough time get away before police response time."

"True, but suppose a cop car just happens to roll into the parking lot to pick up some fresh donuts or something. In that case, what will you do from your cover position to maintain the safety of the participants and the security of the objective?"

"I understand," Ronnie said, smiling. Travis thought that giving them, especially Ronnie, a more active roll in the planning stages of the job would not only give Ronnie a much needed boost of confidence, but they would be better able to anticipate issues.

"Now, you both have your assignments. I expect a report of any contingencies in two hours," Travis announced.

"Two hours! How about we get back to you with our contingency plans in a couple of days? That will give us time to go over the whole job," Jackie offered.

"No. We haven't got that kind of time."

"Why is that?" Ronnie asked. "When you planning on runnin' this job?"

"Tomorrow morning. We meet here at 7:45 sharp. Any questions?"

Neither Ronnie nor Jackie said a word. They had complete confidence in Travis and trusted his judgment as well as his planning skills.

"Good. Let's get to it then. Who got some weed?" Travis asked, remembering that Mystique had smoked up all of his.

"I do," Jackie said.

"Then we'll reconvene at Jackie's house in two hours."

In two hours, they met at Jackie's house. In the time that Travis gave them, Jackie had worked out three possible escape routes complete with scenarios for why each was the proper course of action. Ronnie was also hard at work. As Travis had asked, Ronnie had planned for customers attempting to enter and exit the store, what to do if anyone came into the field of operation. As for police involvement, his plan was simple. "If a cop car just happens to roll into the parking lot to pick up some fresh donuts or something, we'll just have to kill the muthafucka."

Travis wasn't happy about that option. In all the robberies that they had run, they never killed anybody. But it was something that was inevitable. He could only hope it wouldn't come to that.

"Is everybody satisfied with the plan?" Travis asked.

"I think we've covered all the bases," Jackie said.

"Like the *white boys* on Wall Street used to say, I think we've got all our ducks in a *row*," Ronnie said in his best white boy imitation.

"Good, then we meet here at 7:45 sharp."

Chapter Nine

On Monday morning, Me'shelle got out of bed at 6:30, put on her spandex workout clothes and hit the treadmill for her usual five-mile run. While she was running, she thought about what Bruce had said to her the day before. *How you gonna live with yourself when I'm dead?*

Naturally, she was concerned about her brother, but she was more concerned about Brandy. Bruce could take care of himself; he always had. Brandy, on the other hand, was just a child and not accustomed to dealing with the type of people that her father came in contact with. Lost in her thoughts for Brandy's safety, Me'shelle stumbled and pulled a muscle in her thigh.

She turned off the treadmill and limped to the phone. She planned to say that she would be a little late for work because the injury was causing her to move slowly. Instead, she decided that she desperately needed a mental health day. She called the school and told them that she would be in the next day if she was feeling better. Me'shelle knew she had to do something to get Brandy out of that situation, so she left the possibility open for another day off if she needed to take it.

Me'shelle got her heat wrap and went back to bed. She lay there thinking, ignoring the pain as best she could as she considered her options to save Brandy. After about an hour, the pain in her leg became more intense. She could no longer ignore it. She got up and paddled her way to the medicine cabinet. When Me'shelle grabbed the empty bottle of Motrin, she realized that she had forgotten to get some more when she was at the grocery store. *Probably too busy thinking about that fine-ass Travis Burns,* she thought.

Slowly and painfully, Me'shelle got her leather coat and prepared to go to the grocery store to get some Motrin to ease her pain. *Maybe Travis will be doing some early morning shopping.*

That same morning at 7:45 sharp, Jackie and Ronnie arrived at Travis's place in two stolen cars. Jackie drove an old Toyota Tercell, and Ronnie was in a Ford Galaxy 500 that would be used as the escape vehicle. The night before, Jackie had also stolen an Infinity Q45 and parked it on the escape route.

They knocked on the door. Travis came out right away and they proceeded to the grocery store. They arrived at the store and assumed their positions adjacent to the front of the store, waiting for the armored truck to arrive.

"Sound check. Mr. White?"

"Check, one, check two."

"Acknowledged. Mr. Green?"

"Sound check, one, two."

"Acknowledged. Time check," Travis said.

"Eight-thirty," Jackie replied.

"Eight-thirty, check," Ronnie said.

"Acknowledged. Weapons check," Travis said.

"One pump shotgun, two nine millers, check," Jackie said.

"One AK-47, two nine millimeters checked and ready," Ronnie said.

"Acknowledged. Equipment check," Travis said.

At that point, Jackie turned on the C-Guard. "C-Guard engaged," she said.

Ronnie took out a cell phone and checked the screen for a signal. "Signal at one hundred percent." He tried to make a call. "Call cannot be completed."

"Acknowledged. Maintain operational silence," Travis said then they waited.

At 8:45, the armored truck turned into the lot and parked in front of the store in perfect position. The bagman exited the vehicle and went into the store. Once again, Jackie engaged the jamming device. "C-Guard engaged," Jackie said.

"Acknowledged," Travis shot back. From that point, they waited. Minutes seemed to pass like hours as they sat patiently waiting for the bagman to reemerge from the store. Then, all at once, Travis's heart began to pound as he watched a red Honda Civic pull into the lot and park two cars down from Jackie. He looked on in horror as Me'shelle got out of the car and limped gingerly pasted Jackie's car.

"Damn, she's fine," Jackie said.

"Maintain operational silence," Travis said nervously.

"Acknowledged."

Travis became excited at the sight of Me'shelle in spandex and black leather, but his excitement turned once again to horror at the thought of what could happen. What if something went wrong or she came out of the store while they were taking the objective? Travis couldn't take the risk of anything happening that would place Me'shelle in danger.

"Abort!" Travis said frantically.

"What?" Ronnie turned to Travis. "What you mean abort?"

"Repeat your traffic, Mr. Blue," Jackie said.

"Abort! Abort!"

"Acknowledged, Mr. Blue. I'll meet you at the drop-off point," Jackie said as she started up the Toyota and exited the lot.

"What's wrong, Travis?" Ronnie asked as he started up the car.

"I got a bad feeling about this. We need to abort," Travis said to Ronnie.

"What kind of feeling? You see a cop or something?"

"It just doesn't feel right, Ronnie, okay?" Travis screamed.

"Okay, okay, chill the fuck out, Travis. We out of here."

As Ronnie left the parking lot, Travis looked back at the store and saw Me'shelle come out, talking to the bagman. This confirmed his greatest fear and provided justification for his actions.

Ronnie and Travis drove in silence to the drop-off point where Jackie was waiting in the Q45. Once they abandoned the Ford, Jackie drove to Murray's house to drop the car and pick up some money. Jackie and Ronnie remained outside while Travis went in to make the transaction.

"What was up with that?" Jackie asked Ronnie.

"I don't know. One minute he was cool, and the next thing he's hollerin' 'Abort!' like he lost his damn mind. Then he got all quiet. I don't know what's up with Travis," Ronnie said.

"Maybe he saw something," Jackie said.

"Maybe he's losing his nerve."

"Maybe, but whatever it is, we gonna have to watch Travis," Jackie said. " 'Cause I never seen him act like that."

"I have. Saturday night at the party. You didn't notice how he really wasn't into it?"

"Yeah, but I didn't think nothing of it, 'cause when I came out of the room, he was fuckin' the shit out Mystique," Jackie said and laughed as Travis came out of the house.

"Yo, look, I'm sorry about what happened. I just got a really bad feeling, that's all. It won't happen again," Travis said, but in the back of his mind he knew different.

It's time to find a way to make it out the game.

Chapter Ten

At 9:30 p.m., Bruce Lawrence parked his car across the street from The Spot and turned off the engine. The Spot was a private club run by a guy named Rocky, who also dealt for Chilly. It was the kind of place where ballers, wannabe ballers, thugs, low-rent gangsters and those hangers-on who just wanted to be down hung out. Chilly had told Bruce to meet him there at 10:00, but when Bruce arrived, he saw Chilly's car already parked down the street.

Bruce had known Chilly for years, and Chilly liked or at best felt sorry for Bruce. This gave Bruce the advantage of being able to go directly to Chilly for product instead of having to deal with his more ruthless underlings.

He sat there for a while wondering what he was going to do. As usual, he didn't have all of Chilly's money.

After he gathered his courage, Bruce got out of his car and went inside. The place was jammed, and the music was loud. Bruce made his way though the crowd, looking for Chilly without success. Finally, he decided to ask somebody where Chilly was. "He's in the back. In Rocky's office, waitin' for you."

That was the worst.

Bruce felt like he had a better chance of leaving alive if he talked to Chilly with a lot of people around. He'd seen people go in the office and not come out. Bruce began to think that maybe Me'shelle was right. Maybe he should go home, get Natalie and Brandy and leave the city until things cooled out. He could take the money he had and go down south to Columbia, flip that money and come back when he had all that he owed Chilly.

He turned around, headed for the door and walked right into Derrick Washington, Chilly's top lieutenant.

"Bruce, my man!" Derrick hollered over the music. "You're goin' the wrong way. Chilly's in the back. Come on."

Bruce followed Derrick as they made their way though the crowd, cursing all the way. Derrick opened the door to the office and stepped aside to let Bruce go in. *This is not good,* Bruce thought as he looked around the room filled with everybody he didn't want to see and one other man he had never seen before. Rocky was seated behind the desk and Chilly was sitting in one of the two chairs in front of the desk, with a young lady standing behind him.

Chilly was talking to the stranger, who sat quietly listening and nodding his head. The man looked like he didn't belong there nor did he want to be there, and Bruce could tell that he was scared. Suddenly, the man got up and started for the door. Just before he reached Bruce, Chilly called out to him. "Jake!"

The man stopped and turned to face Chilly.

"It's been six months, Jake. I need to start seeing some results. You understand me, Jake?"

The scared man nodded his head.

"I didn't hear you, Jake. Do you understand what I'm sayin', Jake?"

"Yes, Chilly, I understand you perfectly," the scared man answered and rushed quickly past Bruce and out the door.

All eyes were now on Bruce and Derrick. "Look what I found tryin' to make it out the door," Derrick said.

Chilly looked up and smiled when he saw Bruce standing there. He whispered something to the young lady and she left the room. When she closed the door behind her, Chilly motioned for Bruce to come forward. "What's up, Bruce? Come here and have a seat."

"What's up, Chilly?" Bruce said slowly.

"I know you got something for me," Chilly told him. "And I'm really not in the mood for your usual list of bullshit excuses."

Bruce reached into his pocket and handed Chilly the money he had for him. "It's only fifteen hundred. I know I owe you four, but I just need a couple of days to get rest." Bruce had another $1,500 in his pockets, which he would give up if it became absolutely necessary.

Chilly dropped his head. "You know what, Bruce? I knew this was a bad idea when I first started it. I should have passed you off to one of these muthafuckas years ago, but I felt some type of loyalty to you because you looked out for me with Gee when you was still working at the bank. You had a good thing goin' there, but you fucked that up because you couldn't keep your hands out that drawer. You're a fuck-up, Bruce, but I ain't tellin' you anything that you don't already know."

"I'm sorry, Chilly."

"Sorry for what? For being a fuck-up or for not havin' my money? Probably both," Chilly said and stood up. "You wanna know something, Bruce? It ain't even about the money. Shit, this little four grand we talkin' about ain't gonna make me one bit of difference. It's the fact that I trusted you, showed you respect, and this is how you've chosen to repay that, with more of your usual lyin'-ass bullshit."

"I know I'm fuckin' up, Chilly. But you know it ain't always been like this. I made money for you," Bruce pleaded his case.

"Made money for me? What, you think you the man 'cause you move an ounce or two every once in a while? Is that what you think? Shit!" Chilly yelled and slapped Bruce in his head. Everybody in the room laughed. It made Bruce feel like a fool—a fool who was about to die for four thousand dollars, most of which he and Natalie smoked themselves.

"I ain't the man, Chilly. I know that. All I'm sayin' is give me a few days to make my money back on what I got in the street. Chilly, please, that's all I'm askin' is for you to do that for me," Bruce whined.

Chilly looked at Bruce for a long time without speaking. He looked around the room, knowing that everybody was waiting to see how he was going to handle this matter not of money, but of respect.

Chilly stood over Bruce. Without a word, he punched Bruce in the face, knocking him out of the chair. When Bruce tried to get to his feet, Chilly stepped up and kicked him in the gut. "Help him up," Chilly commanded, and his orders were obeyed. "Hold him."

Chilly hit Bruce again. "I'm gonna give you a few days to make back the money on what you got in the street," Chilly whined the way Bruce did to the sound of more laughter. He hit Bruce again. "But this is as far as I'll carry you. Next time you fuck me," Chilly said as he hit Bruce again, "you die for it. And by the way, you can consider this money the interest on what you owe me. Next time I see you, you need to be handin' me four grand. You understand me, Bruce?"

"I understand."

After hitting Bruce a few more times, Chilly instructed his men to drag him out though the crowd to the front door and throw him out in the street.

Bruce lay in the street, thankful to be alive. He had counted on Chilly remembering his loyalty. What he wasn't counting on was the ass kicking he got, but he should have. There were too many people in the room for Chilly to just let Bruce walk out still owing him money.

Bruce made it to his feet and moved slowly to his car. Once he got inside, he knew what he had to do.

Chapter Eleven

Early Saturday morning, Travis was back in his spot outside the grocery store waiting for Me'shelle. It had been a very long week, one filled with questions not only from himself, but from Ronnie and Jackie as well. They weren't blatant with their questions or their accusations, but Travis knew they were thinking that he had lost his nerve. And maybe he had.

Even before he had seen Me'shelle, he knew that something had to change, but now things were different, much different. He had sacrificed not only the money but his honor and integrity with Ronnie and Jackie for Me'shelle. It wasn't because he was in love with her or anything like that. It was simply because he couldn't risk anything happening to the woman that he dreamed of every night before he got a chance to know her.

So he waited.

This time, Travis didn't have to wait long. At 9:47, he saw Me'shelle driving her car into the parking lot. He immediately jumped out of his car and hurried into the store. He wanted to be in there when she got in, instead of having to walk up on her like he was following her. Of course he was, but she didn't need to know that. Maybe one day he'd tell her, but it wouldn't be that day.

But where should he wait for her? The magazine rack? He turned his cart and started down the aisle. *Nah,* he thought, *too obvious. And suppose she doesn't come down that aisle.* Then it hit him. He could hear the smile in her voice as she said, "I see you have plenty of fresh fruits and vegetables." Travis turned around and walked as quickly as he could, still remembering the discipline of looking down each aisle as he passed. Once he reached the produce aisle and turned, Travis ran his cart right into Me'shelle's.

"In a hurry to get some where?" Me'shelle asked.

"No," Travis said. He was embarrassed, caught off guard and happy all at the same time. "Just trying to see to you again."

"See that. I knew you were following me," Me'shelle said and smiled.

"Huh," he said quickly, looking guilty. "How did you— I mean, I'm not following you."

Me'shelle looked at Travis strangely and then to the empty cart. "I was only kidding."

"Oh."

"So, how've you been?" Me'shelle asked.

Travis paused for second and looked in Me'shelle's eyes. Then he smiled and said, "Do you really want to know?"

"Yes, I really want to know." Me'shelle smiled back.

"So, you want me to tell you the truth?"

Me'shelle laughed. "Yes, I really want you to tell me the truth."

"[illegible]ndle the truth?" Travis asked

"Yes, Travis, I really can handle the truth," Me'shelle said, loving the fact that Travis seemed to have a sense of humor.

He took another step closer. "Well, Me'shelle, the truth is that ever since you rammed your shopping cart into me, I've thought about nothing but you. Each time I close my eyes I see your face and I dream the most delightful dreams of you each night when I sleep. The sound of your voice echoes in my ears all the time. So please, Me'shelle, tell me, can I take you out to dinner, could we go to the movies, take a walk in the park, have a cup of coffee together? Anything, Me'shelle, as long as you let me get to know you."

"Wow," was the only answer Me'shelle could come up with behind all that. She had to admit that in the last week she had spent more time than she believed she could have thinking about Travis. If she wanted to be honest with herself, and at times like this she usually didn't, she came to the store that day hoping to see him. It would only be fitting to tell him the truth since he broke out with his own little confession. But that wasn't about to happen. All that stuff was probably just a line anyway. "Dreaming about me, huh?"

"Every night."

"What kind of dreams?"

"Me'shelle, you'll have to go out with me to find that out."

"I don't know, Travis. Like I said, I really don't like going out with men who try to pick me up in grocery stores," Me'shelle told him, even though she remembered how he walked off the last time she said that.

"If it's being in the grocery store that's bothering you, we could go outside," Travis said and smiled.

"You know what I'm talkin' about, Travis. I don't go out with guys with pick-up lines. Even really good ones like yours."

"You know, Me'shelle, I can understand why you would say that. A beautiful woman like *you* probably gets guys hitting on her *all the time.*"

If you only knew, Me'shelle thought.

Me'shelle was a very beautiful woman. Most men were afraid to step to her for fear of rejection. That was the reason she had been alone these last 583 days. She didn't want to be Sister Mary-Me'shelle, but she was a lady. And her aunts had taught her that not only doesn't a lady allow men to pick her up in grocery stores, she never approaches a man. "A lady waits for a strong, self-confident black man to approach her, and always in a polite and mannerly way," Aunt Miranda always told her. It was a policy that she agreed with in principle, but it was that policy that earned her the name Sister Mary-Me'shelle. The truth of the matter was that she was lonely. And besides, it was getting cold outside and Me'shelle missed feeling the warmth of a man's body to curl up against on cold winter nights . . . or summer nights, or any nights, for that matter.

"I tell you what, Travis. Are you doing anything this evening?"

"No," Travis said quickly, though he promised Mystique he would come to the club that night since he'd been avoiding her all week.

"Do you want to meet me somewhere?"

"Yes, definitely. You pick the place and I'll be there."

"Okay. Why don't you meet me at the Starbucks on Metropolitan Avenue?"

"What time?"

"Is six good for you?"

"That would be perfect," Travis said gladly.

"Good, then I'll see you at Starbucks at six."

"Six o'clock it is. I'm looking forward to talking with you, Me'shelle," Travis said as he started to walk away, leaving his shopping cart behind.

"Travis," Me'shelle called to him. He stopped and turned around. "You forgot your cart."

Travis walked back toward her. "Me'shelle, seeing you made me forget what I came here for. But I guess I can put it back where I found it," he said and walked away again, leaving Me'shelle with a big smile on her face. For the first time since Trent told her that he thought they should start seeing other people, Me'shelle had a date.

As she continued her shopping, she thought about what she would wear on a date to Starbucks. *It's only Starbucks. That means it'll just be coffee and maybe some pastry. What does a lady wear to meet a gentleman for coffee and pastry?* She giggled to herself.

Travis arrived at Starbucks a little before 6:00 and stepped up to the counter. He looked over the menu of coffees and ordered a Mocha Valencia then waited impatiently for Me'shelle to arrival. Six o'clock came and went without incident. By 6:30, he had finished his coffee. He stood up and was just about to leave when Me'shelle walked through the door.

"Have you been waiting long, Travis?" she asked as if she were only a minute or two late.

"About a half an hour," Travis said. He wasn't sure which emotion was stronger, the anger he felt about waiting half an hour for her to show up, or joy that she was standing in front of him. Travis settled on the combination. "I hate waiting, but you are worth the wait. You look incredible tonight."

Me'shelle had decided to wear tight black jeans, a white turtleneck and her black leather jacket. "Thank you very much, Travis. You're looking very handsome yourself. What time did you get here?" she asked.

"About a quarter to six."

"It wasn't that bad," she said, looking at her watch. "It's only five after."

"Who taught you to tell time? It's six-thirty." Travis held out his arm so she could see his watch. She glanced at it and took a very deep breath. Hearing her breathe like that aroused Travis, but he maintained his composure.

"I'm sorry, Travis. My watch must be slow."

"It's cool. You're here now. Don't sweat it."

"You forgive me?" Me'shelle asked.

"Only if you promise to be a fascinating conversationalist."

Me'shelle smiled. She took another deep breath. Each time she did it, a chill ran through his body. Her sexuality was overwhelming. "I tell you what, Travis. I promise to be as fascinating a conversationalist as you are. You see, it takes two to tango. Just like it takes two to have an intelligent conversation. But I think it's only fair to warn you that I'm a sucker for an intelligent conversation."

"So am I," Travis replied, trying to sound intelligent and sure of himself. They walked to the counter together and ordered. "I'll have another Mocha Valencia." Travis looked at Me'shelle. Her eyes were driving him insane.

"And the lady will have?"

"Caramel Macchiato."

Once the coffee was prepared, Travis and Me'shelle took a seat at a table by the window. "I never had Caramel Macchiato before. What's in it?" Travis asked.

"Foamed milk with espresso, vanilla and real caramel. It's delicious. Have some?"

"No. I may try one next time I'm here," Travis said as he watched Me'shelle take a sip of her coffee. The sight of her lips on the cup moved him in ways no woman had ever moved him before—not even Mystique, and she had ways of moving a man. This was different.

Travis tried to rationalize that he was probably feeling this way because he had dreamed and fantasized about this woman so much. Now that he was finally here, he was probably just making more of it than there actually was. Travis quickly dismissed that thought.

Me'shelle was different.

"So talk to me, Travis. Tell me who you are."

"There's not much to tell. I came up right here in the Bronx. I went to college at University of Connecticut and became a programmer. Now I work for myself," Travis said, telling her as much of the truth as he could. He didn't think it was a good time to tell her that he was the leader of a robbing crew. "So, who are you, Me'shelle? I want to know everything about you."

"Well, let me see. I'll give you the short version. How about that?"

"Okay." Travis smiled.

"I was born in Queens, and my family moved to the Bronx when I was young. I'm a teacher. A third grade teacher, to be exact. But to be honest with you, Travis, I really don't like talking about myself. If you stay around me long enough, you'll find out everything you ever wanted to know."

"I hope it's a very long learning process. I think I'd enjoy getting to know you slowly."

"So, you're not one of those men who expects to have sex with me tonight? Who, after I sleep with him, slowly loses interest in me because my body is really all he was interested in?" Me'shelle asked, motioning with her hands as she said 'my body.'

Travis smiled and leaned forward, taking in with his eyes all of the body he could see above the table. "Was that a question or a statement?"

"It was definitely a question and a statement," Me'shelle said and smiled.

"Can I answer you honestly?"

"I think that you should."

"Me'shelle, you are the most beautiful woman I've ever known. And I've known some bad ones."

"Why thank you, Travis," Me'shelle beamed.

"You're welcome, Me'shelle. And to be very honest with you, I would love to make love to you. I've dreamed of making love to you." Travis let out a little laugh. "And a few other things that I can't and don't want to explain."

"But in time, I wanna hear about those too. I think that our dreams are an expression of what we really think and feel."

"I think so too. That's why I'm sitting here with you. But like I was saying, I would love to make love to you right here, right now."

Me'shelle closed her eyes for a second and quickly got a mental image of herself seated on the table with her arms around Travis's neck, her legs wrapped around his waist and Travis pumpin' it to her slowly. She opened her eyes and smiled.

"But I think that I want to know you, Me'shelle," Travis continued. "I want to know more about you than you know about yourself. And I want you to know all about me, so when I do make love to you—and I am going to make love to you—I'll be making love with you and to you, Me'shelle. Not just Me'shelle's body."

"Pretty sure of yourself, aren't you, Travis?"

"You said be honest. And besides, if I don't believe in myself, how can I ever hope to get you to believe in me and what I say?"

"I guess you can't." Me'shelle raised her coffee cup. "Here's to getting to know each other. I just hope that you mean what you say."

"Me'shelle, trust me. I mean everything I say," Travis said, pressing his cup against hers. "To getting to know you slowly."

With the flirtation and statement of intentions out of the way, they talked their way through coffee, doing much more talking than drinking. After a second cup and more conversation, Travis walked Me'shelle to her car. She unlocked the door but didn't get in. They talked at the car for another hour or so until Me'shelle attempted to drag herself away.

"I have to go." She laughed as she leaned against the car. Travis leaned shoulder to shoulder on the car next to her. Standing this close to Me'shelle excited him.

"Well, if that's the case, I'll make it easy for you. I'll say good night. I enjoyed my evening, Me'shelle."

"So did I," she said.

"Can I call you some time? I'd like to see you again."

"Why don't you give me your number and I'll call you," Me'shelle said. Travis quickly wrote down his number and handed it to her. "Well, Travis, thank you again. I really have enjoyed talking to you."

"So, does that mean you'll call me?"

Me'shelle smiled and opened the car door. "Maybe sooner than you think," she replied and got in.

As she drove away, Travis looked at his watch. They had been talking almost non-stop for more than three hours. Travis walked to his car thinking, *Now, that was an interesting conversationalist.*

Chapter Twelve

Sunday went as all Sundays did for Me'shelle. She got up early and hit the treadmill. She didn't fall this time, even though her thoughts were of Bruce. She hadn't seen or heard from him since she told him she wouldn't give him any more money to support his habit. His words rang in her ears once again. *How you gonna live with yourself when I'm dead?* Me'shelle pushed the thought out of her mind. She went to her aunt's house for Sunday dinner and while she was there, Bruce called to speak with her.

"What's up, Me'shelle?"

"Bruce, where have you been? I was worried about you. Is everything all right?"

"Worried about me, huh? But not worried enough to help me out, huh, Me'shelle? Anyway, I'm fine. We're all fine. We're down south."

"Down south? Down south where?"

"We're in Columbia, at Grandma's house," Bruce replied.

"Good. That's where you should stay. It might keep you out of trouble for a while."

"Yeah, maybe. But we'll just be down here for a couple more weeks until I get my shit back to where it needs to be."

"So, you're coming back?"

"Yeah, Me'shelle, I'm a New York City boy, and it's a little too country down here for me. Some of these niggas still rockin' Jheri curls. The women are cool, and fine as hell, though."

Me'shelle laughed. "Maybe slow and country is what you need to slow your ass down. Give yourself a chance to get yourself back together. Stop smoking that stuff before it kills you or gets you killed. And what about Brandy? Is she in school?"

"No," Bruce said flatly.

"Don't you think she needs to be?"

"Yeah, but she wasn't goin' to school too tough while she was up there."

"That's why you should have let Aunt Juanita get custody of her. Brandy doesn't need to be livin' that life with you and your dope fiend wife. She needs a chance, Bruce. Don't you see that she's on the wrong path now?"

"Yeah, yeah, sister Mary-Me'shelle. I understand all that. But I didn't call you to get a lecture. I just called to let you know where we were, that we're all right and that we'll be back in a couple of weeks."

"Well, thank you, Bruce. You know I was worried."

"You worry too much, Me'shelle. You should worry about findin' you a man before that pussy dries up and nobody wants your ass," Bruce said jokingly.

"You are so gross, Bruce, but you always have been. And for your information, I had a date last night."

"You're kiddin'. Well, it's about time you stop waiting for big head Trent to realize he made the biggest mistake of his life, leave the tittie woman alone and come back to you. It's time you get on with your life. So, who is this nigga?"

"His name is Travis Burns."

"Travis Burns . . . Travis Burns. Where have I heard that name before?" Bruce wondered aloud.

"I doubt you know him. He's not like the lowlifes you run around with. He's a programmer," Me'shelle said.

"Whatever, Me'shelle. Look, I gotta go. I don't wanna run up Grandma's phone bill."

"Okay, Bruce. Kiss Brandy and Grandma for me and tell them that I love them. And snatch the pipe out of Natalie's mouth and slap her upside the head for me," Me'shelle said.

"Bye, Me'shelle." Bruce laughed, thinking that she was right. Natalie did smoke too much and was the reason they were in the spot they were in.

"Bye, Bruce."

When Me'shelle got home, she took a long, hot bath and got ready for bed. Once she had made herself comfortable in bed, she called Travis. "Hello, Travis?"

"Yes."

"This is Me'shelle. How are you?"

"I'm fine, Me'shelle. How are you today?"

"I'm fine. Did I catch you at a bad time?" Me'shelle asked.

"No, not at all. I'm glad you called," Travis said, thankful that he told Mystique he was tired and didn't let her come get in the bed with him as she requested. "I was just sitting here working out the bugs in a program I'm going to run in the morning." He was actually working on the final details of the grocery store robbery that they planned on running in the morning. "But I was really just keeping myself busy, sitting by the telephone waiting for you to call."

"You know, Travis, you say the nicest things. Do you say things like that to every woman you meet?" Me'shelle asked.

"No, I don't. I don't meet women like you every day. There's something special about you, Me'shelle. I can't quite put my finger on it or give it a name, but it's something."

"So, tell me about these dreams of yours."

"No."

"Why not?"

"Because they're silly."

"Last night you said those dreams were the reason you were sitting there with me."

"They are, but they're still silly."

"Come on, Travis. I promise I won't tell anybody about them. It will be our little secret."

"Okay," Travis said sheepishly. "But you have to promise to share a secret with me. You promise?"

"Yes, I promise." Me'shelle giggled. It felt so good to laugh again.

"Okay. Don't laugh, okay?"

"I will if it's funny."

"After you attacked me with your cart, I used to have these dreams where I'd try to talk to you but something would always keep me from getting to you. So, one night I dreamed that I was on the D train and it's rush hour. You're on the train, too, but you're sitting across from me.

"There's a man sitting next to you. The next stop is Times Square and the man gets up and goes for the door. You say, 'Come sit next to me, Travis,' but when I get up, the doors open up and everybody rushes on the train and I can't get to you.

"So, when we get to Thirty-fourth Street, the doors open and some of the people get off, and now there are these two white girls sitting where you were. I look around for you and you're standing on the platform. I try to get off, but I run into the guy from the seafood counter at the grocery store. Once I get around him, the doors close in front of me. But even though the doors are closed, I can still hear you saying, 'Well maybe you should look where you're going.' "

By then, Me'shelle was laughing all over herself.

"Then you laugh, like you're doing now, and the train pulls off and your image fades away."

"You have got to be kidding me, Travis. You're just making this up, right? Tell me you just made that up," Me'shelle said, still laughing.

"I swear that I actually dreamed that about you," Travis said, laughing along with her.

Me'shelle tried to compose herself, but it wasn't happening. "You know, when you said you dreamed about me, I thought that you were going to say it was something sexual. You know, like we were doin' it on top of the Empire State Building or something like that. But I really wasn't prepared for us on the train," she said, still laughing.

"See, I knew you would laugh. And just so you know, some of my dreams of you were very sexual in nature, but they were far more creative then doin' it on top of the Empire State Building."

"Tell me about it."

"No."

"Why not?" Me'shelle laughed.

"Because you promised to tell me a secret about you," Travis said, hoping that was his way out of this conversation.

"You'll know all my secrets soon enough, Travis."

As the night wore on, Travis and Me'shelle talked. They talked about a little of everything. They had impassioned discussions on the state of black America. Like most black people, they agreed when identifying the problem, but came down on different sides of the fence when the conversation turned to a solution. Me'shelle, who had a somewhat liberal ideology, felt that the government should play more of a role in resolving some of the issues. Travis believed that black people, especially black men, should take personal responsibility for their condition and look inward to resolve those issues.

"There should be more programs to help people make their lives better," Me'shelle argued.

"You're talking about this government, right? This government do something to help black people? Live in reality. We need to stop going to Massa's house, tappin' on the back door, beggin' Massa, 'Please, give your niggras something.' No, Me'shelle, we as a people need to do it better, smarter and for ourselves. Take responsibility for our destiny."

"You're right. We should be doin' it a lot better than we are. But they caused our condition and maintain the environment where it is permitted to exist unchecked. They should do something to reverse it," Me'shelle pleaded, but Travis would have none of it.

"Where are your eyes, those beautiful eyes? Are they so clouded that you can't see that it's permitted to exist, as you say, by design? Do you think that politicians don't realize the impact of some of their decisions on black people? You think they don't know what's going on? That's why revolution is the only way."

"Revolution, Travis? Don't you think that's just a tad radical?"

"I'm talking about revolution of the mind. Free our minds of the slave mentality. An economic revolution; take control of the money that flows so freely out of our hands and into somebody else's, never to be seen or heard from again."

"That's right. Hit them where it hurts. Take money out of their pockets. It's the only thing they understand anyway."

Travis smiled. "Until we can look them in the eyes and trade greenback for greenback, we gets no respect."

"We're gettin' pretty intense for our first telephone conversation," Me'shelle said, but she loved it. Their conversation was stimulating her in more ways than just intellectually.

"I know how to end any discussion on the state of black America. Guaranteed to work without fail every time," Travis said.

"How's that?" Me'shelle asked.

"What should we do about it?" Travis asked.

Me'shelle didn't have an answer to that question. "You're beginning to interest me, Travis."

"Really? Tell me why."

"I don't know. You're not like most guys I've met. Not that I meet a lot of guys, but they're not at all like you."

"Yeah, but why, Me'shelle? What makes me so different?"

"You're very confident and self-assured, but not to the point of being arrogant. You know what I mean? It's like you know what you know and that's enough for you. It's not like you need to prove it to the world. You understand what I'm sayin' now?"

"I think I like that. I think I like you, too, Me'shelle, my belle."

"What did you call me?"

"Me'shelle, my belle. It's a line from an old Beatles song. The next line is in French, but I don't remember how it goes."

"My mother used to call me that when I was younger."

"I'd like to meet your mother some day," Travis said.

"She died when I was seven. Both my parents are dead."

"I'm sorry."

"My father died a few years ago," Me'shelle said with some sadness in her voice. Then she remembered what her aunt said about him being happy to get back to his Sabrina. "But they're together in a better place. What about you?"

"I lost my father a few years ago, too. My moms lives in Florida."

Me'shelle glanced at the clock by her bed. "Ooh, Travis, it's after one in the morning."

"Really?"

"Yup. We've been running our mouths for four hours."

"I guess we have a lot to talk about," Travis said.

"I guess we do. I guess we should say goodnight. I have to be at school at seven forty-five. I got spoiled last week."

"Really? Why was that?"

"We had a teachers' work day and I didn't have to be there until nine, but I ended up not going at all because I hurt my leg."

"How'd you manage that?"

"I slipped and fell off the treadmill," Me'shelle said. That answered Travis's question about why she was at the store at 8:45 that past Monday. And then the conversation took off in another direction. This happened twice more before Me'shelle said, "Look, it's almost three in the morning and I have to get up in three hours."

"But you are going to school in the morning? I mean, you're not going to fall off the treadmill and skip school, right?" Travis asked to be sure he wouldn't have to abort the job again because Me'shelle came to the store.

"No, I promise to be more careful this time and make it to school. I won't be any good, but I'm going."

"Good. So, I'll let you go to sleep."

"Good night, Travis."

"Goodnight, Me'shelle," Travis said and hung up the phone.

The next sound Travis heard was Jackie yelling, "Yo, Travis! Wake up! You gonna make us late."

"What?"

"Get the fuck up out the bed, nigga, and let's go do this," Ronnie shouted.

"Damn. What time is it?"

"It's almost eight, man. We gotta go," Jackie said.

"Yo, Travis, what's been up with you?" Ronnie asked. "It's like lately you haven't been up for it like you used to be. You ain't losin' your nerve, are you?"

"Where did that come from? Because I overslept, now you think I lost my nerve and shit? Give me a fuckin' break," Travis said as he got up and began to get dressed.

"It ain't just that, Tee. You been second-guessin' yourself, and you panicked last week," Jackie stated. "We just wanna know what's up."

"I did not panic. It just didn't feel right to me, that's all."

"Well, today I think I should call the job," Ronnie said. "Me and Jackie will go after the bagman. You set the jammer and cover the driver."

"So, it's like that?"

"This how it gotta be, Tee," Ronnie said. "Something ain't right about you, man. Maybe you lost your heart, maybe not. But this just how it gotta be today."

"What do you say, Jackie?"

"I think Ronnie's right. You have been actin' kind of funny lately. And whether you wanna admit it or not, you did panic last week. It didn't get no better than we had it last week, but you aborted. And you still can't say why, other than it didn't feel right."

Travis looked at his partners for a moment. He started to protest and proclaim that he had to call the job like he always did, but he knew they were right. He had aborted the job because he saw Me'shelle walk across the parking lot. He could have and probably should have waited to see how her presence was going to play into the mix of the job. After all, they had planned for the contingency of some customer entering their field of operations. He could have remained calm, but he panicked and called abort.

"Okay, if that's the way it's gotta be, then that's the way it is," Travis said. *Besides, Me'shelle promised to be careful on the treadmill and go to school. No reason to abort the job this time . . . I hope.*

Just as they had a week earlier, they arrived at the store and assumed their positions adjacent to the front of the store, waiting for the armored truck to arrive.

"Sound check. Mr. Blue?" Ronnie said.

"Sound check, one, two."

"Acknowledged. Mr. White?"
"Check, two, three, baby."
"Time check," Ronnie said with authority in his voice.
"Eight-thirty," Jackie replied.
"Eight-thirty, check," Travis said.
"Acknowledged. Weapons check," Ronnie said.
"Two loaded nine millers, check," Jackie said.
"One AK-47. Two nine millimeters check," Travis said.
"Acknowledged. One pump shotgun. Equipment check," Ronnie said.

Travis turned on the C-Guard. "C-Guard engaged," he said.

Jackie took out a cell phone and checked the screen for a signal. "Signal at one hundred percent." She tried to make a call. "Call cannot be completed."

"Acknowledged. Maintain operational silence," Ronnie said and they waited.

At 8:45, the armored truck turned into the lot and parked in front of the store in perfect position. The bagman exited the vehicle and went into the store. Travis engaged the jamming device. "C-Guard engaged," Travis said.

"Acknowledged," Ronnie said.

Travis looked out the window of the Geo Prism Jackie had stolen, waiting for the bagman to exit the store. He looked over at Ronnie and Jackie in their Pontiac. He checked his watch and thought, *Any second now*. The bagman came out with four bags. "Subject exiting store."

"Acknowledged, Mr. Blue. Assume cover position one and stand by," Ronnie said.

"Acknowledged, Mr. Green." Travis exited the vehicle and moved on the armored truck, as Ronnie and Jackie moved to intercept the bagman approaching the rear of the truck. Once Travis was in position, the driver saw him and attempted to call for backup.

When the bagman reached the rear of the truck, he saw Jackie and Ronnie coming toward him with guns drawn. He dropped the bags and reached for his gun. As he pointed the weapon, Jackie fired from both nine millimeters over the head of the bagman, hitting the truck. The bagman dropped his weapon and took cover on the ground behind the truck.

Meanwhile, the driver, who was unable to get anybody at the base station, started to get out of the truck. He jumped down from the truck with his gun drawn.

Travis stepped up. “Drop it!” He pointed the AK-47 at the driver. Ronnie, however, did not wait to see if the driver was going to comply with Travis’s order. Ronnie raised the pump and fired, hitting the driver in the chest.

Jackie quickly kicked the bagman’s gun under the truck and got the four bags. “Objective secured, Mr. Green,” Jackie said and went for the Pontiac. Both Ronnie and Travis maintained their cover positions.

Travis kept his AK-47 trained on the driver. There was a big hole in the vest he was wearing. From where Travis was standing, he couldn’t tell if the bullet went through. The driver was still moving, but that didn’t mean anything.

Jackie drove by and picked up Ronnie, who opened the rear door for Travis. He jumped in as the vehicle passed. They drove to the drop-off point and parked behind an Infinity X4 SUV. “What’s up with the SUV, Jackie?”

“Special request from Murray,” Jackie answered as they exited the Pontiac, took off their trench coats, and got in the SUV.

No one said a word while they traveled to Murray's. Jackie drove, Travis sat in the back seat with his head down, and Ronnie sat up front. Travis noticed how heavily Ronnie was breathing. "You all right, Ron?"

"I'm cool," Ronnie answered. But he wasn't. As much as he talked about it, this was the first time he'd ever shot anybody, and it had him shaken. Ronnie didn't know if the driver was dead. He tried to force the image from his mind, but he kept seeing the driver knocked off his feet from the impact of the 12-gauge round.

When they arrived at Murray's house, Travis and Ronnie got out and went straight to the clean vehicle. Jackie drove the SUV around the back of the house and went inside to make the deal with Murray. Since it was all prearranged, Jackie returned quickly with the twenty grand Murray had promised for delivery of the vehicle.

Once they got back to Travis's house, they sat around the dining room table and watched as Travis counted the money. They knew it was a lot, but they really weren't prepared for what Travis was about to say. "There is four hundred and fifty-six thousand dollars here."

"What?" Jackie and Ronnie both sat with their mouths wide open.

"That and the twenty grand Jackie got for the SUV, minus the forty-seven six we gotta give Freeze, leaves us with one hundred and forty-two thousand, eight hundred dollars each," Travis said to the sound of silence.

Chapter Thirteen

At noon, Travis sat by the phone waiting for a call. He had paged Freeze hours ago and still hadn't heard from him. He was restless and just a bit nervous. This was the biggest job they had ever run, and that worried him. What Travis thought would be a quick hit for some easy cash turned out to be nearly half a million dollars.

He reached for the television remote and turned to channel 7. As expected, it was the top story. Travis listened as the reporter spoke of the daring daytime robbery of an armored truck, which left one man hospitalized with injuries related to gunfire. Travis interpreted that to mean the bullet hadn't gone through the vest. The driver was only hurt by the fall he had taken from the impact of the bullet. Travis was glad that the man wasn't going to die.

Then something happened that caught him completely off guard. The entire robbery was captured on film by the store's parking lot cameras. Travis got up and poured himself a drink. How could he have missed the cameras in the parking lot? As much time as he had spent watching that lot, how could he have missed that? Then he began to ponder the possibility that he could have been caught on tape during one of his many surveillance runs through the parking lot.

The knockout punch came. A uniformed police sergeant appeared on camera to say that the three masked suspects involved in this robbery appeared to be the same three suspects in a jewelry store robbery last month in Manhattan.

Travis was hot, and he knew that he didn't want to be sitting around with $142,000 of stolen money in the house. In the past, he was able to get money into his account in the Caymans though one of Ronnie's Wall Street contacts. This was too much cash, though, to trust in anybody's hands but his. Travis paged Freeze again, and this time he called right back.

"I need to see you," Travis told Freeze.

"Yeah, I know. Met me at the 205th Street train station in thirty minutes," Freeze said and hung up.

Travis packed up the money, a few clothes, got the title for his car, and headed out the door, cursing all the way. *How the fuck could you have missed that?* Thirty minutes later, Travis was standing on the platform at the 205th Street train station, which was the last stop on the line, waiting for Freeze to arrive.

When the train arrived at the station, Freeze got off and approached Travis. The two men embraced as black men do, and Travis discreetly handed Freeze an envelope. "That's forty-seven six," Travis said.

Freeze smiled. "You're hot."

"I know this."

"Who did the shooting?"

"Ronnie," Travis replied, knowing how Freeze would take it.

"Figures. You need to lay low for a while."

"What I got to do is get this money out of the country as soon as possible. I need to go to the Cayma—" Freeze cut him off quickly.

"I don't need to know all that. You get to Miami. When you get there, you go to a private charter service called Pete's. You talk to Pete personally. You tell him that Mike Black sent you, and if he gives you any shit, which he won't, remind him that he owes Black a favor You understand?"

"I understand."

"Good luck," Freeze said then got back on the train.

Travis drove south doing the speed limit until he was too tired to go any farther. He got off of Interstate 95 at David McLeod Boulevard, Exit 160-A in Florence, South Carolina, and checked into a Red Roof Inn for the night.

When he got settled into the room, Travis called to check his messages. Both Jackie and Ronnie had called him several times, wondering where he was. Each wanted to talk for obvious reasons, which they didn't go into over the phone.

Me'shelle had called, too, and she left her number. This made Travis smile for maybe the first time that day. As much as he wanted to call her right away, he thought it would be best to call Jackie first. He went to a pay phone and called Jackie. "I'll call you back in ten minutes," she said.

Jackie went to a pay phone and called Travis back. He explained that he was out of town on business and would return in a day or two. "We'll all get together and talk things through when I get back. In the meantime, try to relax. Everything is gonna be fine. But maintain all security protocols until further notice."

"Okay, Tee. I'll do that, but this is fucked up."

"I know, Jackie, I know. How is Ronnie?'

"He is on fire," Jackie replied. "But I'll keep him in check until you get back."

"Do that. And keep him away from Freeze," Travis said and hung up the phone. Then he went back to the room and called Me'shelle. "Hello, Me'shelle. This is Travis. I hope it's not too late to be calling you."

"Well, actually it is, Travis, especially on a school night. But for you I'll make an exception this one time. How are you?"

"I'm good," he lied. "Out of town on business. I should be back in a day or two."

"Really? Where are you?"

Travis paused. "In South Carolina, but I'll end up in Miami." He didn't think it was necessary to tell Me'shelle where he was going or why. However, he did give some thought to the mountain of lies he was building.

"I've never been to Miami," Me'shelle said.

"Well, if this wasn't a school night, I'd invite you down, show you the town."

"Can I have a rain check?"

"But of course. Any time. Any time you want to go anywhere, all you have to do is say so," Travis boasted.

"So, you got it like that, huh?"

Travis looked over at the suitcase filled with money and smiled. "I do all right. I'm not a rich man or anything like that, but I can afford to do most of the things that I want to do."

"It's not like that for me. Don't get me wrong; I love kids and I love teaching them. I get real satisfaction knowing I have a hand in shaping their futures, so it motivates me to do the best job I can. I just wish it paid more."

"Maybe I'm just stupid like that, but I think you and all teachers have the most important job in the world. I think your job is much more important than some guy who calls himself a CEO, whose biggest decision is what time to tee off. I think you should get paid based on level of importance. But like I said, I'm just stupid like that."

"No, I don't think so. I think you got it right. But anyway, you're not gonna have me up all night talkin' my head off like you did last night. I'm going to say good night. Call me tomorrow, but please, make it a little earlier, okay?"

"Okay, Me'shelle. Maybe when I get back you'll do me the honor of having dinner with me."

"I would be happy to."

"Good night, Me'shelle"

"Good night, Travis."

Me'shelle drifted back to sleep thinking of traveling to new and different places. She had never been anywhere except Columbia to visit her grandmother during the summer. Those trips ended when her mother died. She had planned to go to Jamaica with her girlfriends one summer, but that was the year her father died and she just wasn't feeling it. Since then, Me'shelle hadn't left New York, not even across the bridge to New Jersey.

It wasn't that she didn't want to go anywhere or that she was afraid to fly or anything like that. She just never had the time. When she wasn't teaching during summer break, Me'shelle would volunteer to work with children in one program or another. It was her way of giving back.

She also never had anyone who wanted to travel with her. During her years in a relationship with Trent, he was the one who never wanted to go anywhere. He would always ask, "Why do we need to leave New York when everything you could ever want to do is right here?"

She fell asleep with a smile on her face, thinking about how eager Travis seemed to travel with her.

Meanwhile, back in the Bronx, Jackie met Ronnie at Cynt's. When she got there, Ronnie was sitting alone at the bar, not surrounded by dancers as he normally would be after a job.

Jackie stepped up to the bar and motioned for Sammy. "Henny straight up, and one for my friend here," she said. As Sammy went off to pour the drinks, Jackie turned to Ronnie. He had been there for hours and had already had his share of Hennessey. "I talked to Travis."

"Where the fuck is he?" Ronnie asked.

"Somewhere in South Carolina."

"What the fuck is he doing there?"

"Says he down there on business and he'll back in a couple of days."

"This nigga gone and we in some fucked up shit up here!" Ronnie said.

"You ain't gotta get loud about it. I know the shit is fucked up."

"We were on the fuckin' news, Jackie. The fuckin' news. How the fuck could he have missed some fuckin' cameras in the fuckin' parking lot, Jackie? You tell me that shit. Travis is slippin'! You hear me?"

"Yeah, I hear you. Your voice carries. Keep it down before you get us put out of here. These niggas don't need to know our business."

"Fuck that. Let them try to put my ass out this muthafuckin' place, as much money as I spend off in this bitch. That nigga is slippin' and he gonna get us all fucked up."

Jackie leaned close to Ronnie. "Let me ask you a question. You were in that lot twice. Did you see any damn cameras? I didn't."

"No, but that ain't my fuckin' job."

"I went there while we were in the planning stages and I didn't see anything."

"Travis is supposed to see all that shit and plan for it."

"He can't see everything, Ronnie. That's why he brought us in on the planning, so we could be on the lookout for shit like that too."

"I don't give a fuck," Ronnie said. "Look, Jackie, Travis been actin' real funny for the last couple of weeks. He missed that camera shit, and now he's gone. What's up with that?"

"You sayin' he did that shit deliberately then bounced on us?"

"That's how it looks to me."

"That's because you're drunk, Ronnie. You've known Travis just as long as I have, so you know he's not like that. We've gone too far and too fuckin' long together," Jackie said, grabbing Ronnie by his shirt, "for you to believe some shit like that. Come on. Let me take you home." Jackie pulled Ronnie's arm. He jerked it away.

"I can walk," Ronnie said, stumbling off the barstool.

"Yeah, just not straight." Jackie laughed.

"All I know is that nigga ain't right, and if he ever come back, we gotta watch him."

Even though he was tired, Travis still couldn't sleep. He tossed and turned all night, only drifting off to sleep for a while before waking up again to look at the clock. At

7:00 a.m., Travis was back in the car. He had breakfast at a nearby IHOP then headed for Miami.

As soon as he arrived in Dade County, he called Pete's charter service. Unfortunately for Travis, the woman who answered the phone said that Pete wasn't available and wouldn't be until the next day. "Do you want to leave a message for Pete?" the woman asked.

"No."

After getting the address and directions, Travis continued his ride south on I-95 and got off at Biscayne Boulevard. He checked in at the Riande Continental, the hotel where he usually stayed when he was in Miami. Once he was satisfied that his money was secure, he changed his clothes and walked across the street to the Bayside Marketplace.

He went to the Latin Grill, which featured Cuban style cuisine. He sat alone enjoying a zesty Palomilla steak while he contemplated his situation. Finally, Travis began to relax. He recognized that if he continued to make decisions in his current state of mind, he would make the kind of mistakes that would get him caught. He convinced himself that there really was no need for the panicked state he was in. With a clearer head, Travis realized that this trip was going to take longer than he thought it would. *And why not spend a couple of days in the Caymans?*

After he finished his steak, Travis wandered around the marketplace and picked up a few things to wear in the Caymans. As he was passing the Silver Palace, a necklace caught his eye. He went in and bought it for Me'shelle. He stopped in the Hard Rock Café, then Fat Tuesday's, and had a drink in each before ending up at Sharkey's. While he was there, Travis met and had a very interesting conversation with an attractive Hispanic woman named Marita, who was having drinks at the bar.

As he was getting ready to leave, Travis told Marita that he was staying at Riande Continental. He gave her the room number. "If you're not doing anything later this evening, stop by."

He started to go back to his room to relax but ended up at a strip club called Black Gold on Biscayne Boulevard. Once that grew old, he headed back to his room and called Me'shelle.

They stayed on the phone talking for over an hour. Travis told her that he had bought her a souvenir and would give it to her over dinner when he returned to New York.

"Thank you, Travis. You know you didn't have to do that."

"I know, but I wanted to. As soon as I saw it, I thought that you would like it."

"Oh, really? What is it?"

"It's a surprise," Travis said.

"Well, that will give me something to look forward to." Me'shelle paused. "Along with dinner," she said quickly.

"For a minute there I thought that you were looking forward to seeing me," Travis said, hearing the smile in her voice.

"Maybe just a little. I like talking to you. I don't think that I've ever enjoyed talking to somebody as much as I've enjoyed talking to you."

"Well, Me'shelle, the feeling is mutual."

"Well, Travis, I'm going to say goodnight now," Me'shelle said.

MOB

"Do you have to hang up now?" Travis asked just as a he heard a knock at his door. He had a good idea who it was. "But I understand that you have to mold young minds in the morning, so I'll let you go. I'll call you tomorrow." The knocking continued and got louder.

"Okay, Travis." Me'shelle yawned. "Good night."

Travis hung up the phone and went to open the door. He swung the door open and as he expected, Marita stood before him.

"Can I come in?"

Chapter Fourteen

At 9:00 the next morning, Travis had said goodbye to Marita, checked out of the hotel, and was standing in a used car lot. The dealer looked over the Thunderbird and offered Travis a thousand dollars for it. "Sold," Travis said then signed over the title. He thought it best that he get rid of the car just in case the police reviewed the tapes of the parking lot and were looking for his car.

He caught a cab to Pete's charter service and went inside. He approached the man behind the counter. "What can I do for you?" Pete asked with his typical *not another nigger* look on his face.

"I'm looking for Pete," Travis said

"That's me. What can I do for you?"

"Mike Black sent me. I need to charter a plane to the Cayman Islands."

Pete looked at Travis strangely, then it hit him. "Oh yeah, Mike Black," Pete said when he remembered who Mike Black was and how Angelo Colette said to treat him. "You tell Mr. Black that I'll be more than glad to take you there."

"He'll be glad to hear that," Travis said, laughing to himself because Mike Black wouldn't know him from a can of paint.

"When do you want to leave?"

"As soon as possible."

"Any cargo going or comin' back?"

"Just my luggage."

Pete looked strangely at Travis again, wondering how these niggers made money. Trips of this sort were usually in and out, coming back with cargo. *These guys act like they're going to take a vacation.* "Do you want me to wait for you?"

"No." Travis thought for a second or two before instructing, "Come back for me on Friday morning if that's not too much trouble."

"No problem." He told Travis his fee, and Travis paid in cash. Pete counted the money twice. "Have a seat. I'll come get you when the plane is gassed and ready for takeoff."

Once the plane landed at the airport in George Town, Grand Cayman Island, Travis asked Pete if he knew someplace nice where he could stay. "Naw," Pete said. "I don't know a place to stay here." Travis took a look at Pete in his beat-to-shit flight suit and his two-day growth of beard, and wasn't surprised. "Wait a minute. I do know of a place. It's called The Pools. It's in Kaibo in Rum Point on the north side of the island. They got them beachfront condos out there. I flew a business exec down here a couple of months ago. Older guy, probably cheatin' on his wife. Anyway, that's where him and his little chippie stayed. She was a one of them high-class pretty blond gals. So I figure it must be someplace nice."

"Thanks. I'll check it out, Pete. I'll see you Friday morning."

After a lengthy ride around the coastal areas of Grand Cayman Island, the taxi driver made it to Rum Point. The cab pulled up in front of The Pools. Travis was very surprised and very impressed. *He wasn't expecting much from Pete's* referral of someplace an old man visited with his mistress. He went inside and the clerk described the property.

“The Pools feature fully furnished and smartly equipped one bedroom, one bath vacation properties. Our rooms are specifically designed with a private screened pool on your lanai, with ultra large sliding doors that fully open up the bedroom, living area and kitchen to a magnificent view of the beach and North Sound. You are about fifteen steps from the pool to the warm, relaxing water and soft, sandy white beach. It is located on the very end of The Pools development, making for a very private setting. Your room will be shaded under palm trees, and enjoys consistent trade winds that come across from Rum Point. Would you care to see a unit, sir?”

“Yes, definitely. Lead the way,” Travis said and followed the attendant.

Once he reached the condo, he went on to explain, “The condo has a king-sized bed in the master bedroom, with a large sleeper built into the living area couch, making for comfortable accommodations for up to four adults.”

“I don’t plan on having that much company.” Travis smiled.

“But it’s good to have and don’t need, yes? Come, let me show you, the unit has cable TV, stereo, and a phone. There are ceiling fans in the bedroom and living area, along with central air conditioning. The condo has a fully equipped kitchen with all the modern appliances. The laundry room has a full size washer and dryer, and the condo comes equipped with linens and towels, along with basic toiletries for your use. Chisholm’s grocery is just a seven minute drive down the road.”

“I’ll take it.”

Once Travis was finished with the check-in process and was alone in the condo, he stepped out on the lanai to look at his private screened-in pool. He gazed out at the beach and exclaimed, "This is the shit!"

When he calmed down, he thought about calling Jackie or Ronnie to see what was up. Then he thought it was a better idea to page Freeze. Freeze called him right back on his cell phone.

"What's up?" Freeze asked.

"You tell me."

"It's all good in this corner of the world. Your crew been up at Cynt's the last couple of nights. I hear your boy Ronnie was drunk. I talked to Jackie for a minute last night. Her fine ass says it's all been good on her end. Every time I see her I think what a waste. She don't fuck no men?"

"Not that I know of," Travis said and smiled.

"What a fuckin' waste. Anyway, you back in town yet?"

"No. I'm in the Caymans. Just got here, in fact."

"Pete take good care of you?"

"Yeah, man. No problems there. He's coming back for me on Friday," Travis said.

"Good. Anything else?"

"No. I just called to holla, see what was up. We'll talk when I get back."

With that call out of the way, Travis found time to relax. He gave some thought to catching a cab back into George Town to rent a car, but decided against it. Instead, Travis walked to Chisholm's grocery to pick up a few things he'd need for his stay.

He took a cab back to The Pools and put in a call to Veronica Evans. She worked in investment and special services at National Commercial Bank, where Travis kept his money. In her position she handled demand and time deposits in all major currencies, investment advisory services, and spot and forward trading in the foreign exchange markets. Travis had talked with her many times over the past two years, and there was always a very sexual undertone to their conversations.

When Travis told her that he was on the island, Veronica asked him to meet her for dinner in George Town at a restaurant called Paradise. "It is the best place to enjoy the true Cayman sunset overlooking the harbor at Eden Rock," Veronica told him.

Travis was excited to meet the woman who had the most adorable West Indian accent he'd ever heard. He waited at the oceanfront bar for her to arrive. "Travis?" Veronica said as she approached him at the bar.

As soon as he heard her voice, Travis turned around quickly and stood up. "Veronica?"

"I know it was you the minute I see you sitting there. You look exactly like you sound," Veronica said.

Travis looked her over and a smile slowly came across his face. "Please, have a seat," he said. Veronica sat down next to him at the bar. "You don't look anything like I pictured you."

"What you think I look like? No, let me guess. You thought I was a little skinny something, right?"

Travis smiled and nodded. "That's exactly right."

"Everyone I have conversation with by phone is surprised when they see me." Veronica laughed. She wore her hair in short dreadlocks, which seemed to fit her attractive face and full lips. Her dark skin was radiant in the island sun. But what brought the smile to Travis's face was her body. Her hips and her chest screamed for attention. Veronica stood five feet ten inches tall and had the type of body that used to be called a *brick house*. She was very well put together, dressed in a blue-skirted business suit and white blouse, which by this time was buttoned down.

"So, tell me the truth, Travis. Are you disappointed in what you see?" she asked, leaning forward to give him a view of her ample cleavage.

"Not at all." Travis leaned closer to her. "In fact, seeing you makes me wish I had made this trip much sooner," he said, smiling all over himself.

For the next hour or so, they had drinks at the bar and Veronica told Travis about life at the bank. "NCB is a subsidiary of National Commercial Bank of Jamaica. I was transferred in when a mutual fund company acquired just over seventy-five percent of the share holdings in the bank," she said.

"Jamaica. Is that where you're from?"

"Yes. I am from Saint James Parish."

"Saint James Parish? I've never heard of that."

"It very near to Montego Bay," Veronica answered.

"I've been to Jamaica a few times."

"Have you now? What part you been to?"

"I've been to Montego Bay, to Kingston, and Negril."

"You know, as many times as you've been there, you really not been to there 'til you go with somebody who from there. You see, you probably spend all of your time at whatever resort you went to. Am I right?"

"You're right. We went on the little resort sponsored shopping trip, but they try to have enough going on so you stay in the resort."

"They don't want you rich Americans spending too much of your money outside the gate. Maybe somebody else make some money other than them," Veronica said.

After a bit more small talk, they were seated at a table with a view of the setting sun for dinner. "Do you know what you want?" Travis asked as they looked over the menu.

Veronica smiled at Travis. "I always know exactly what I want."

"And what might that be, Veronica?"

"A very juicy cut of filet mignon," Veronica replied, looking into his eyes. "It's called Filetto Al Pepe Verde, and it's served with our homemade peppercorn sauce," she said slowly and deliberately. "What about you?"

"I'm was thinkin' about the New Zealand rack of lamb. But you've got me feelin' the Mermaid Surf n' Turf platter. You know, that big steak and jumbo shrimp combination, grilled to perfection, served with a guacamole sauce," Travis said, keeping the tone of the flirtation.

After dinner and not so polite dinner conversation was finished, Travis asked about the nightlife.

"There's a place called Bamboo that's nice. It's located at the Hyatt Regency Hotel."

"What kind of place is it?" he asked.

"You go there for an upscale kind of sophisticated atmosphere. It's a sushi bar and lounge. Do you like sushi, Travis?"

"I love to eat sushi, but not right now."

"Or there's The Matrix. They have a DJ that plays hip-hop and reggae. Or we could go to Bed."

"I beg your pardon?"

"Travis, honey, if you could only see the look on your face." Veronica laughed. "Bed is a cozy little lounge on the Harquail Bypass, where the drinks are served by waiters in silk pajamas."

"You are too much, girl."

"No, me just enough."

Travis and Veronica ended up at The Next Level on West Bay Road near the Marriott, where the pair danced to reggae music. It was a little after 1:00 in the morning when Veronica arrived in Rum Point and pulled up in front of Travis's condo to drop him off.

"Do you want to come in?" Travis asked as he got out of her car. He leaned in the window. "It's a long ride back."

"But it will be a longer ride if I come in," Veronica said. "I must work in the morning, and we have business to transact at the bank."

Travis laughed. "Okay, Veronica. I'll see you tomorrow."

Chapter Fifteen

The following morning, Travis arrived at the bank dressed like a tourist, complete with a camera around his neck. After a bit of flirtatious small talk and comments about Travis's attire, Veronica personally assisted him in depositing $140,000. Once the transaction was complete, Veronica asked Travis what his plans were for the day. He had made arrangements to take a bus tour of the island, after which he planned to relax at the beach by the condo.

"You can take my car, as long as you come back for me at five," she offered.

Travis gave it some thought, but declined her offer. "I really don't feel like driving here. That's why I didn't rent a car. The whole left side driving thing is kind of freaky to me, you know."

"I understand. To be honest, most of our accidents are from you Americans renting cars. So, can we get together tonight?" Veronica asked.

"Oh, no doubt. Why don't you come by the condo tonight? I'm sure we'll find something to get into."

"That's sound good to me. Say around nine?"

"Sounds like a plan is coming together. See you around nine, Veronica," Travis said as he headed out of the bank. "Oh yeah. Bring some swimwear."

From then on, Travis was a tourist. The money was now safely in his account, which brought the balance to just over $200,000. He stopped at the first bar he found and had a couple of strong tropical drinks before proceeding to the tour bus.

While waiting to board the tour bus, Travis struck up a conversation with two British women who were visiting the island from York, a borough of North England. Once the tour began, the group was driven around the island to the many points of interest. Travis and his English companions took quite a few digital photos of themselves and the sights.

"The Cayman Islands were first sighted by European explorers on 10 May, 1503," the tour conductor told the group, "owing its existence to a chance wind that blew Christopher Columbus's ship off course." He continued to tell the story of the islands' discovery, and the origin of the name Cayman Islands. "By 1530, the name Caymanas was being used. It is derived from the Carib Indian word for the marine crocodile, which is now known to have lived in the islands. This name, or a variant, has been retained ever since." He went on to describe the settlement of the islands, including their history of slavery. Travis appreciated the history lesson, but was looking forward to relaxing that afternoon.

Once the tour concluded, Travis spent the rest of the afternoon hanging out on the beach with the two English women. Once the sun went down, he made his way back to Rum Point. He looked at the clock and thought this would be a good time to call Me'shelle.

"Well, this is a surprise."

"How you doing, Me'shelle?" Travis asked.

"I'm doing fine. I guess I don't have to ask you how you're doing. I know you're having a good time. So good a time that you forgot to call me yesterday," Me'shelle said. Then she flipped it. "I'm just trippin' with you, Travis. I'm glad you're enjoying yourself in Miami."

"Actually, Me'shelle, I'm not in Miami."

"Where are you? Back in New York?"

"No. I'm in the Cayman Islands."

"What? You're in the Cayman Islands? What are you doing there?"

"Just tying up some loose ends from the last job I did."

"Oh, now I'm mad at you. Did you know it snowed here today? It never snows this early in the winter. It was just a few inches, but still, it snowed. So, you're down there, having fun in the sun while I'm here in the snow. You're probably calling me from the beach right now, aren't you?"

"No, Me'shelle, I'm not on the beach. The sun went down about an hour ago. But the condo I'm staying in has a screened-in lanai with my own private pool."

"I hate you, and I never want to see you again," Me'shelle said.

"Oh, so it's like that?"

"No." Me'shelle smiled. "But it should be. I don't like the cold."

"You wanna come down here for the weekend? I'll send you a ticket."

"No, Travis. I don't know you that well."

"Are you sure, Me'shelle? I could call my guy and tell him not to come until Sunday. There's a couch that turns into a bed. You could have the bedroom. I promise to be a perfect gentleman."

"Your offer is tempting, Travis, but I don't think it's appropriate for me to come to the islands to meet, not to mention stay with a man I barely know."

"I can respect that."

"I know a lot of women who would jump at the chance to fly to the Caymans to stay with a handsome man in a condo with a private pool."

"So do I," Travis said quietly.

"I heard that. So, why didn't you?"

"Why didn't I what? Bring a woman down here with me?"

"Yes. Why didn't you?" Me'shelle asked. "Or are you one of those people who doesn't like to bring sand to the beach?"

"No, it's not that." Travis thought carefully about what his answer would be. He really wanted to answer her question honestly. "I'm here alone for two reasons. One, I'm here to handle some business. Two, there's nobody in my life I feel enough for to want to bring them along on a trip like this."

"Then why did you invite me?"

"Because I think there's a chance that you just may be somebody I could feel that way about," Travis answered. He thought about what he just said, then he thought about Marita, his one-night stand in Miami. The last time he talked to Me'shelle he rushed her off the phone to let Marita in.

He looked at the clock next to the bed. It was 8:30 p.m. In thirty minutes, Veronica would be there, and he had every intention of stripping her juicy body down. Then he thought about Mystique. What was he going to do with her? *Is this how a man acts when he thinks he's found the one?*

"I don't know about all that, Travis," Me'shelle said as if she heard the question. "I like you. I enjoy talking to you more than I've enjoyed talking to anybody in a long time." She thought about Trent. Wasn't this how things started with him too? *Maybe this is how it always begins.*

When they met, Me'shelle thought Trent was the most fascinating man she'd ever met. Two days later she was bent over her couch and Trent was inside her. After a few months, his stories got old and all sounded the same. Before they broke up—*you mean before he dumped you for the tittie woman*—he seemed like the shallowest man she'd ever met. But she thought she was in love with him. Maybe it was just that she got comfortable with him and didn't like being removed from her comfort zone. Me'shelle had spent a lot of time thinking about that very thing, and she didn't have the answer—at least not yet.

"I'm not saying that I'm the answer to all your questions, but can I tell you what I'd like to do with you, Me'shelle?"

"Go ahead."

"I'd like to have a chance to take my time and see if you can be all that I think you are."

"I like the part about taking your time. That sounds really good to me. I've rushed into relationships before and I've gotten my feelings hurt every time. So, as much as I like you, Travis, I'm going to take it really slowly with you."

"Are you still gonna have dinner with me when I get back?"

"No doubt. I'm looking forward to it," Me'shelle said.

"So, if I call you from Miami, will you pick me up tomorrow night from the airport?"

"It depends on what time, but yes."

"Good," Travis said happily. "I'll call you from Miami."

"Okay."

MOB

"Good night, Me'shelle, my belle."
"Bye, Travis."

a story by roy glenn

Chapter Sixteen

Travis hung up the phone, stretched out on the bed and closed his eyes. It wasn't long before he had fallen asleep. He was awakened suddenly by a loud noise. He looked at the clock; it was 10:30. He got up and made his way to the door.

"I bet you thought I wasn't coming," Veronica said.

"No. To be honest with you, I fell asleep," Travis said as his eyes began to focus on the woman standing before him with her arms extended. She wore a white cotton dress and carried a bottle of champagne in one hand and a big purse in the other.

Veronica handed the bottle to Travis. "A little something to celebrate your last night on the island," she said as she passed.

"Dom Perignon '93."

"I see you already have on your trunks. Why don't you pour us a glass and wait for me in the pool?"

Before Travis could say another word, Veronica disappeared into the bathroom. Travis shrugged and went in the kitchen to pour himself a glass of Henny. He'd noticed that there was a champagne bucket in the cabinet. He filled it with ice, got two glasses, and headed out the sliding door to the pool.

He dimmed the light around the pool and turned the water temperature up just a bit before he stepped in. He poured the champagne and sat patiently in the pool slipping Henny, waiting for Veronica to make her appearance.

Finally she appeared, still wearing that same white dress. Veronica came though the door and walked slowly toward the pool. "Did I take too long, Travis?" she asked as she let the dress drop to the ground. "I brought a bikini with me as you asked me to." She stepped into the water. "And I had started to put it on, but I say, for what? So I can take it off in a few minutes?"

Travis handed her a glass of champagne and Veronica immediately poured it out across his chest. She slowly ran her tongue across his chest until she consumed every drop, all the while rubbing the bulge in his trunks. Travis leaned his head back and closed his eyes. Me'shelle's image appeared in his mind's eye. He heard Me'shelle say, *Pleasure me, Travis*.

Travis reached between Veronica's legs and ran his hand through her hair as he fingered her clit. Veronica stood up and reached for the bottle. She poured herself a glass and took a sip. "This is very good champagne," she said then put down her glass.

She walked to the middle of the pool as Travis watched. Then she smiled and went under the water, swimming toward him. Once she got to him, she pulled off his trunks before coming up for air.

Veronica stood in front of him, gliding her hand up and down his staff. Travis grabbed her hips and lost himself in her chest, licking and gently sucking her huge, dark nipples.

She reclaimed her glass, took another sip, and poured the rest on her chest for Travis to lick off. Veronica straddled Travis and eased herself down on his length. She rode Travis slowly while he continued to feast on her nipples. Travis began to feel her legs trembling on his thighs, and he pushed harder. Veronica bared down on him and increased her pace. She could feel that she was about to climax, and she wasn't ready to. She reached out and touched his face with both hands and kissed him.

Veronica stood up and held out her hand. "Let's go inside," she said.

She led Travis out of the water and into the bedroom. She kneeled down on the edge of the bed.

"Damn, you have a pretty ass, Veronica," Travis said, sliding his hands across it.

"Thank you, Travis."

Travis placed his hands on her wide hips and entered Veronica slowly. No matter how hard he tried, he still couldn't get the image of Me'shelle out of his mind. He was gliding in and out of her slowly. Veronica was very wet, and she had excellent control of her muscles.

Veronica rolled over, and Travis eased her on her back and entered her. He placed the weight of his body on his arms and Veronica arched her back, rotating her hips in perfect unison with him. Moving slowly, then fast, then slowly again. Her body began to quiver as she stretched out her legs, seeming to anticipate his movements. Their heartbeats quickened along with the pace, until their bodies shook and she screamed, "Oh, Travis!"

Chapter Seventeen

New York's Kennedy Airport was as busy as it's always been. Travis stood in the lobby looking out the window, wishing he had brought a heavier coat along when he left for Miami on Monday. He had called Me'shelle from Miami and told her that he would be arriving at 7:35 that evening. Me'shelle promised to be there to meet him in the baggage claim area. Now it was steadily approaching 9:00 and there was no sign of her.

Several times he'd considered calling Ronnie or Jackie to come get him, but he didn't want to call them and have Me'shelle pull up right after he hung up the phone. Besides, it was only Me'shelle that he wanted to see. Travis checked his messages both at home and on his cell phone to see if Me'shelle had left a message, which she hadn't.

After two hours of creeping along, traffic on the Van Wyck Expressway finally broke loose. This was one of the few times that Me'shelle regretted not having a cell phone. She knew that Travis was probably standing outside waiting for her to get there. Or maybe he had given up on her and called somebody else to pick him up, and was sitting at home that very minute. She drove just a little faster than she normally would in an attempt to get there that much quicker. Not that it would make much difference now. By the time she got there, she would be almost two hours late.

While she was stuck, creeping along in gridlock traffic, she thought about the conversation she had with

Travis the night before. She'd meant what she said about taking it slow with him. If that was the case, why did she agree to come to the airport to pick him up? He could have just as easily gotten somebody else to come for him. She understood why he would want her to; he was trying to get with her. But it was her own reasoning that momentarily escaped her. The answer was simple: she was tired of being alone, and she wanted to see him.

Me'shelle looked in the rear view mirror. *So, you can talk that 'take it slow with Travis' shit all you want to, but you and I know what's goin' on. And that is where my soliloquy ends.*

When she rolled up on the terminal at 9:30, Travis was walking toward the cabstand. *What is he doing out here without a heavier coat?* Me'shelle slammed on her brakes and jumped out of the car. "Travis!"

He turned around and saw her waving her arms wildly. He smiled a satisfied smiled and started walking quickly toward her car. Me'shelle opened up the trunk then quickly got back in the car. Knowing he'd be cold, she turned the heat up just a bit more.

Travis threw his bags in the trunk and took out the box he had for Me'shelle. He closed the trunk and got in the car. "Hello, Me'shelle," said a very cold Travis.

"Well, hello, mister island man."

"Thanks for coming to get me, Me'shelle."

"I'm sorry I'm so late. Traffic getting here was terrible. Major accident."

"I thought you had forgotten about me or flat out changed your mind about coming to get me."

"I wouldn't do you like that. I'm a woman of my word," Me'shelle answered as she drove off. "Are you hungry?"

"Starving."

"What do you have a taste for?"

Travis looked at Me'shelle. He wanted to say, "You."

"I was thinking about Italian," he said.

"I know a place that has the best Italian food in the world," Me'shelle said.

"Really? What's it called?"

"Mario's."

"On Arthur Ave. I know the place, and yeah, the food is good there."

Traffic on the way back to the Bronx was just as heavy as it was coming. The long ride gave them time to talk. Me'shelle asked about his trip, and Travis told her about everything he did in the Caymans. He did, however, leave out the part about Veronica in the pool the night before. Then Me'shelle asked Travis the inevitable question. "Do you have a girlfriend?"

"No," was Travis's simple and quick answer.

"Okay. Since I know how you men are, I'll rephrase my question and ask it again." Me'shelle smiled and Travis smiled back. "Are you currently having sex with anybody?"

Travis considered his answer before opening his mouth. "Currently, no," was his answer. "What about you, Me'shelle? Are you dating somebody now?" he asked before she could get out the next question.

"No, Travis, I am not dating or having sex with anybody."

"Why not?" Travis asked quickly.

"The last guy I was dating decided that we should see other people."

"You mean he wanted to see other people."

Me'shelle smiled. "Exactly."

"Which is why you want to take your time with me. You want to make sure that I'm not the same kind of asshole."

"You are so smart," Me'shelle said. "Now, tell me what 'currently no' means. Oh, you didn't think that I forgot that gem of an answer, did you?"

"No, Me'shelle, I know you're too sharp to let one slip by you."

"So, why'd you try it?"

"Just to see."

"And the answer is?"

"I'm not currently having sex with anybody, because I decided to stop seeing the woman I was having sex with. I didn't think it was going anywhere," Travis answered.

"How come? Sex wasn't good?"

"No, the sex was good, but that's all there was. You know what I'm sayin'? I mean, we'd talk when it was necessary, but mostly we'd talk about having sex."

"If that's all there was, then why did you keep seeing her?"

"I don't know if you know this about men, but we'll go through a lot of things we normally wouldn't for good sex."

"You men are so shallow like that," Me'shelle said and rolled her eyes.

"I guess you're sayin' that women aren't like that?"

"No, that's not what I'm sayin'. I know women who will jump though some flaming hoops for some good dick. Excuse my French. But not all of us are like that. If a woman has a good man and the sex ain't that great, she'll stay with him because he's a good man."

"But then she'll creep on him with the guy with the good dick. Excuse my French."

"Touché."

It was after 11:00 by the time they reached the Whitestone Bridge. Since it was going to be too late for Mario's, Travis asked Me'shelle to take him straight home. He'd pick up a couple of slices from a place around the way. Once they got to Travis's house, he turned on some music.

"That's what I missed the most while I was gone."

"What's that?"

"Jazz."

"Who are we listening to?" Me'shelle asked with a bit of a frown on her face.

"Wes Montgomery," Travis replied proudly as he sat down at the dining room table and prepared to eat his pizza.

"Never heard of him."

"He's on guitar. I take it you don't really like jazz."

"Some of it's okay. I mean, like Kenny Gee, David Sanborn, stuff like that. But this is . . . I don't know."

"This is real music. Guys like Miles Davis, John Coltrane, Thelonious Monk, Horace Silver, these guys put their whole heart and soul into their music. Kenny Gee wishes he could play the sax like Coltrane."

Me'shelle laughed. "If you say so. I guess I'd have to hear some."

"Stick around and you will," Travis said. "I almost forgot." He went and got the small box out of his pocket. He returned to the table and handed the box to Me'shelle. "This is for you."

Me'shelle looked at the box and knew it was jewelry. She opened the box. "Travis, it's beautiful." The necklace Travis bought her was platinum with a half-carat diamond. “Is this the little souvenir you said you were bringing me?”

“Yup,” Travis said with his mouth full of pizza. “Do you like it?”

“Yes, it’s beautiful. Thank you so much. How did you know I love platinum?”

“I didn’t. I just thought it would look beautiful on you.”

“When you said you were bringing me a souvenir, you know, I was expecting a T-shirt with some stupid sayin’ on it or a bag of sand or whatever.”

Travis got up, took the necklace from Me’shelle and put it on for her. “I was right. It does look beautiful on you.”

“I don’t think the words ‘you shouldn’t have’ are enough for this, Travis. How much did this cost?”

“A gentleman never tells.”

Chapter Eighteen

Early the next morning, Travis paged Freeze. He wanted to find out what was going on before he spoke to Ronnie and Jackie. When Freeze called back, he told Travis to met him at Cynt's at 1:00. Since he wanted to talk to Freeze alone, he called Jackie and told her to meet him there at 2:00. Then he called Ronnie.

"What's up, Ronnie?"

"It's about time you came back to the real world. When did you get back?"

"Last night," Travis said.

"How was the island?" Ronnie asked. Travis noted the cool tone.

"It was great. Weather was nice. I had a good time."

"Did you meet Veronica?"

"Yeah, we hung out a couple nights. She was real cool."

"Well, what does she look like?" Ronnie asked.

"Yo, she doesn't look anything like she sounds. She's a big, juicy, fine-ass muthafucka."

"Really? So, I know you had a good time with her. I know you like them juicy. Which reminds me, your girl Mystique has been askin' for you every time I go to Cynt's. Said you don't call her no more," Ronnie said, trying to sound like a woman.

"What you tell her?"

"Not a damn thing," Ronnie said and laughed. "She gets real funky when she don't get what she wants, don't she?"

"She sure does," Travis replied and laughed.

"So, what's up, Travis?"

"I know we need to talk and that you got a lot of questions."

"I just asked the only question I got."

"Then the answer is it's all good. So, why don't you meet me at Cynt's at two? We'll talk there. Cool?"

"Cool. If you say it's all good, then that's all I need to hear," Ronnie said.

After Ronnie hung up, Travis called for a cab. In addition to going to Cynt's, he had a few other things he needed to get done. Before anything else got done, Travis had to do the one thing that had been bothering him for the past week.

Travis stood in front of the grocery store looking for the camera that somehow he missed while he was planning the job. As discreetly as he could, he walked out into the parking lot, looking on top of the building for mounted cameras. There were none. *They're here somewhere.* Travis thought back to the job itself and the brief piece of footage that he saw on television. He thought about the angle from which the footage was shot and where the camera had to be in order to get that shot. *The lights.*

Travis stopped at the spot where he had the correct angle and looked up at closest light pole. Then he walked back in front of the store and picked up the pay phone to call another cab. From that spot, almost exactly where the armored truck was parked, he could see them. They were small, built into the pole. With the morning sun shining, they almost looked like reflectors, but now he was sure that they had to be cameras. They were perfectly positioned to get an excellent shot of everybody exiting the store.

When his cab arrived, Travis got in and headed for Cynt's. *Easy to miss, but you should have seen them anyway.*

Freeze had arrived at Cynt's early and was there, waiting for Travis when Wanda came in.

"What brings you up here so early in the day, Freeze?" Wanda asked and sat down next to him.

"I was just about to ask you that," Freeze replied.

"Cynt asked me to stop by to discuss a legal problem she's having."

"What problem she havin'?"

"Calm down, Freeze. She said it was a personal problem. If it's something that you need to know about, I'll tell you. So, what are you doing here?"

"I got to meet somebody here at one. And I had to bring some money up here so they could open the tables."

"Why?"

"It was a weird night in the NBA. A lot of upsets," Freeze said then pushed the newspaper in front of Wanda.

"Knicks beat the Lakers, huh?"

"Yeah, that's the one that broke us. Everybody made that sentimental bet on the Knicks to win."

"Shit happens," Wanda said. "We aren't that bad off, are we?"

"Nothing we can't handle, but we need to bust 'em on down at football this weekend or everybody's envelope gonna be a little light this week."

"That's how it goes," Wanda said. "Who are you meeting with?"

"Travis Burns."

Wanda rolled her eyes and sucked her teeth. "The wannabe robber."

"No, baby, my nigga's the real thing."

"Yeah, right."

"I didn't notice you complainin' or callin' him no wannabe when he personally made your envelope a little fatter. My nigga is smart; he's organized, he's disciplined, he's got his crew under control. They execute their jobs like clockwork, and he's a good earner. So, tell me the truth, Wanda, why don't you like him?"

"Think about what you just said: smart, organized, disciplined, in control. He reminds me too much of Mike Black."

Freeze thought about it for a second. "Now that you mention it, he damn sure does."

When Travis arrived at Cynt's a little early, he was surprised to see that Freeze was already waiting for him. He expected Freeze to keep him waiting like he usually did. Wanda saw Travis coming toward the table. "Here comes your nigga," she said mockingly. "I'll leave you two to talk." Wanda got up from the table and headed for the stairs to the offices for her meeting with Cynt. She passed Travis on the way. Travis smiled as men did when they saw Wanda walking toward them.

"Hello, Travis," she said and kept walking.

"Hello, Wanda," Travis said nervously. *What's up with that? Wanda never speaks to me.*

Travis sat down at the table with Freeze. "So, what's the word?"

"The word is good. I got it on good information that the cops don't have a clue on who ran that job at the grocery store. They assume that the same people that ran that job ran the jewelry store job, but they got no leads on either case. I know there was some concern about the video surveillance of the parking lot, but they gone over it a bunch of times and they remain clueless. But that's a cop's nature."

"How do you know all this?"

"Don't you know? I know everything," Freeze said flatly. "But in this particular case, I know a little cutie that's bangin' the lead detective on the case. He tells her everything and then she tells me. That pillow talk is a muthafucka." Freeze laughed. "But I still think you should chill for a while." He stood up.

"That's what I got in mind," Travis said as Freeze walked away.

It was a little before 2:00 when Ronnie got to Cynt's. He wandered around the club looking for Travis and finally found him sitting in the back corner with Mystique. She was burning up his ear when Ronnie came toward them. Once Mystique turned and saw Ronnie coming, she stood up and slapped the shit out of Travis. "You ain't shit," Mystique said and walked away.

Ronnie came to the table laughing his ass off. "What's happenin', player? Havin' some problems with your people today?"

"Something like that," Travis said, rubbing his face. "I told Mystique that I didn't want to see her anymore."

"I guess that wasn't what she wanted to hear."

"I guess not. Like you said, she gets real funky when you tell her no," Travis said and laughed a little. "So, what's up with you?"

"I'm cool," Ronnie said as Jackie joined them at the table. "What's up, Jackie? You're just in time. Travis was just about to tell me the deal."

"Well, let's hear it. How bad are we?" Jackie asked.

"We aren't bad at all. Cops aren't looking for us, and since we didn't leave them any, they have no clues that will lead them to us," Travis said confidently.

"What about the parking lot footage they were showing every day on the news?" Jackie asked.

"Consider that your fifteen minutes of fame," Travis said. "There's nothing on that tape to lead them to us."

"What about while you were doing surveillance? Won't that lead them to you?" Jackie asked.

"Jackie, I'm tellin' you, they got nothing they can use, and more to the point, they don't have anything that points to me. I even sold the Thunderbird in Miami while I was down there. I'm tellin' you, we're good on this," Travis said. He looked at Ronnie, who was surprisingly calm and quiet. "You don't have any questions, Ron?"

"Nope. Jackie got all the questions now. You answered all my questions when you came back to the city and told me it was all good. You woulda stayed your ass in the Caymans if there was any problems at all."

"You're right. I probably would have. The Caymans is nice."

"Oh, so you woulda left us to twist in the wind for it?" Jackie asked.

"Hell no. I knew you were talkin' to Freeze. He woulda gave you the heads up if it wasn't all good."

"That is something I do have a problem with," Ronnie said. "Why we gotta give that nigga so much money?"

"Ronnie, how you think I got to the Caymans? What did you think, I walked up to the counter at Miami International Airport with a bag full of money? I flew down there on a charter plane. Freeze put me on to a guy named Pete. He flew me in and out of there, no customs, nothing like that.

"How you think I know that the cops ain't got nothing on us? Freeze got that handled. He got an in to the cops. Like I told you when we started, we give Freeze that money for his protection and services," Travis explained as Wanda came down the steps and walked across the floor. "And we pay for the legal services of that fine-ass muthafucka there," he said and pointed at Wanda.

"God damn, that woman is so fine," Jackie said.

"I see all that," Ronnie said, seeming to ignore Jackie's observation about Wanda. "But I still think we give that nigga too much of our money, so forgive me if I bitch a little. We gave that nigga damn near fifty grand of our money. And while we're talkin' about money, why you feel the need to run to the Caymans to get rid of your money? Why didn't you just let the white boy handle it like he always does?"

"I didn't feel comfortable giving him that much money," Travis said. "I didn't want him to make no connection to the job. Y'all all right with your money?"

"I just feed it to him a little at a time. He didn't make no connection. He thinks we're big time drug dealers anyway," Ronnie said.

"Why does he think that?"

"Boy is a fiend for X. Every time I see him, I give him enough Ecstasy to freak half the women in New York."

"So, what next, Travis?" Jackie asked.

"Best thing we can do for the next couple of months is keep a very low profile."

Chapter Nineteen

Over the next couple of months, all three kept as low a profile as they could. Thinking that it would improve his chances of getting with Jackie, Freeze was instrumental in getting her a few modeling jobs. But she was gambling more now than she usually did, so she was spending the money as quickly as she made it. Ronnie started working on making his next fortune from home as a day trader.

Travis got called for a contract programmer job, and went to work three days a week. The contract was in Long Island and the building was next to a bank. Although the idea of getting out still had a haunting pull on him, Travis couldn't resist the temptation of planning their next job—if there was to be a next job.

From his office window, Travis could watch the comings and goings without even trying. He opened an account at the bank to deposit his checks. While he was in the bank conducting business, he observed the layout of the bank and studied their procedures.

Travis spent most of his time, though, getting to know Me'shelle, and he was loving every minute of it. Their time together had been like one long conversation. It was an old fashioned courtship. They spent a lot of time together, slowly getting to know one another. They talked a lot, went to the movies, to concerts, to plays and they danced. They both loved to dance.

During this courtship, Me'shelle learned something about herself: "I love to eat out." In fact, she loved to go out period. While she was with Trent, they never went anywhere. He was a homebody. She finally concluded he was just too cheap to want to go anywhere. Trent would show up at Me'shelle's house in time for dinner, which she would always have to cook, with a couple of movies and some microwave popcorn.

"You know what I wanna try?" Me'shelle asked Travis.

"What's that?"

"Jerk chicken."

"You've never had Caribbean food?"

"Nope. I've got a rich southern heritage. That's where my family's from. My aunt cooks southern food. But I've heard so much about Caribbean, I just have to try it."

"That's cool. I know a little place on Sixteenth Street called Maroons. You'll love it. They serve both southern and Caribbean food. I always have Aunt Sarah's stewed oxtails."

"You go there a lot?"

"Not really, but it is one of my favorites," Travis replied.

They had their first fight at Foley's restaurant on Seventh Avenue. It all began one day when Mystique showed up at Travis's house unannounced and uninvited, while they were on their way out.

When Travis came out of the house, Mystique was coming up the walkway. He froze in his tracks.

"Travis, you and I need to talk, baby," Mystique said and put her hands on his chest. "I'm sorry that I slapped you. I really miss you."

"I told you it's over between us," Travis said.

"I just want things to get back to the way they were," she said. That was when Me'shelle walked out the door. "Who the fuck is this bitch?"

Me'shelle didn't like being called a bitch, but she kept her cool and let Travis handle his business.

"This is Me'shelle," Travis said.

"So, is this the bitch you dumped me for, Travis?"

I ain't gonna be too many more bitches, Me'shelle thought.

"This cidity bitch!"

"That's it," Me'shelle said as she stepped toward Mystique. Travis tried to step in between them, but he was too slow. Before he knew it, Me'shelle was all up in Mystique's grill. "Who the fuck are you callin' a bitch?" Me'shelle said. "I only see one bitch here, and it damn sure ain't me, bitch."

Mystique rolled her eyes and put her hands on her hips. "Don't you know I will kick your ass, bitch?" she threatened.

Me'shelle started taking off her earrings. "Well, come on wit' it then!" she challenged. Travis grabbed Mystique and carried her away from Me'shelle. "No, let the bitch go, Travis!" she shouted, but that wasn't about to happen.

It took about ten minutes for Travis to convince Mystique to leave, but to Me'shelle it seemed longer. She watched them talk from the window to observe their body language. When he came inside, he had to convince Me'shelle that they should still go to Foley's for dinner. Me'shelle was mad as hell, but what she was more was hungry, so she agreed to go.

She wasn't even all that mad at Travis, although she let him think that she was. She was mad at Mystique and madder at herself. They said little if anything on the drive downtown. Me'shelle simply looked out the window.

When they got to the restaurant and were seated, the waiter came to take their order. Me'shelle had barely looked at the menu. “For starters, how about some Boston clam chowder, with chunky potatoes and frizzled onions?” the waiter asked.

“That sounds good to me,” Travis told him.

“And for the lady?”

She didn’t answer.

“Me’shelle?” Travis said.

“That’s fine,” she said. By this time she had moved beyond Mystique and was trippin’ on how quickly she snapped and was ready to go at it ghetto style. *I can’t believe you took off your earrings and was ready to fight that woman*. She looked at Travis; he had a look on his face that was concern and sadness at the same time.

“Are you ready to order your entrée, or do you need more time?”

“Give us a minute, would you, please?” Me’shelle asked. Once the waiter left, she turned Travis. “We need to talk about this.”

“Yes, we do.”

“So, who was that woman?”

“She’s the woman I told you about.”

“The one with the good sex. Are you still seeing her?”

“No. I haven’t seen her in two months. I’ve been with you every day for the last month and a half.”

“Yeah, but you still could be seeing her. You go home every night.”

“Yeah, I do.”

“So, are you still sleeping with her?”

“I told you, Me’shelle. No, I’m not seeing her, sleeping with her; I ain’t doin’ nothing with her. If I wanted to see her, I would. And I wouldn’t be spending all my time with you. All I want to do is be with you, Me’shelle,” Travis said as he reached for her hand.

The waiter returned and they paused the discussion long enough to order. "I'll have the Seafood Castellane pasta, but hold the roasted tomatoes," Travis said. Me'shelle ordered the grilled Red Snapper with roasted sweet potato cakes.

By the time their food arrived, they were still at it. "Well, tell me this then: When did she slap you?"

"The day I told her that it was over," Travis answered.

"Come on, now. You said you haven't seen her in two months. You're gonna sit there and tell me that it took her all that time to finally show up to talk about it?"

"I guess so. She's been callin' every day, but I don't answer the phone when she calls, and I don't call her back."

"Wait a minute. I'm at your house practically every day. Has she called while I was there?"

"Yes, but I turned the ringer off." Travis smiled. "So we wouldn't be disturbed."

"How many other women call you?"

"None. I'm only interested in being with you, Me'shelle. Please believe that." Travis paused. "But it hasn't been easy."

"What do you mean?"

"I mean I want to make love to you, Me'shelle."

"I want you, too, but I told you I didn't want to rush into that with you." Me'shelle took a deep breath.

Travis loved it when she did that. The sound she made, the way her breasts would rise each time, excited him. "I love it when you do that."

"Do what?"

"When you breathe like that. It does something to me every time." Travis smiled.

Me'shelle took anther deep breath. "Stop it, Travis." She paused. "I won't make you wait too much longer. I promise. But this feels so right between us, and I just want to be sure."

"I can understand that. 'Cause it feels right to me too."

Me'shelle smiled at Travis.

"What?"

"Our first fight."

"I think we came through it all right. Neither of us got up and left the other one sitting here. But I'll tell you one thing."

"What's that?" she asked.

"There's a whole other side to you. I got to start checkin' you out a little bit closer."

Me'shelle smiled. "What are you talkin' about, Travis?" she asked, but she knew what was coming.

"Well, come on wit' it then. No, let the bitch go."

"Okay, so I went ghetto style on her. I can go for mine when I have to. Don't let these manicured nails and this nice dress fool you. I'm still a Bronx girl from around the way."

The following week, Travis and Me'shelle planned to go to Cabana Carioca, a Brazilian restaurant on West 45th Street. They were on their way out the door when his phone rang.

"Hello," Travis answered.

"Travis, this Ron, man. Look, I need a big favor."

"What's that?"

"I need you to do something for me."

"What's that?"

"I'm at the train station at two-fifth street. I get off the train and all my windows is busted out and all my tires are slashed."

"Oh, shit! Which woman did you piss off?"

"I'm pretty sure it was this bitch named Pauleen. I know she's the one who did it, 'cause we was on the phone arguing before the train pulled up here."

"Do I know this woman?"

"You know Pauleen, Travis. I know you know her. Don't you remember? You introduced me to her one night at some club we were at."

"You ain't talkin' about Freeze's girl Pauleen."

"That's her."

"You're fuckin' Freeze's girl? Have you lost your fuckin' mind, Ronnie? How long has this been goin' on?"

"About a year," Ronnie replied.

"You're kiddin'. Does Freeze know about it? What the fuck am I sayin'? Freeze knows everything," Travis said, realizing that was probably why Freeze didn't like Ronnie. It also explained his constant threats to kill him. *Just business my ass*. "Okay, Ron, I'll be down there to get you."

"No, no, Travis, that ain't what I need. Don't your boy Freeze have his hooks into a body shop?"

"Yeah."

"And I know they got to have a tow truck. So, call your boy and get me the hook-up," Ronnie said.

"You're fucking his girl and now you want him to hook you up on the repairs?"

"Yeah. When you really sit and think about it, it's only fair. It's his girl that caused the damage. She's on his card; he should cover the whole bill. But I know that ain't happenin', so the hook-up will satisfy me."

"You're crazy, but I'll get it done for you," Travis said.

"Thanks, Travis. You da man," Ronnie said and hung up.

Travis called Freeze and got the hook-up on the repairs for Ronnie. He did, however, leave out the part about him being responsible for the damage because it was Pauleen who did it. Travis called Ronnie back and told him to ask for David. "And tell him Freeze told you to call." Afterwards, while he went on his dinner date with Me'shelle, she asked questions about what she had just heard.

"Why you want know so much?" Travis asked.

" 'Cause there's a whole other side to you, Travis. I gotta start askin' some questions."

Me'shelle had questions for Travis the whole night. Travis was all right with it because they were all questions he could answer honestly, without giving up more information than he was willing.

While they munched on Clams Bulhao Pato appetizers, Me'shelle asked about Freeze.

"Freeze is a guy I went to junior high school with. He's a very dangerous man, but I do things for him and he looks out for me when I need things," Travis answered.

After the appetizers, Me'shelle ordered the Mariscada, a seafood combination in red sauce. Travis had the broiled filet of salmon. Over dinner, Me'shelle wanted to know who his friends were. "Are all of your friend like—what's his name? Ronnie?"

"What do you mean?"

"I mean do they all mess around with your other dangerous friends' women, who bust out windows and slash tires?"

"No. My only other close friend is Jackie. She's nothing like Ronnie."

"She?"

"Yeah, Jackie is a woman."

"Should I be jealous of your friendship with her?"

"No, you have no worries there. For one, me, her, and Ronnie grew up together, and two, Jackie gets more pussy than I do. Excuse my French."

"She's gay?"

"She doesn't like to be labeled, but yes, she is at best bisexual."

"You and her ever do it?"

"Not since we were experimenting kids," Travis answered, knowing there was a little more to that story. He didn't think Me'shelle needed or would really want to hear all the details.

"What's she like?"

"She carries it like a lady, if that what you were asking. If you didn't know she was into women, you'd never guess by looking at her. But if you're asking what type of person she is, she's the exact opposite of Ronnie. Right now, Ronnie's working on making a fortune as a day trader—very high-energy position for a very high-energy guy. Even though Jackie is working now as a model, she's a chemist. She prefers to work alone in a very quiet kinda atmosphere."

"And you're somewhere in the middle. But I like that about you, Travis. I think it's very sexy."

"Do you really?"

"Yes. I think you're a very sexy man." Before Travis could bite on that hook line, Me'shelle asked, "So, tell me, Mr. Burns. How are we going to spend the rest of the night?"

"Well, Ms. Lawrence, we're going to a place called Smoke on 106th and Broadway. There's going to be a jazz album release party there, so there may be a star or two in the house," Travis said.

"That sounds nice."

After the show was over, Travis took Me'shelle home and she invited him in. "But just for a minute," she said. Me'shelle went into her bedroom briefly, then to the kitchen to pour them each a glass of wine. She joined Travis on the couch. They talked about their evening and the time that they had spent together. It had been almost a month since the incident with Mystique, and they were now able to look back and laugh about it.

"You know the only thing that was missing from the evening?"

"What was that?"

Me'shelle moved closer to Travis. "This." She kissed him on the cheek then touched his face. Travis turned to Me'shelle, drawing her to his lips. "Our first kiss," she said.

"I hope it's the first of many."

"It will be," Me'shelle said as she stood up. She held out her hand and Travis accepted it. He stood up, ready to say goodnight and tell Me'shelle what a wonderful time he'd had with her that evening, as he always did. But Me'shelle placed her finger over his lips and said, "Shhh."

She quietly led Travis into her candlelit bedroom. She kissed him again, and he let his hands roam freely over her body. Their bodies shook from the excitement of the lovemaking that both had anticipated for so long.

Travis unzipped her dress and started to slide it off her shoulders, but Me'shelle stopped him, moving his hands back to his sides. She undressed Travis slowly, kissing and caressing him as she removed each article of clothing. "Lay down," whispered in his ear.

Travis lay across the bed and watched Me'shelle deliberately and seductively slide her dress down her body until it hit the floor. She turned around and slid her thong off her hips and let it drop next to her dress. Travis knew he was in heaven.

Me'shelle reached behind her back, unhooked her bra and slid it off her shoulders. When she was naked, she lay down in bed next to Travis. He ran his hand across her breasts and teased them with his tongue, sliding it slowly around her beautiful, dark circles, but never touching her nipples. When Me'shelle spread her legs, Travis fingered her clit. He felt it getting harder under his touch. Me'shelle moaned her approval.

Travis guided his tongue along her eyebrows then kissed her eyelids. The sensation of hands gave way to the sensation of her lips, soft and wet, against his chest. As he lay on his back, eyes closed, he enjoyed the taste of her tongue darting playfully in and out of his mouth and across his chest.

She began gliding her hands across his skin to his now throbbing hardness. She reached out and slowly began to massage it. Me'shelle kissed him passionately as she continued to stroke his erection. Travis reached out for Me'shelle and gently moved her body so he could taste her. He ran his tongue along her lips and proceeded to lick her clit. She moaned her pleasure while continuing to slide her hand up and down his shaft.

Me'shelle repositioned herself and straddled his torso as Travis looked on with great anticipation She lowered herself onto him. While she took his erection into the wetness between her thighs, they stared into each other's eyes. They moved in unison; each movement was agonizingly slow and deliberate to heighten their mutual pleasure.

Me'shelle rolled off of Travis. He watched her crawl around on the bed and enjoyed the perfection that was Me'shelle's ass. Travis crawled over beside her and ran his hands along her back, around her perfect ass, then squeezed her firm thighs. Me'shelle spread her legs and he fingered her clit and played with her lips.

Travis got up on his knees and entered her from behind. Her pussy was so soft, so wet; he could barely control his passion. He felt her ass buck, pounding against him. He felt the muscles inside her tighten around him.

Me'shelle smiled and touched his face, then she curled up in the fetal position. Travis ran his hand over her shoulder and down her arm. Her skin was soft and smooth. He paused to admire each curve, studying each nuance of her body.

Me'shelle began to move in response. She rolled into his arms and kissed his lips. He tasted her tongue. It glided slowly and smoothly over his. Travis broke their embrace and spread her legs. He kissed her inner thighs and once again tasted the wetness between them. Me'shelle held his head in place as his tongue slithered along her lips, making circles around her clit. Her grip grew tighter, her stomach muscles locked and her head drifted back in quiet ecstasy. This had definitely been worth the wait.

Chapter Twenty

After spending two months in Columbia, South Carolina, Bruce and his family finally returned to New York. The trip was productive, as Bruce had put together all the money he owed Chilly. Naturally, it took longer than it should have, because as soon as they made the money, they would smoke up half of it. When they came through the door, Brandy went straight to her room and closed the door. Bruce and Natalie went to their bedroom.

The first order of business was to call Chilly so Bruce could bring him his money. However, each time he called, Bruce was told that Chilly was unavailable. This made him nervous. He was always able to talk to Chilly whenever he needed to. He even tried to call Chilly at home. He talked to Chilly's wife, Gee, but she hadn't seen him since he left the house that morning.

Bruce paced nervously around the bedroom of the house his father left him. "What's wrong, Bruce?" Natalie asked as she got undressed. She took off her bra and put on her nightshirt.

"This is the fifth time I called Chilly and muthafuckas keep feedin' me this unavailable shit," Bruce answered.

"Maybe he don't care about the money no more."

"That's what worries me, Nat. If Chilly don't want the money no more, then Chilly's gonna want something else. I told you we were fuckin' around down there too damn long. We shoulda came back when we had all the money the first time, but your ass had to start smokin' it up."

"Me? I seem to remember you were there smokin' right along with me, so don't give me this shit about me smokin' it up."

"So, it wasn't you beggin' me to re-up so we could have a little piece to do? You know, just you and me. That wasn't you?"

"You coulda said no."

"And even if I did just say no, how many nights did I come back after being out all night making money and find you down in Grandma's basement smokin' up whatever your searchin' ass could find?"

"Well, you shouldn't have left it there for me to find!"

"Who the fuck you yellin' at?"

"I'm not yellin'. I'm just sayin' if it wasn't there, I couldn't smoke it. You shoulda took the shit out the house with you."

"If that ain't the stupidest shit I ever heard!"

Natalie got quiet when Bruce started yelling.

"What I look like out in the street with all the dope on me? An easy-ass mark, waitin' to get his ass robbed or killed!"

"Well, maybe you shoulda just left me a little piece to hit on. Then I wouldn't have to go searchin'."

"I guess you don't remember we tried that one night. And what did you do? Huh? What did you do? Your ass went searching though the house, tearin' shit up until you fuckin' found it!"

"What you expect me to do? That little shit you left me!" Natalie screamed.

"Fuck this. This shit ain't gettin' us nowhere, Nat. I just need to get this nigga his money before he sends somebody after us."

"Us? What the fuck you mean us?"

"Us means you and me, Nat. Like it or not, we in this together. He come after me, he come after you too."

"Does that include Brandy?"

Bruce thought about the question. He walked over to the window and looked out. Everything that his aunts and Me'shelle told him about getting Brandy away from the life he was living came rushing home. "I guess it does." He started down the hall to tell Brandy to pack her shit; she was going to stay with Me'shelle.

"That's fucked up. How you gonna drag us into your shit? That's too fucked up, Bruce. I'm gonna need a little hit to take my mind off this shit," Natalie said.

Bruce looked at Natalie for a second or two. He wanted a hit too. He went to get his stash out of the closet, he took out a box that contained two pipes and his cooking paraphernalia, and went in the bathroom. Natalie got up and followed him.

Bruce opened the box and pulled out a test tube, a single-edge razor blade, and a $25 bag of cocaine.

"Pretty skimpy quarter," Natalie commented.

"Not much cut on it," he replied, lifting a box of baking soda and a rolled dollar bill from the box. He laid the bill on the counter and emptied the contents of the bag onto it. "You wanna cook?"

"No."

Bruce paused and looked in her direction, chopping lightly. "Nothing but a habit, huh?" Bruce laughed. "Maybe Me'shelle's right. Maybe I do need to snatch the pipe out your mouth and slap you upside your head."

"Fuck Me'shelle's wannabe-a-saint ass," Natalie said as Bruce shook a little baking soda onto the dollar then mixed it in with the razor.

Bruce lit a candle. A teaspoon of water followed the mix into the test tube. Bruce held the tube over a flame watching carefully as it began to sizzle. He moved the tube away from the fire, poured in a little more water and shook the test tube. “Me’shelle said she was datin’ some nigga.”

“Nobody wants Me’shelle’s think-she’s-so-fuckin’-smart ass. Not after they fuck her anyway. She’s so smart until she’s stupid,” Natalie said, taking a pipe from the box and adjusting the screens.

“She’s smart enough to know this shit gonna kill us or get us killed. Maybe we should try to get off this shit.” Bruce poured the water slowly out of the test tube into a strainer. He placed the white rock of cocaine on a small mirror and sat on the edge of the tub. “Came back nice for a skimpy quarter.”

Natalie didn’t comment. She picked up the razor blade and cut off a piece of the rock. “Got any torches?”

“No,” he said, breaking the rest of the rock into smaller pieces. Bruce took the other pipe out of the box. “Use a lighter.”

“No. I don’t like the way it tastes.”

Bruce put a piece of the rock in the pipe. He took a quick hit to light it then pushed a lighter in front of her. “Even if we did have torches, we don’t have anything to burn with except rubbing alcohol, and I know you don’t like the taste of that.”

Reluctantly, Natalie picked up the lighter and lit her pipe. She watched the bowl of the pipe fill up with smoke. She paused a moment and thought about Brandy before lighting the pipe again.

Bruce and Natalie stayed in the bathroom smoking for the rest of the afternoon and well into the evening.

Bruce made several trips back to the closet to raid his stash until it was gone.

Chapter Twenty-one

"Why don't you just take a couple hundred that you got for Chilly and go get some more?" Natalie asked as she walked out of the bathroom and lay down on the bed.

" 'Cause I ain't tryin' to live like that. Don't you understand these muthafuckas ain't no joke?" Bruce asked, slowly following her.

"Why not? I know you got more than you owe Chilly."

"Did you hear what I been tellin' you? I ain't tryin' to do that."

Just then, a loud knocking at the front door startled them. "Go see who that is," Bruce said.

"Yeah, but I still don't see why you can't take some of that money and go do what you gotta do," Natalie whined as she got up to answer the door.

Bruce lay down on the bed, but got up immediately and went back in the bathroom. He checked to see if any pieces of rock had fallen on the floor. Not finding any, he began to think about getting some of that money and going to do what he had to do, as Natalie suggested. Then he heard Natalie scream.

"Stop! You can't come in here like that!"

Bruce rushed out of the bedroom to find four masked men in the living room. Two of them were holding Natalie while she screamed her ass off and struggled to get free. One man was tearing up the living room. The other just stood there. "Shut her the fuck up," he said as Bruce came into the room.

"What the fuck is this?" Bruce screamed. "Let her go!"

"Chilly sends his regards," the man said then punched Bruce in the face. Bruce hit the ground hard, but got right up. The man hit him again, and Bruce went down. This time he stayed there.

One of the men who was holding a still struggling Natalie tore the shirt off her back, leaving her naked except for her panties. He quickly ripped the shirt in half. He spun Natalie around and hit her hard in the face then used the shirt as a gag to keep her quiet. He tied her hands behind her back and started to fondle her breasts.

Brandy heard the commotion in the front room and immediately knew what time it was. She had feared this day would come. She locked her door and went into her closet to hide, quickly pulling clothes off the hangers and pouring all of her dirty clothes on the floor. She lay on the floor and tried to pull as many clothes as she could on top of herself. She lay there, shaking and listening.

"Where the fuck is the money, Bruce?"

"I got the money, man! There ain't no need for all this!"

The man stepped up and kicked Bruce in the face. "Where is it?" he asked and kicked him again, this time in the gut. The man pulled out a .45 with a silencer and pointed it at Bruce.

Bruce screamed in pain. "It's in my bedroom. I'll get it. Just don't hurt her," he begged, watching the two men feeling on Natalie. His next thought was for Brandy.

The man with the gun signaled for the one who was searching for the money to go look in the bedrooms. He went down the hall and stopped in front of Brandy's door. "It's locked!" he yelled when he turned the knob. He kicked it in, then went inside and began to look around.

There was terror in Bruce's eyes when he saw the man go in Brandy's room. "Not that room! The other one!" A feeling of relief came over Bruce as he watched the man come out of Brandy's room and go into his.

"Where?" the armed man asked.

"In the closet. In a shoebox on the shelf."

"You hear that?" the armed man yelled.

The searcher went into the closet and found the box. He opened it up and got the money, counting it as quickly as he could. Once he was finished counting, he yelled, "I got it!" and stuffed some of the money in his sock.

"Bring it here," the armed man commanded.

The searcher came out of the room and brought the money to the armed man. "How much is it?" he asked Bruce.

"There's five thousand dollars there. The four grand I owe Chilly and another grand for making him wait. But you can keep the other grand. Just leave my wife alone," Bruce pleaded.

He began to slowly count the money. His eyes narrowed and he counted it again. "There's only forty-five hundred here, nigga."

"I swear, man, I had five grand in that box," Bruce said. Both he and the armed man looked at the searcher.

"Where the rest of the money?" He pointed his gun at the searcher.

"That's all there was, man. He's lyin'," the searcher insisted.

"I don't think so. Why would he lie? You got that money, muthafucka!" He shot the searcher once in the face.

"Oh, shit!" Bruce said. Natalie' eyes bucked open and Brandy put her hand over her mouth at the sound of the blast.

The armed man turned to one of the men who was holding Natalie. "Search him. It doesn't take two of y'all to hold that bitch."

Before doing as he was told, one of the men stuck his hand in Natalie's panties. "I'll be back for you, baby." Natalie struggled to break free, but it did her no good.

He rolled the searcher over so he wouldn't have to look at his face. He went though his pockets and found nothing. "He ain't got it."

"Check his socks and in his drawers," he commanded.

Once again, his orders were followed. "You were right. Nigga had it in his sock."

"Y'all got what you came for, man. Why don't y'all just go? Tell Chilly I'm sorry. It will never happen again," Bruce said.

"Search the joint. Make sure there ain't no more money up in this bitch."

"There ain't no more money here, man."

"No, Bruce, I think there is. You're in too big a hurry for us to bounce. There's something else in here."

The man went off and began his search in Brandy's room. Bruce closed his eyes and prayed that Brandy had left the house while they were getting high. When he opened his eyes and looked at Natalie, she was completely naked, bent over a chair. Her captor was standing behind her.

"Look what I found!" he said, dragging a kicking and screaming Brandy by the arm. He threw her on the couch. "I found her fine, young ass hiding in the closet."

"So, that's what you was hidin', huh, Bruce?"

"Please don't hurt my baby, man. Please," Bruce begged with tears rolling down his cheeks.

"You need a little something to remind you that Chilly ain't nobody to be fuckin' around with, Bruce. Fuck them bitches."

"No!" Bruce yelled. "Don't do that! I won't fuck with Chilly's money no more!"

Bruce watched as the man pulled Brandy's pants off. She struggled to resist him. He hit Brandy in the head several times, then pulled down his pants and put his hand over her mouth. Bruce jumped up from the floor in an attempt to pull the man off Brandy, but before he could get to him, the armed man beat Bruce back down to the floor.

While the man kicked away, Bruce looked at Natalie. As her assailant forced himself inside her, Bruce saw the pain and anguish in her eyes. He heard her muffled cries. Then he looked at Brandy.

He tried again to get off the floor, but his attempt was met by the barrel of a gun. "Open your eyes, nigga, and see what happens when you fuck with the wrong nigga." The man kicked Bruce in the face.

Brandy reached out and grabbed the lamp next to the couch. She hit her attacker in the back of his head with the base of the lamp. It stunned him long enough for Brandy to push him off.

"Run, Brandy!" Bruce yelled.

But Brandy was way ahead of him. She ran out the front door.

"Go after her!" the armed man yelled. Natalie's attacker went out the door after Brandy. Natalie tried to run out too, but before she made it to the door, the armed man grabbed her and threw her to the floor.

Brandy didn't look back. She ran into the streets, screaming as loudly as she could. "Help me, please! Somebody help me!"

She heard the sound of footsteps coming up quickly behind her as she rounded the block. One old man came out of his house. "What's going on out here?"

"Mind your business, old man," Brandy's pursuer warned. The man backed into his house. By that time, Brandy was out of sight. He turned around and went back to Bruce's house.

"Where is she?" the armed man asked as he finished having his way with Natalie.

"I couldn't catch her," he answered, fearing the outcome.

"Fuck it. Let's go." He looked at Bruce, who was lying on the floor crying but still glad that Brandy had escaped. At the same time, he knew his fate.

The armed man raised his gun and pointed it at Natalie. "Watch your woman die." He fired twice then turned the gun on Bruce.

Chapter Twenty-two

When Me'shelle arrived at school, there was a message waiting for her to call a number at Jacobi Hospital. When she spoke with the nurse, she was told that the night before, the police brought in a young woman. She was found wandering the streets wearing only a black T-shirt and socks. Cold chills ran through Me'shelle's body as she asked the young woman's name. She knew it could only be Brandy.

"That's just it, Ms. Lawrence. She wouldn't tell us or the police her name. She's in shock, and she's been talking with the counselor this morning. We were able to get your name and number out of her, but not much else."

Me'shelle left school immediately and went to the hospital. The doctor on duty told Me'shelle that Brandy had been raped and she was still in shock. They allowed Me'shelle to see her, but only for a while, as Brandy had become very agitated and had to be sedated.

She sat at Brandy's bedside, crying while she held her hand until the nurses forced her to leave. When Me'shelle came out of the room, two officers and the rape counselor were waiting to talk to her.

They sat and questioned a tearful Me'shelle for about half an hour, but there wasn't much she could tell them.

"What relation are you to the victim?" the officers asked.

"I'm her aunt. Her father is my brother. Have you called her parents?" Me'shelle asked.

"No, ma'am. Yours was the only name I could get out of her in the state she's in," the counselor said.

"Can you give us the address and phone number of her parents?" the officer asked politely.

Me'shelle gave the police the information they requested and one went to try to call the house. Meanwhile, the counselor continued to ask Me'shelle questions she could not answer. When the officer returned, he informed Me'shelle that there was no answer at that number. They were getting off their shift, but had called in to have a car sent over to Bruce's house.

When the doctor returned to check on Brandy, the counselor went back in with her. Me'shelle went to the pay phone to call her aunt. Miranda was horrified, but not surprised by the news. Me'shelle began to cry once again and Miranda tried in vain to calm her down. She promised to call Juanita, then they would come to the hospital. Then Me'shelle called Travis, but she got no answer.

Me'shelle sat restlessly outside Brandy's room until the doctor and counselor came out. Before continuing her rounds, the doctor assured Me'shelle that Brandy was going to be fine physically. "But she may complain of a general soreness and aches throughout her body. She may also complain of pain in the specific areas of the body that were targeted during the assault. These pains may be the result of actual physical trauma, or may be a psychosomatic response. Both reasons are equally valid and real. We'll keep her under observation for a while, but your niece is going to be fine. However, I strongly recommended that you talk with the counselor about what she could expect next."

"Hi," the counselor said as the doctor walked away. "I didn't get a chance to introduce myself. My name is Judith Franklin, and as the doctor said, I'm a rape counselor."

"Me'shelle Lawrence," she said and held out her hand.

"How are you feeling?" Judith asked, giving her a hug.

"I'm all right," Me'shelle assured her. The truth was that she blamed herself for not doing more to get Brandy out of that environment. She thought about all the times she'd threatened to pack Brandy's things and take her away from Bruce and Natalie, but never did.

"I'm going to assume that since you were the only person Brandy would tell us about that the two of you are close."

"Yes, we are," Me'shelle said quietly.

"I think it will be very helpful to Brandy for you to play an important role in her recovery."

"I will. I'll be there for her no matter what." It was a commitment Me'shelle made to herself.

"I'm glad to hear you say that," Judith said with a reassuring smile that seemed to have a calming effect on Me'shelle. She and Me'shelle sat down and Judith continued. "I want to take a minute to talk to you about some of the things that you can expect with Brandy."

"Okay, Ms. Franklin."

"Please, call me Judith."

"Judith it is. And please, call me Me'shelle."

"The first and most important thing, Me'shelle, is that although every survivor's experience will be unique, many will have one thing in common: Rape Trauma Syndrome, or a cluster of emotional responses to the extreme stress experienced during the sexual assault. More specifically, it's a response to the profound fear of death that almost all survivors experience during an assault."

"I can't even imagine what that must feel like or what she's going through."

"Well, the trauma that Brandy is experiencing generally occurs in two phases: the acute or initial phase, which usually lasts anywhere from a few days to a few weeks after the assault, and the reorganization phase, which can last anywhere from a few weeks to several months after the assault. Each phase is characterized by particular emotional and physical concerns that most survivors experience."

"Like what?"

"In the acute phase, the survivor experiences a complete disruption of her life, responding to the fear of death she experienced. Survivors may display any of a number of contrasting emotional responses. A survivor may cry, shout, swear, or she may laugh nervously, which is called expressed style. Or as in Brandy's case, sit calmly or be silent, which is controlled style."

"Which one is better?"

"No response is inappropriate," Judith said passionately. "Brandy may exhibit characteristics of both styles. Responses vary depending on any one of a number of circumstances. Any emotion is appropriate because everyone has their own unique way of responding to events in their life."

"What can I do to help her?"

"Just be there for her. Right now, Brandy's initial response to the assault may be shock and disbelief. Many survivors may appear numb."

"That's what scares me. I've never seen her like that. Brandy is always so lively. Now she looks so distant."

"That's not inappropriate behavior. Actually, this response might provide an emotional 'time-out,' so to speak. It could be a time for her to acknowledge and begin to process the experience. If the assault was particularly brutal, Brandy may experience an extreme shock response and completely block out the assault."

"I know that can't be good for her."

"No, it's not, but it's something she may experience, and you have to be prepared to deal with it. Following the shock and disbelief, she may experience a variety of emotions. Brandy may feel angry, afraid, or lucky to be alive. She may feel humiliated, sad, confused, vengeful, or degraded and dirty. She may begin washing compulsively, particularly in the lower body, in response to feeling dirty. All of these responses are normal."

"And these feelings, how can I help her deal with them by simply letting her go?"

"Whatever a survivor is feeling is valid because they're feeling it. It's how they express their reaction to assault."

"Is there anything else that I can expect?"

"You may notice disruptions in her usual patterns. Brandy may not be able to eat or sleep, or may eat more than usual and be unable to stay awake."

"Should I sleep near her to let her know I'm there? I mean, she may have a horrible nightmare and wake up hysterical. Then what?"

"Survivors may report nightmares in which they relive the assault. Sexual assault is such a traumatic event that the survivor may dream about it in some way throughout her life. Oh my, look at the time," Judith said when she glanced at her watch. "I have got to get going." She stood up.

"Thank you for all of the information, Judith."

"You're welcome, Me'shelle. I hope that it's helpful to you and your family. What Brandy needs most now is love and support. With that and time, I believe she'll be fine," Judith said and handed Me'shelle a card. "Please call me when she's able to talk, or have one of the nurses contact me. And if you have any questions or I can help in any way, just let me know."

"I will," Me'shelle answered as the counselor walked away. She went into the room to check on Brandy, who was sleeping peacefully. Me'shelle made a commitment to herself that no matter what Bruce and Natalie had to say about it, Brandy was coming home with her. She would take a leave from work and watch over her niece. She had stood by too long and allowed too much to happen. It had to stop, and it had to stop now.

After she checked on Brandy, Me'shelle went to call Travis.

Chapter Twenty-three

Early that morning, Travis surprised Jackie and Ronnie with the announcement that he had another job planned. This was just what they both wanted to hear. Ronnie had made some bad investments and had to dip deep into his reserve to cover his losses. Jackie was deep into her reserves as well, as her gambling losses began to pile up.

Travis had decided to tell them that this would be his last job. Since the first day he began thinking seriously about it, he knew that his decision to get out would have a profound effect on his relationship with them. They knew something was going on with him, but up until this point, he was able to convince them his recent changes in behavior were all about him working again and nothing more.

And for a while that was fine. Jackie had gotten wrapped up in doing a little modeling and Ronnie seemed happy and content to be trading stocks again. But now, with their recent financial misfortunes, Travis felt responsible somehow and obligated to do this last job.

When Jackie and Ronnie arrived, Travis laid out his plan to take the bank he had been surveying. "Aw'ight, listen up. Our next job is going to be the taking of the First American Bank," Travis said. He laid a diagram of the bank on the table.

The house phone rang, but Travis ignored it and handed Jackie a map of the area around the bank. "On Friday, this branch has a larger than usual amount of cash on hand to process payroll checks from the offices in the area. When the bank opens on Friday morning, there's a small rush, which ends at approximately 10:15 a.m. Then there's a lull that lasts until approximately 11:30, when the lunch rush begins. That's our window. Our target time is 10:30. We will observe standard operating procedures as well as wearing standard operating gear, with business attire under our jumpsuits."

Travis turned his attention to the diagram of the bank. "The security is stationed outside of the bank, supposedly as a deterrent to robbery. His standard patrol pattern is simple; he walks circles on the sidewalk around the outside of the bank. He goes into the bank every fifteen minutes for a period of time that never exceeds ten minutes. He will enter the bank here at the north door, and will exit here at the south door," Travis said, pointing to the diagram.

The phone rang again, and once again Travis ignored it.

"Jackie will be positioned there and will advise on his entrance. Once he is in the bank, Jackie will move into position at the north door and stand by for the word 'go.' Ronnie, you and I will assume an ambush posture at the south door. When the guard exits the building, Ronnie will disarm and secure him while I cover. Once he's secure, the word is 'go.'

"Inside the bank there will be six employees: five females and one male. There are four teller positions and three offices directly adjacent to them. During our target window, at least two of those positions will be manned, but all positions will be stocked.

"Once inside, I will cover the room, and, if it's all right with you two, control the operation. Agreed?"

"Agreed," Jackie said.

"Ronnie?"

"You da man," Ronnie said.

"All right. The timeline is two minutes. Once we're inside, your first objective is to move everybody to the center of the room. Ronnie, you clear these offices while Jackie moves everybody out from behind the counter, but you'll maintain your position behind the counter and prepare to go for the money in the teller positions only.

"Ronnie, in the first office you'll find the bank manager. She will have a key on her waist; secure it. Once we have accounted for and have secured the guard, all six employees and however many customers are there, Ronnie will join Jackie behind the counter.

"You should have approximately one minute to get the money in the drawers and from the rolling cart, which will be behind the counter. Ronnie, that key will open the cart and any of the cash drawers that are locked. Take the cart first, Ronnie, while Jackie clears the teller positions.

"Jackie, once Ronnie has the cash from the cart, you will give him your bag, and you will exit the building trough the south entrance and prepare for our escape. Ronnie, you proceed to take any of the drawers that were locked."

This time his cell phone rang and Travis answered it. "Hello."

By the time she got Travis on the phone, Me'shelle was crying again, and it was very hard for Travis to understand what she was saying. "Slow down, Me'shelle. Are you all right?" Travis asked as he walked away from the table.

Jackie looked at Ronnie. "Who the fuck is Me'shelle?" she said softly and with a bit of attitude.

"How the fuck should I know?" Ronnie answered.

Travis was only able to make out the words 'rape', 'Jacobi Hospital' and 'please come.'

"All right, Me'shelle, just calm down. I'm on my way," he said and hung up.

Travis turned to Jackie and Ronnie, who both stood before him with questioning eyes. "What's up, Tee?" Ronnie asked.

"Who the fuck is Me'shelle?" Jackie asked.

"I gotta go, y'all."

"You leaving? In the middle of plannin' a job?" Ronnie asked in disbelief. "I don't fuckin' believe this shit. What's so fuckin' important that you got to drop everything and run out?"

"Who the fuck is Me'shelle?" Jackie asked again.

"I'll answer all your questions when I get back, but I gotta go. Y'all can stay here if you want to or bounce. I'll get with y'all later," Travis said and left the house.

"Ain't that a bitch," Ronnie said.

"It damn sure is. And who the fuck is Me'shelle?" Jackie asked.

Chapter Twenty-four

When Travis arrived at the hospital, he looked around for Me'shelle. The duty nurse led him to Brandy's room, where he found Me'shelle sitting quietly at her door. Travis sat down next to Me'shelle and the two sat quietly in the hallway holding hands. Me'shelle began to cry again, and Travis squeezed her hand a little tighter. Her thoughts were on Bruce and Natalie. Where were they, and why hadn't either of them come to the hospital to see about their daughter? *Probably off somewhere getting high.*

When her aunts arrived, Me'shelle cried as she told them how Brandy was doing and what she knew. Travis stayed back and allowed the family their space. "Has anybody heard from Bruce?" Juanita asked.

"Nothing. The police said they were going to send a car by the house, but I haven't heard anything else about that either," Me'shelle replied.

"Him and Natalie are probably off somewhere getting high like they always do," Miranda said, then she cried. "Can we see her?"

"I don't know. You'll have to check with the nurses. They said that Brandy was very agitated and they had to sedate her. They wanted her to rest."

Juanita started walking toward the nurses' station. "We'll see her."

While Juanita went off to talk with the nurses, Me'shelle introduced Miranda to Travis.

"I'm sorry to have to meet you under these circumstances. Me'shelle talks about you and her aunt

Juanita all the time. She has a lot of love and respect for you both," Travis said.

Miranda looked at Travis and rolled her eyes. "Did she teach you to say that?"

"No." Travis laughed a little. "She really does talk about the two of you all the time."

Juanita returned from the nurses' station. "We can see her now, as long as we don't wake her. I promised to call one of them if she wakes up."

"Aunt Juanita, this is Travis Burns, the man I've been telling you about. Travis, this is my aunt Juanita."

"It's a pleasure to meet you. I was just telling your sister that Me'shelle talks about the two of you all the time, and how she has so much love and respect for you both," Travis said

Juanita rolled her eyes just like Miranda did. "Huh. So you're the reason that Me'shelle can't come have Sunday dinner with us old ladies anymore," she said, looking at Me'shelle. "You know, the ones that she has so much love and respect for."

"I guess I am," Travis said softly.

"Let's go see Brandy, Juanita," Miranda said. Juanita followed her to Brandy's room. Before they entered, she stopped and turned back to face Travis. "I guess that means that you have to come to Sunday dinner with her now, since she can't seem to do anything without you," she said.

"It may be the only way we get to see her again," Juanita added then the pair disappeared into the room.

Travis turned around and reclaimed his seat. "That didn't go well."

"Yes, it did," Me'shelle said as she sat down next to him. "I think they like you."

"What makes you say that?"

"When they first met Trent, Aunt Juanita told him he had a big head, and Aunt Miranda, well, she didn't even speak to him. They were both looking forward to meeting you. I told them that you were the perfect gentleman and that you know how to treat a lady."

"I'd never have known it from that response."

"They invited you to dinner, Travis."

"So they can fatten me up for the kill. A punishment for taking their Me'shelle away from them."

As the day wore on, Me'shelle left Travis sitting in the hallway while she went in the room to be with her family. When she came out and sat down, Me'shelle noticed two men at the nurses' station. The nurse pointed in her direction and the two men came down the hall.

"Who are they?" Me'shelle asked.

"Cops," Travis answered.

"How do you know?"

"I can spot 'em a block away." Travis wasn't really feelin' being this close to the cops, but he didn't want to leave Me'shelle's side or look suspicious to the cops. They both stood up to meet the officers.

"Ms. Lawrence?"

"Yes."

"I'm Detective Richards, and this is my partner, Detective Kirkland. We just came from your brother's house, and I'm sorry to have to tell you this, Ms. Lawrence, but your brother and sister-in-law are both dead," he said

Me'shelle fell into Travis's arms and began to cry.

"They were murdered some time last night, we believe," Richards continued. "The murders may be drug-related. I understand that your niece was raped. Do you know if she was in the house last night?"

"I don't know. The doctor told me she's in shock and hasn't told anybody anything," Me'shelle answered.

"Yes, I know, but I thought that maybe you could tell us something."

"I don't know," Me'shelle said tearfully. "I don't know."

While Detective Richards tried to get answers from Me'shelle, Travis noticed Detective Kirkland staring at him. He couldn't help but wonder if there was any possibility that this cop recognized him. Travis avoided making eye contact with Kirkland, choosing instead to focus his gaze on Me'shelle and Detective Richards. The detective's eyes on him made Travis nervous, but he tried not to show it.

Kirkland put his hand on his partner's shoulder. "I know this is a bad time for you, Miss Lawrence, but we're going to need you to come in and talk with us." With that, Richards took out one of his cards and handed it to Me'shelle. "So, when you feel up to it, please give me a call."

Kirkland continued to stare at Travis as Richards turned and walked away. "Don't I know you from somewhere?"

"No. I don't think so," Travis answered.

"What's your name?" Kirkland asked. Richards turned around and returned to his partner's side.

"Travis Burns."

Kirkland looked Travis up and down then finally walked away.

Me'shelle looked curiously at Travis. "What was that all about?" she asked, wiping away her tears

"I have no idea," Travis answered as he watched the two detectives leave. But now he was worried.

Me'shelle called her aunts out into the hallway and told them about Bruce and Natalie. They cried together while Travis looked on helplessly. He was really shaken by his encounter with the detective. The thing to do now was to remain calm and page Freeze. He would wait a half an hour before he got up and left the area.

"What was that all about?" Detective Richards asked when they got on the elevator. "You know that guy?"

"Nah," Kirkland answered. "Never seen him before in my life."

"You think he might be involved?" Richards asked.

"I don't know, and to be honest, I really don't think he is. But you know how these things are, Pat. At this point, we don't have shit. So, sometimes you gotta shake shit up and see what falls out."

Chapter Twenty-five

Travis paced back and forth outside the hospital, waiting for Freeze to call him back. It had been almost two months since Travis had spoken to him. When Freeze called back, Travis told him where he was and what was going on, then informed him of his encounter with Detective Kirkland.

Freeze listened to what Travis had to say and told him not to worry. "Kirk is a homicide cop. His thing is drug-related murders. You wouldn't be on Kirk's radar. But he's a smart cop, as far as cops go, so stay out of his way."

"I plan to do just that," Travis said, but it was clear that he was still shaken by it all.

"So, what's goin' on, Travis? I haven't seen you around lately. You into something I should know about?"

"Been taking your advice and keeping a low profile."

"That's good, but you could still come by the spot and holla at a nigga. Let him know you all right and shit."

"You're right, Freeze. My bad. I'm just gettin' into some other things lately."

"So I heard. Your girl Jackie tells me you don't hang with them like you used to. Says you always busy, got something to do or whatever."

"It's fucked up, but she's right. But I got with them both this morning. You know, told them what they wanted to hear."

"You and me go back some years, don't we?"

"We sure do."

MOB

"Hey, you remember the time we hopped the turnstile and that cop grabbed you just before you could make it on the train?"

"Yeah, I remember that. He took me to the precinct to teach me a lesson. My pops had to come get me and shit."

"I remember you said he was sweatin' you pretty hard to tell him who was with you. But you was a man about it and kept your mouth shut."

"I wasn't about to give you up. I got caught and you didn't. But the next time you see who went over the turnstile first." Travis laughed, but Freeze didn't.

"You always was loyal . . . and smart too. So, I gotta ask you a question, and I want you to think about what I'm askin' and answer me honestly."

"No doubt."

"I don't even like havin' to ask you this, but I got to. And understand if it was anybody but you, Travis, I would just come to my own conclusion and do what I gotta do."

"Ask me what you wanna ask me, Freeze."

"Hang up the phone and turn around," Freeze said.

Travis turned around quickly and saw that Freeze had pulled up in front of him and was sitting in his truck waving for Travis to come to him. Travis walked toward the truck. "Get in," Freeze said.

After they exchanged pleasantries, Freeze drove off. Travis noticed that Freeze had a gun sitting in his lap. "What you wanna ask me, Freeze?"

"I need to know what's goin' on with you. See, a man in your position, havin' done the things that you've done, who don't hang out with his partners no more, only does it for two reasons. Either he got caught and he's talkin' to the cops about givin' somebody up, or he got a woman."

Travis laughed. "Her name is Me'shelle."

"I'm glad you said that."

Travis looked at the nine in Freeze's lap. "I am too."

"You really diggin' this ho?"

"Yeah, really."

"She the one whose niece got raped?"

"Yeah."

"She know anything about what you do?" Freeze asked, trying to get a sense for how much, if anything, Me'shelle knew.

"Nothing. As far as she knows, I'm a programmer."

"How long you plannin' on keeping up that front?"

"I don't know."

"You know she's gonna feel betrayed when she finds out. Let me give you some advice: be real with her about who you really are and what you really do," Freeze said as he pulled up in front of the hospital again. "I know this might not be the best time, but I want to meet her. Bring her to Cuisine for dinner one night. We've made a lot of changes since the last time you were there, so call ahead for reservations."

"I'll do that. Maybe we'll do that tonight if she's up to it. Me'shelle loves to eat out," Travis said as he got out of the truck.

As he walked inside the hospital, he thought about what had just happened. It scared him. He knew Freeze would have shot him if he felt he had rolled over. Travis thought about how much the detective's conversation had scared him, and now this. He thought back to how he panicked and ran to the Caymans after he saw himself on television. He was starting to realize that he wasn't built for this life. Travis knew that he had to get out.

Chapter Twenty-six

It was late when Me'shelle finally left the hospital. She asked Travis drive her to Queens to stay with her aunt. She didn't want to be alone, and felt she needed to be with family at a time like this. Travis understood, and dropped Me'shelle off at the door. "You sure you don't want me to come in and sit with you for a while?"

"No, that's all right. It's late and I just feel so drained. Besides, she's probably already gone to bed."

"Can I at least walk you to the door?"

"Of course you can."

Without another word, Travis quickly got out of the car and came around to open Me'shelle's door. She thanked him and they walked hand in hand to the front door.

"Good night, Travis, and thank you for being there for me today."

"Where else would I be? I always wanna be by your side, Me'shelle."

"I just wanted you to know that it meant a lot to me, that's all. I really needed your strength today," Me'shelle said. Travis gave her a hug.

"I know today wasn't easy for you. Anything you need, anything at all, you just have to ask. Okay?"

"Okay." She kissed him on the cheek. "Good night, Travis."

"Good night," Travis said as Me'shelle un-locked the door.

She stood in the doorway and watched Travis get in his car. Once he had driven away, Me'shelle went in the house.

Her intention was to go straight upstairs to bed, but those plans changed when she walked past the living room and found that both Juanita and Miranda were still up waiting for her.

"Hello," Me'shelle said quietly. "What are you two still doing up? I hope you weren't waiting up for me," she said as she plopped down on the couch next to Miranda.

"We were just sitting up talking," Miranda said. "But we were kinda waiting for you to get here."

"So, how are you, Me'shelle?" Juanita asked.

"I'm okay. I just feel drained, that's all."

Miranda looked at Me'shelle; she did look drained, which was to be expected. But Me'shelle was like a daughter to her, so she could tell that there was something else. "You should get some rest. It's been a long day. We all should."

"We wanted to make sure that you were all right. I know this day couldn't have been easy for you," Juanita said.

"Losing family never is, Juanita," Miranda said.

"I know that, Miranda. All I'm saying is that the violence involved with what happened hasn't been easy for any of us to take. I know it's been hard on me . . . Even though I knew this day would come."

"Juanita!" Miranda shouted.

"What?"

"We don't need to talk like that."

"Miranda, would you listen to how you sound? Yes, we do need talk like that. We have to talk about what happened and what we're going to do next. What arrangements need to be made, that type of stuff. What's going to happen with Brandy? I know we're all very concerned about that. But what's most important is that we all do one thing. We all need to deal with the fact that Bruce and Natalie were murdered and poor Brandy was raped." Juanita stopped suddenly. "Do you think Brandy saw her parents get killed?"

There was silence in the room as the three searched each other's faces and contemplated the questions Juanita had posed.

Since there was no way of knowing until Brandy was well enough to tell them, Juanita went on while Miranda and Me'shelle just shook their heads. "It probably happened because of something that Bruce was involved in."

Finally, Miranda cut her off. "You're right. We do need to start dealing with the fact that—I still can't bring myself to say it. We need to deal with what happened, but do we have to do it now?"

"The soon the better. And there is never a better time than now. Look at you, Miranda. You can't even say it. They were murdered. Brandy was raped."

"We know," Me'shelle said softly. "Bruce and Natalie are dead. They were murdered. My brother is dead." Me'shelle began to cry and Miranda touched her hand. "He's with Mommy and Daddy now. I know we all have to deal with it, and we will, but give us time."

Juanita could feel the anguish in Me'shelle's voice and in her tears. The feeling took her back to her sister's death and to all the pain she felt. She thought about all the death Me'shelle had to deal with in her life. "If I came on a little too strong, I'm sorry," she said.

"You always were just a little insensitive, Juanita. From the time we were little," Miranda scolded.

"I was not."

"Yes, you were. Anything is liable to come flying out of your mouth."

"You must be talking about yourself, 'cause I'm not like that," Juanita came back quickly.

"Yes, you are," Miranda said just as quickly.

While the debate raged on between the two sisters, Me'shelle got lost in her thoughts. She thought about Juanita's question. Did Brandy see what happened to Bruce and Natalie? Could that be part of the trauma that Brandy was trying to reconcile? Whatever the case, if Brandy saw them or not, it didn't change what Me'shelle was feeling.

It's my fault. I could have helped them, but I didn't. Now Bruce and Natalie are dead, and Brandy is traumatized.

And for that, Me'shelle blamed herself.

After a while, the combination of her thoughts and her aunts bickering became too much for her, so Me'shelle excused herself and said goodnight.

Being alone in her room was no better. The next morning, she lay across the bed, still fully dressed from the night before, staring out the window. It was going on 7:00 in the morning and she still hadn't gotten very much sleep. She'd spent the night thinking of Bruce. When she did drift off to sleep, her dreams were the same as her waking thoughts.

"Please, Me'shelle, just get me the money."

"No, Bruce, I'm not gonna do that. I'll take you and Natalie to a treatment program to get yourselves together. Brandy can stay with me until you two got it together, but I won't ask them for any money so you can get high."

"You don't understand me, Me'shelle. They're gonna kill me if I don't have it by Friday. Please, Me'shelle, you're the only one I can come to."

"Bruce, if somebody is gonna kill you, the best thing for you to do is leave Brandy with me and you and Natalie get out of town. I'll buy you two bus tickets to anywhere you want to go."

"Thanks for nothing, sis. But how you gonna live with yourself when I'm dead?"

It was those words, *How you gonna live with yourself when I'm dead?* that echoed in Me'shelle's mind throughout the night and haunted her dreams.

She wondered how she would live with herself knowing that Bruce came to her for help and all she did was offer him a bus ticket. If she had only given him the money when he asked for it, none of this would have happened.

But it did happen, and Me'shelle would have to put that behind her. Brandy would need her now, and she would be of little use if she couldn't cope with her own issues. She thought about Brandy being raped, most likely by the same men who wanted money from Bruce and killed him for it. The thought made her angry, not only with the rapist, but with Bruce and Natalie for not protecting her.

She was angry with herself as well. She thought about her constant pleas to get Brandy away from that environment where things like this could happen. Now she knew she should have done more than just talk.

Stop it!

Chapter Twenty-seven

After Travis left Me'shelle in Queens, he made the long ride back to the Bronx. When he arrived at his house, he was surprised to see Jackie's and Ronnie's cars still parked in the same spots.

He walked though the door and was met by Jackie's eyes, cutting through him like a knife. "Wake up, Ronnie. Travis is back," she said, shaking Ronnie out of his sleep.

"What's up, y'all?" Travis asked as he sat down on the chaise.

"What's up? That all you gotta say? What's up?" Jackie said.

"You wanna tell us about it, Tee, or what?" Ronnie asked.

"What do you want to know?"

"Let start with who the fuck is Me'shelle?" Jackie asked. "I think that will be a good place to start."

"She's a friend of mine."

"No shit," Ronnie said, bouncing up off the couch. "She must be a damn good friend for you to run out on us while we in the middle of planning a job."

"Yeah."

"Yeah? What the fuck does that mean?" Jackie asked. "You gonna have to break this one down for us, Travis, 'cause I really ain't feelin' this *yeah* shit."

Travis stood up. "Is there any weed left?"

Jackie smiled. "Ronnie tried to smoke you out, but I saved a blunt for you." She pulled a blunt from her cleavage and handed it to Travis. He lit the blunt and proceeded to explain to Jackie and Ronnie, in much more detail than they expected, his relationship with Me'shelle. He described the day they met at the grocery store when he came back from Connecticut. He told them about the dreams he'd had, and how those dreams led him to stake out the grocery so he could see her again. He explained why he aborted the job when he saw Me'shelle walking across the parking lot. "You remember her, don't you, Jackie? You thought she was fine." He even admitted that when they did actually run the job, the reason he overslept was because he had been on the phone with her all night. Lastly, he told them that her brother and sister-in-law had been killed and that her niece was raped.

"Now you know the reason I haven't been around much these last couple of months. I've been with her every day. Which reminds me, Jackie. Why you have to go and tell Freeze that?"

"Tell Freeze what?"

"That I haven't been around much."

"It's the truth. You haven't been around much."

"Yeah, well, you made him think I was talkin' to the cops."

"What?" Jackie said. "Travis, I'm sorry. I just mentioned to him that you didn't hang out like you used to, that's all."

"You know how paranoid that nigga is, Jackie," Ronnie said. "Don't ever tell that nigga shit unless you have to."

"He rolled up on me today, wanted to know what I was into. Had a nine in his lap," Travis told them.

"You think he was gonna kill you?" Jackie asked.

"If he thought I was talkin' to the cops, yes. He would've shot me twice in the head and had his upholstery cleaned."

"Damn, Travis, I'm sorry," Jackie said again.

"When did you have time to see Freeze anyway?" Ronnie asked. "I thought you was at the hospital all day with what's her face."

"I called him to ask about this cop name Kirkland. He's the cop investigating Me'shelle brother's murder. He came to the hospital."

"What you want to know about a cop for?" Ronnie asked.

"He said I looked familiar to him. So I asked Freeze about him."

"What! A cop said you look familiar?" Ronnie shouted.

"Shit! This is not good. Do you think he recognized you from the parking lot film?" Jackie asked.

"I don't think so. Freeze said he's a homicide cop. He doesn't think he'd be interested in us."

"Fuck what that nigga think. Fuckin' Freeze don't know every fuckin' thing," Ronnie said. "You got to pull away from this woman, Travis."

"Why?"

"If the cops are investigating her brother's murder, they gonna start lookin' at everyone around him. That includes his sister, and if you're hangin' around her, that means you too."

"He's right, Travis. You've got to leave her alone before this shit goes any further," Jackie added.

"I can't do that," Travis said and dropped his head.

"Do you love her?" Ronnie asked.

"Yes."

Jackie bounced up from the couch and left the room. Travis and Ronnie watched her storm into the kitchen then looked at one another.

"What's up with that?" Travis asked.

"I don't know, and right now, Travis, I really don't give a fuck. Travis, listen to me. Whether you love her or not, you have got to let her go. I mean back all the way up off her. You already got that nigga Freeze trippin' on you about the cops, and if they start lookin' at you, they start lookin' at us, and that ain't good, Travis."

Travis sat quietly.

"Do you hear what I'm sayin'?" Ronnie yelled.

"Yeah, Ronnie, I hear you and I know you're right."

"Damn right, I am. If the cops get onto you, they have the manpower and the resources to get you, and if Freeze thinks it will lead to him, he'll kill you, me and Jackie."

"I'll back up off her."

"Don't fuck around on this one, Travis. I'm serious."

"Okay, Ron. Shit. I said I'd back up off her. At least until things quiet down on her brother's murder," Travis said.

"No, Travis, you really ain't hearin' me. How you know when things quiet down? Huh?"

Again Travis sat quietly.

"That's what I thought. And even without the cops fuckin' with you, you still got Freeze to deal with. So, I'm tellin' you that you are going to leave her alone."

"Who are you to tell me what I gotta do?" Travis asked angrily.

"I'm your best fuckin' friend, Travis, that's who I am. And I'm the one who'll go down right along with you if it comes to that. Now, I don't wanna go to jail, and I damn sure don't want Freeze to kill me."

"You think I do?" Travis asked.

"No, I don't think you do, and I know Jackie don't either. So, what I'm tellin' you is to think about whether you being in love with this woman is worth riskin' any of that. I know that it's not."

"It's not, Ronnie. I know that. But it ain't easy."

"Yes it is, Travis. Us stayin' alive and not gettin' caught, that's what hard," Ronnie told Travis in a sober tone. "I'm glad we got that settled. And I'm glad to know that you didn't lose your nerve. And I'm sorry for thinking it. Who knew that all the time you were just pussy whipped?" Ronnie said and sat down.

"Yeah, who knew?" But Travis knew what the truth was, and now was the time to tell him. "Maybe I have lost my nerve, Ron."

"What are you talkin' about?"

"I've been thinking about making this my last job."

"Because of this?"

"No. I've been thinking about it for a while now. Ever since the jewelry store job. But now with all this happenin' with the cops and Freeze . . . I don't know."

"I do." Ronnie yawned and stood up. "You're just trippin' about Freeze with a nine in his lap, and I'm too tired to argue with you about it. Now you can go in there and see what Jackie's trippin' about."

Travis went into the kitchen and found Jackie sitting at the table, drinking Hennessey. He got a glass and joined her. "So, what's up?" he asked as Jackie filled his glass.

"Nothing. I'm just being stupid."

"So, tell me what's up anyway."

"No. You're gonna think I'm being stupid."

"No, I'm not."

"Yes, you are. Because I am."

"What's up, Jackie?"

"I'm jealous."

"Jealous? Jealous of what?"

"You're in love with another woman, Travis, and I'm jealous 'cause it's not me. Sounds pretty stupid coming from me, right?"

"I don't get it, Jackie."

"I don't get it either. And that's what so stupid about it." She drained her glass and poured another. "I guess I've gotten comfortable with the idea of you being my man."

"You lost me."

"Travis, you've been my man for years. Every time I needed to show up someplace with a man, it's always been you. Prom, college parties, office parties, family gatherings, whatever. It's always been you. Shit, my parents still wanna know when we're getting married. Don't ask me why, but somewhere in the back of my mind I thought . . . " Jackie paused. "I don't know what I was thinking. Stupid, right?"

"Damn, Jackie. I never knew you felt like that."

"Neither did I. Not until I heard you say you loved her. You've never taken a woman seriously." Jackie laughed. "Neither have I. But to hear you say that you're in love with her, that just caught me off guard. But I'm cool."

They sat quietly at the table looking at one another. Jackie smiled at him as Ronnie came into the kitchen. "You two kids got your shit worked out yet?" Ronnie asked as he poured himself a glass of Henny.

"I don't know," Travis said and turned to Jackie. "Do we, Jackie?"

"Like I said, I'm cool."

"Good, 'cause we got a job to do in a couple days, and both of y'all need to have your minds right."

Chapter Twenty-eight

A teary-eyed Me'shelle picked up the telephone once again and dialed Travis's number. The last day and a half hadn't been easy for her, but she got through it. With help and support from her aunts, she went to the morgue to identify Bruce and Natalie's bodies and made arrangements for their funeral. Natalie's family hadn't had anything to do with her in years, so when Me'shelle called them, her father's only response was, "Let me know where you bury her."

After taking care of that painful business, Me'shelle stopped by the hospital and sat with Brandy. While she was there, Detective Richards came to question Brandy, but she was still in shock. She acknowledged their presence in the room with her eyes, but never spoke. When he asked Brandy if she understood that her parents were dead, she just stared at Me'shelle and tears flowed from her eyes.

After the police left, Me'shelle told Brandy about her day and the arrangements she'd made for her parents. Then she read an article from *Vibe* out loud for Brandy before visiting hours ended and she had to leave.

Through it all, Me'shelle had been calling Travis both at his house and his cell phone. His cell was off, so the calls went straight to voicemail. He hadn't answered the house phone. She had left several messages and Travis hadn't chosen, up to this point, to call her back.

Travis sat next to the phone, as he had been for the past day and a half. He would see her name come up on caller ID each time, and let it go to voicemail. Then he would sit and listen to her message. He could hear the longing in her voice and could feel the pain. He felt tortured, caught between his loyalty to Ronnie and Jackie and what he felt for me Me'shelle. Travis felt like he was doing the right thing, but why did it feel so wrong?

"Please call me, Travis. I really need to talk to you, to hear your voice. I love you, Travis, and I miss you so much," Me'shelle said and hung up the phone.

"I miss talking to you, Me'shelle. But I can't," he said out loud.

She had never said she loved him before, and hearing it now had an effect on him. A single tear rolled down his cheek. "I love you so much, Me'shelle, but I can't."

Travis wondered why he was putting himself through this. It was bad enough that he couldn't talk to her, but why did he have to sit there and listen to her tear-filled messages? He could have just as easily left the house, left town, gone to Connecticut. At the very least, he could have turned off the answering machine.

He wanted to feel this pain, but he was growing weary of it.

Twenty minutes later, the phone rang again. Once again, it was Me'shelle. No longer willing to deliver or endure any more pain, he answered. "Hello, Me'shelle," Travis said softly.

"I'm so glad you answered. Where have you been? I've been calling you. Didn't you get any of my messages?"

For a fraction of a second, Travis thought about telling her that he wasn't going to see her again and why. "I had to go out of town for a minute. I just got back and listened to all of your messages. I miss talking to you, Me'shelle."

"I've missed talking to you so much these last couple of days. I don't know what to do with myself."

"I'm sorry I didn't call you. How are you holding up?"

"Not good, but I'm still standing."

"How's Brandy?"

"I just came home from seeing her. She looked at me when I came in the room and she squeezed my hand a couple of times while I read to her, but she's still not talking. But the hardest thing about this is my brother. I never mentioned this to you, but my brother came to me and asked me for money and I told him no." Me'shelle started to cry. "He said they were going to kill him. If I had only got the money for him, none of this would have happened."

"Me'shelle, you can't blame yourself for what happened."

"I know that I shouldn't, Travis, but it's one of the last things he said to me that's really fuckin' with me."

"What did he say to you?"

"He said, 'How you gonna live with yourself when I'm dead?' "

"Damn. That's some fucked up shit to say to somebody."

"Ain't it, though?"

"I'm sayin', but he probably wasn't expecting to get popped when he said it. Even though they know it's a possibility that it could happen, nobody expects to die. He just said that so you would feel sorry for him and give him the money."

"I know that, but it still bothers me."

"Do you know who he owed the money to?"

"Not really. He used to deal with some guy who calls himself Chilly. And the only reason I say that is because it's the only name I ever heard him say. It might be him, it might not. To be honest with you, I have no idea. I'd been giving him money to support his habit and get people off his back for years. But the one time that I tell him no, he gets killed."

"You can't do this to yourself, Me'shelle. You don't even know if that's what he got killed over. And even if it was, that's how he chose to live his life. You are not responsible for anybody's choices but your own."

"I know, I know. We've had this conversation before, but I still feel the way I feel, and I can only hope that over time I get to the point where I can deal with it a little better."

"I hope so."

"The funeral is the day after tomorrow. Will you come? I need you to be there for me."

Travis wanted to make some excuse for why he couldn't be there. He knew the best thing for him to do was stay away from her as long as it took for the investigation into her brother's murder to play itself out.

"I'll go with you," he said softly." He wanted to be, had to be by her side. "I'll be there for you, Me'shelle," Travis said louder, knowing the implications of choosing Me'shelle over his loyalty to Jackie and Ronnie.

"I want to see you."

"I wanna see you."

"I love you, Travis."

"Yeah, I know. I got your message. I gotta say it felt so good to hear you say it, since I've been in love with you since the first time I saw you. But still, I gotta ask. Are you sayin' it because of what's going on with you?"

"No, it's not that. And I'm sorry that it took all this to get me to say it out loud. But do I love you, Travis. I love everything about you. I love the way you talk to me. I love the way you make me feel. I am so into the way we are together. I feel like you are so much a part of me now. These last couple of days without you have been so hard for me. I love you, Travis. So please, don't think it's only because of this."

"Okay."

"And besides, you never told me that you loved me."

"Not in words, Me'shelle. But you know everything about me screams I love you."

"I know, so stop all this talk. I need you now."

"I'm on my way."

"No. This place reminds me too much of Bruce and that night. I'm coming over there."

"I'll see you when you get here."

Chapter Twenty-nine

Funeral services for Bruce and Natalie Lawrence were a small family affair. Nobody from Natalie's family bothered to show up. Her parents, a deeply religious couple, had disowned her years ago because of the life of drugs and prostitution she had chosen for herself. They were, however, very concerned about Brandy. The doctor thought that in her still very unstable condition, attending her parents' funeral might be too much for her. So, the attendees were Me'shelle and Travis, along with her aunts, Miranda and Juanita.

There were two other guests who came late to the funeral: Detectives Kirkland and Richards. The sight of them made Travis's blood run cold. They sat in the back of the church and waited until Pastor Franks completed his eulogy, then waited outside for Me'shelle.

"Ms. Lawrence," Detective Kirkland said. "I'm really sorry to have to bother you at a time like this. I've left several messages for you, but you haven't returned my calls."

"I've been staying with my aunts these last few days," Me'shelle said tearfully to the detectives as her aunts gathered around to support her.

"Young man," Juanita began. "I don't mean you any disrespect, and I know you got a job to do, but as you can imagine—"

"Maybe he can't," Miranda interrupted with much attitude.

"Miranda," Juanita said quickly, cutting her eyes at her sister. "Detective Kirkland, these last few days have been very hard on my niece and our family."

"I understand that, but I really do need for her to come in and talk with us."

"And I'm quite sure that she will, but today, young man, I'll thank you to show our family some respect and allow us to bury our dead in peace," Juanita said and walked away. The family followed her lead and went straight to the limousine. Travis fought the urge to give him the finger. Pastor Franks did, however, wave a chastising finger at the detectives as he joined the family in the limousine.

After the funeral, Travis kept his word to Freeze and brought Me'shelle to Cuisine for dinner. Although Freeze had mentioned it, Travis was surprised at how much the atmosphere had changed since the last time he was there. Freeze had moved quickly and returned to supper club to its former stature as a place of fine dining and intimate atmosphere.

"Travis Burns. I have a reservation for two."

"Good evening, Mr. Burns. Welcome back to Cuisine," the hostess said. "If you and your guest will please follow me, I have an excellent table waiting for you." She grabbed two menus. Travis and Me'shelle followed the hostess to their table and found a waitress waiting.

"Good evening, Mr. Burns. Welcome back to Cuisine," the waitress said. "We're glad to have you dining with us again," she said as she held the chair for Me'shelle. "My name is Bianca, and I will be your server this evening. Would you like something from the bar?"

Travis looked at Me'shelle. "Just some wine, maybe."

"Would you like to see our wine list?" she asked Me'shelle.

"Yes, thank you."

"I'll be back with our wine list. But before I go, let me just mention that today's special is grilled tilapia with a white wine sauce." The waitress departed.

"Well, Mr. Burns, I take it you've been here quite a bit," Me'shelle said as she looked over the menu.

"Yes. Do you remember me mentioning a friend of mine named Freeze?"

"The very dangerous one. I remember."

"He runs this place. But it's changed a lot since I was last here."

"How so?"

"That reception, for starters. You didn't need reservations before. And it was never this crowded so early in the day. It's a more upscale atmosphere now," Travis explained as their waitress returned with the wine list, accompanied by another server carrying a bottle of champagne and a bucket of ice.

"Dom Perignon, 1982, compliments of the management," the server said as she prepared to pour. "Mr. Burns, Freeze asked me to tell you and your guest to enjoy your meal. He will join you once you've finished," the waitress said after she handed Me'shelle the wine list. "Take your time. Look over both the menu and the wine list, and I'll be back to take your order."

Travis and Me'shelle enjoyed their meal, and as promised, Freeze joined them afterwards for cocktails and conversation. Travis looked up and couldn't believe what he saw coming toward him: Freeze wearing a suit.

"This must be Me'shelle," Freeze said and extended his hand.

"And you must be Freeze," Me'shelle said, accepting it. From that point, the three laughed and talked for the remainder of the evening. At first, Me'shelle was a little apprehensive about Freeze because Travis had told her that he was a dangerous man. But as the evening wore on and the drinks flowed and the conversation turned to this and that, Freeze made Me'shelle feel as comfortable as if they were old friends.

By the time Travis and Me'shelle left Cuisine, she was just a little drunk, and feeling kind of horny. As soon as they got in the door of Me'shelle's apartment, she stripped Travis down and led him into the bedroom and made love to him. Afterwards, she lay in his arms and they talked.

And then Me'shelle dropped it.

"I'm gonna go and talk to those detectives tomorrow," Me'shelle said and placed her head on Travis's chest.

"Have fun."

"Will you come with me? You know, for moral support."

"No."

"Why not?"

"I don't like cops."

"You don't have to talk to them. Just come down there and keep me company," Me'shelle said, running her hand over his chest.

"No."

"You don't even have to go in. Just take me down there."

"No. I told you I don't like cops, so I don't go around them."

"Not even for me?" Me'shelle asked and looked into his eyes.

"Not for you, Me'shelle, not for anybody. I don't mess with cops."

Me'shelle rolled over and grabbed her pillow. She was hurt by his refusal. She didn't think that she had made an unreasonable request. Just be with her.

While Me'shelle drifted off to sleep, Travis lay still and quiet. He knew that he couldn't go anywhere near Detective Kirkland. There was no way he was going to take the chance that he might have been recognized. He watched her as she slept and thought about what Freeze had said to him. *She's gonna feel betrayed when she finds out. Let me give you some advice: be real with her about who you really are and what you really do.*

When Me'shelle awoke the next morning and reached out for Travis, he was no longer in bed with her. She sat up and looked around.

"Good morning, Me'shelle," Travis said. He was dressed and sitting in the chair next to the bed.

"Good morning. You're up early," Me'shelle said, glancing at the clock.

"There's something that I have to tell you."

"I don't think I like the way this is going already," Me'shelle said and covered herself with the sheet. "What do you want to tell me?"

"I want to tell you why I can't go to the police with you."

"Well, don't leave me in suspense."

Travis stood up and began to pace. "I can't go with you because I can't take the chance that that detective really did recognize me from somewhere."

"Where would he recognize you from?"

He stopped and faced Me'shelle. "I robbed the grocery store where I met you."

"What?"

"I robbed—"

"No, Travis, I heard what you said. I just can't believe what I'm hearing. You robbed a grocery store?"

"Yes. And a lot of other places."

"You're kidding, right? I mean, this is all a joke, right, because this can't be happening to me. I can't be in love with a crook," she said as tears began to roll down her cheeks.

"I'm not kidding, Me'shelle."

"How long have you been doing this?"

"Two years."

"Two years, Travis? My God. Why didn't you tell me?"

"It's not the kind of thing that I just up and tell everybody."

"So, why are you telling me now?"

"Because I love you, Me'shelle, and I can't live with this lie any longer. I know it hurt you for me to say that I wasn't gonna go to the cops with you. Now you know why I can't go."

There was silence in the room. Me'shelle sat up on the bed and stared at Travis. To him, it felt like eternity.

"Say something, Me'shelle."

"I buried my brother and his wife yesterday. They were killed for the criminal things they were doing. My niece is in shock, raped, because of the criminal shit that her parents were doing!" Me'shelle said through her tears. "Now you stand there and tell me that you're a criminal too. Get out, Travis. I never want to see you again."

Chapter Thirty

By the time Me'shelle left the police station, she realized something. She hated cops too. Her experience with Detectives Kirkland and Richards wasn't pretty. In the two hours that she spent with them, Me'shelle was made to feel more like she had committed the crime than like the grieving sister of the victim.

When she walked in, she had every intention of giving her full cooperation to the investigation into her brother's murder. She was ready to offer any assistance she could to put the guilty person in jail for what they had done. They had killed her brother and sister-in-law and raped her niece. Me'shelle wanted to see them caught, tried, convicted and put away in jail for life.

She offered them the only bit information that she knew. Bruce was involved with somebody who went by the name of Chilly, and Bruce was worried because he owed money to somebody. But she couldn't say for sure whether he owed that money to Chilly or somebody else. Me'shelle simply didn't know.

That was all she had, and Me'shelle thought she would share that information then be free to go. However, the longer she sat there, the more Me'shelle was made to feel like she was not only involved in whatever Bruce was doing, but was involved in, if not responsible for what had happened. Their interrogation left a very bitter taste in her mouth, one that wouldn't be easily washed away.

When she thought it was over and she could leave, Detective Kirkland started asking about Travis.

"What do you want to know about him?"

Me'shelle wasn't listening while Kirkland asked his questions about Travis. She was lost in her own thoughts, wondering whether she should tell the detectives that Travis was involved in the grocery store robbery. The decision was easy. She was mad about the way the detectives had treated her by that point, so she had no desire to help them with anything. Besides, even though it hurt her to hear what he had told her, Me'shelle still felt love for Travis, and she couldn't do that to him. If they found out on their own, so be it. But she would have no part in it.

Kirkland didn't even remember Travis's name, a fact that amused Me'shelle. She wouldn't help the detective out by saying it. Her mind drifted to what Travis had said to her about not liking police and not wanting to have anything to do with them. She now shared his opinion.

"Miss Lawrence. Did you hear what I said?" Kirkland asked.

"Yes detective, I heard what you said," Me'shelle lied. "But I'm not exactly sure of what you're asking me."

"I don't see where it's such a tough question. Did your friend have any involvement with your brother?"

"The answer is no. But what I don't see is what one has to do with the other."

"It's just a simple question, Miss Lawrence. I wouldn't read anything into it, unless something belongs there." From that point forward, Kirkland asked questions and made statements that implied a relationship between Travis and Bruce where none existed. Not wanting to seem defensive about the subject, Me'shelle went along and answered the questions.

Finally, she'd had enough.

"Look, detective, I've said this before, but I'm going to try to explain it to you one more time so you understand what I'm sayin'. He did not know Bruce or Natalie. Now, I've sat here and listened to you make snotty innuendo after snotty innuendo first about me and now about my friend, and I really don't appreciate it. I've told you what little I know about my brother and what he was into," Me'shelle said and stood up, "so I'm going to go now."

Kirkland and Richards stood up. "Thank you for coming in and talking with us, Miss Lawrence," Kirkland said. Me'shelle didn't respond. She was expecting an apology, but since none seemed forthcoming, she started for the door. "Detective Richards will show you out," Kirkland said and left the room.

While Detective Richards escorted Me'shelle out of the building, he offered up a half-baked apology, which he served cold. He found no takers. Me'shelle walked silently out of the building and got in her car. She understood now why Travis didn't want to go with her to the police station to face the detective. She realized, after the treatment she received, that even though Travis didn't know Bruce, the detective would have tried to push a connection down his throat.

That thought made her feel a little better as she drove herself home. What was still troubling was the fact that Travis was not only a robber, but he had lied to her about it all these months. Maybe if he was honest about it from the start . . . *Get real. If he had told you what he was doing, you wouldn't have given him the time of day.*

She thought about something Travis had told her over dinner when he first started the programming job.

"This is the first programming job that I've had in two years."

"How have you survived for two years without a job?" Me'shelle asked.

"Sometimes real life leads you to make real hard choices that you normally wouldn't." But then the waiter arrived and broke into an elaborate description of the desserts, and she never got around to asking Travis what he meant by that. Now she wished that she had.

What's really bothering you? she asked herself. *Is it what he does for money, or that he didn't tell you?*

She didn't know, but the question had to be answered.

Chapter Thirty-one

The day had come for Brandy to be released from the hospital. It had been decided that she would stay with Miranda until more permanent arrangements could be made for her. Although she was still disoriented, and still plagued by uncontrollable trembling and feelings of coldness all over her body, Brandy's condition had improved. She began to communicate again.

Me'shelle and her aunts arrived at the hospital early. However, when they walked into Brandy's room, they found Detective Richards, the rape counselor, and a police sketch artist in the room with her.

"What in God's name is going on here?" Juanita demanded to know as soon as they came though the door.

Brandy looked up at them and smiled. Detective Richards stood up and approached the three ladies.

"Brandy, I needed to speak with your family for a minute. Is that okay?" Judith, the rape counselor, asked.

Brandy nodded and glanced in Me'shelle's direction. Seeing Me'shelle made her feel better. Brandy spoke slowly. "Can Aunt Me'shelle stay with me, Judith?"

"Well, Brandy, honey, I really need to speak with Me'shelle too. Is that going to be okay? I promise that it won't take long and we'll be right outside. Is that okay?"

"It's okay," Brandy said softly. Judith stood up and started for the door.

"Judith," Brandy called.

Judith turned around. "Yes, Brandy?"

Brandy pointed at the sketch artist. "I don't want to be alone with him." The sketch artist got up immediately and walked out of the room.

"Does he frighten you?" Judith asked.

"No. I just don't want to be alone with him."

"He's gone now, Brandy. But we need his help to catch the men who did this to you."

"I understand."

"I'll stay in here with her," Miranda offered. "I won't do anything to upset her."

Judith looked at Detective Richards and he nodded. Miranda sat down next to Brandy as the others left the room.

Once outside the room, Detective Richards explained that when Judith called and told him that Brandy could answer questions, he grabbed the sketch artist and came right down.

"I'm sorry that I didn't call you, but I kind of assumed one of you would be here," Richards said.

"That doesn't matter," Juanita said.

"That girl is a minor. One of us should have been here before you asked her anything," Me'shelle added.

"Under normal circumstances, I wouldn't have, but you haven't exactly been cooperative, Ms. Lawrence. I thought it best that we go ahead. I haven't asked any questions. I just listened while she told Judith what happened to her."

"Me'shelle," Judith said, "I want to assure you that Brandy has been doing fine with this. She's been able to tell us what happened that night, and was doing very well with the sketch artist.

"Brandy told me that she felt dirty and ashamed. She may have not have been able to be as open if her family was in the room while that was going on."

"But Brandy wants me to stay with her," Me'shelle protested.

"I see that, and since she's already told us all what happened, I'm willing to let you go back in there with us. But just you. And only if you promise to keep quiet and let us do our jobs."

"You act like I don't want you to catch the people who did this to her." Me'shelle was angry at the thought and started to say something else, but then she caught herself. The detective was right. What was important here was for them to get what they needed from Brandy, not her own trampled feelings.

"I'm sorry if I've given you that impression, Detective Richards. I want you to catch them, and I won't do anything to interfere with that. But before we go back in there can you please tell me what happened?"

"Your niece was able to tell us that there were four of them, and that she was listening when one of them killed the fourth man. She heard the men yelling at your brother about money he owed them. She hid in the closet under a pile of clothes, but they found her while they were looking for the money. After they found her, your brother told them where to find his money. She said after they got the money, they raped her and her mother while your brother watched, just to teach him a lesson."

"Oh my," Juanita said. Me'shelle shed tears for her brother.

"She got away when she hit one in the head with a lamp, and her father told her to run. She doesn't know what happened after that."

After hearing the story, Me'shelle wiped her eyes and followed them back into Brandy's room. While she sat there listening to Brandy bravely describing her attackers, Me'shelle's mind replayed the detective's words. *She heard the men yelling at your brother about money he owed them.* Bruce said that if they didn't get them their money they would kill him. She should have given him the money.

Me'shelle looked at Brandy. *I'm sorry. If I had just come off my high horse and gave Bruce the money, none of this would have happened.*

As the tears began to flow from Me'shelle's eyes, Brandy looked over at her. "Don't cry, Aunt Me'shelle," Brandy said to her. "It's gonna be all right."

Me'shelle quickly tried to wipe away her tears. She knew that she had to be strong for Brandy. She would have to put aside her feelings of guilt for the time being.

The next couple of day weren't easy for Brandy, as they were still marked by feelings of coldness and uncontrollable trembling. Brandy complained of an overall soreness of her body and had difficulty walking at times due to the pain she felt. She still had some bruises on her upper body, and she often complained of sudden, sharp pains in her vagina. There were times when Brandy would cry uncontrollably. She had headaches on a daily basis, which she attributed to having been hit in the head repeatedly during the assault.

She didn't talk very much, and would spend most of her day lying across her bed. One afternoon, some of her friends caught the train out to Queens to see Brandy, but she refused to see or talk to anyone. Her family did everything they could to make her comfortable and safe. One of them stayed in the room with her at all times.

She didn't sleep much, and when she did, she would be awakened frequently by nightmares about the assault. "I don't like goin' to sleep, Me'shelle," Brandy told her.

"How come?"

"Every time I sleep, it all happens again. And I wake up feeling all dirty and nasty."

"Is that why you take so many showers?"

Brandy nodded. "Down there especially."

"It's all right, Brandy. I'm not gonna ever let anything happen to you again."

"You don't have to worry about me, Aunt Me'shelle. There's nothing left for me anyway. They made me a dirty ho," Brandy said and began to cry. "Nobody will ever want me for anything."

"Don't say that," Me'shelle pleaded.

"I know I shouldn't feel that way, but I do. There's nothing left for me."

Me'shelle put her arms around Brandy and they cried together.

"I'm scared, Me'shelle. I'm scared all the time."

"You don't have to be scared, Brandy. We'll be here to protect you."

"My daddy used to say the same thing, and when those men came, all he could do was lay on the floor and watch."

Me'shelle had no answer, nothing she could say to reassure her that she would be safe.

"Those men are gonna come after me because I told the police what they looked like. And when they do, there's nothing that you can do to stop them."

Me'shelle continued to sit with Brandy. She knew that she had to do something to make this right. She stayed in the room until Brandy could no longer fight off sleep.

Downstairs in the living room, Juanita and Miranda sat watching television. Me'shelle joined them.

"Is she asleep?" Miranda asked.

"Yes," Me'shelle answered as she sat down on the couch next to Miranda. "But she told me that she's afraid to go to sleep because she's having nightmares about what happened."

"I'll go sit with her," Juanita said. She got up from her chair. "One of us should be there if she wakes up," she said before she went up to Brandy's room.

"You should get some sleep, too, Me'shelle. You've been up just as long as she has."

"I'm all right, Aunt Miranda."

"What's bothering you, Me'shelle?"

"Really, Aunt Miranda, I'm fine."

"I've seen that look before, Me'shelle Lawrence. Tell me what's on your mind," Miranda insisted. Me'shelle rested her head on her aunt's shoulder.

"I have so much on my mind I don't know where to start. But what it is, is that it's my fault that this happened."

"What you talkin' about, Me'shelle? How is this your fault?"

"Bruce told me that somebody was gonna kill him because of the money he owed them. He asked me for the money and I didn't give it to him. I had the money and I could have given it to him. If I had just given him the money, none of this would have happened."

"My God, child. This is not your fault. I don't mean to be speaking ill of the dead, but the truth is that Bruce was a drug addict. He's got money and stolen from all of us to buy drugs. Natalie was selling her body for drugs. There's no telling what else they were doing."

"I know all that, but—"

"But nothing, Me'shelle. You listen to me. Suppose you gave Bruce the money and they killed him anyway.

What then? Would you still blame yourself? 'Cause that's what would have happened. That life he was living was gonna kill him or get him killed. You know that, Me'shelle. You used to tell Bruce that all the time."

"I know what you're saying, and maybe you're right, but that's how I feel, and I got to do something about it."

"Like what?"

"Even if you're right about Bruce," Me'shelle said, ignoring Miranda's question, "I still could have done more to get Brandy away from there."

"That's a cross we are all gonna have to bear," Miranda said sadly.

"When Bruce said they were in Columbia and Brandy wasn't in school, I should have gotten in my car and went to get her."

"We all could have done a lot more for Brandy. All we can do now is be there for her now," Miranda said.

"I was too busy," Me'shelle went on. "I was too busy going out with Travis and eating in fancy restaurants to worry about Brandy and what was best for her."

Seeing where this was going, Miranda said, "I don't mean to change the subject, but I do notice that you haven't mentioned his name, and I don't remember you talking to him in a while."

Me'shelle laughed a little. "That's another thing."

"See, I know my little girl. I knew there was something else. What's bothering you?"

"I found out something bad about Travis," Me'shelle said.

"Really? He seemed like a nice young man. What did you find out about him?"

"I'll just say he wasn't completely honest with me."

"How do you feel about him, Me'shelle?"

"Well, I—"

"Do you love him, Me'shelle?"

"Yes, I think I do."

"Does he love you?"

"He says he does."

"Do you believe him when he says he loves you?"

"Yes, I believe he loves me."

"Me'shelle, what you are going to have to decide is whether whatever you found out about him is so bad that it changes your feelings for him," Miranda offered. "And I don't think it does, 'cause if it did, you wouldn't be going through no changes about it."

"You may be right. But none of that matters now anyway. Right now I need him."

Chapter Thirty-two

After Me'shelle put him out of her apartment, Travis was alone with his thoughts. Even on days when Ronnie and Jackie came over to his house, he was still alone. They told Travis that it was for the best. Ronnie said that his involvement with Me'shelle under these circumstances would only end in disaster for the three of them. "And it ain't worth the risk," he said.

Jackie was pretty quiet, though, offering up an opinion or agreeing with Ronnie when it seemed appropriate. But she felt Travis's pain, and didn't want to minimize it, so she sat next to him and held his hand. What was more pressing to Jackie was the exploration of the depth of the feelings that she had for Travis.

Once Travis had heard enough from Ronnie about how he should be happy that Me'shelle didn't want to see him again, he turned the conversation around to business. He got up and went into the dining room. "We have a job to run in the morning, so let's go over this again. Especially since we were interrupted the first time, I want to be sure we're all on the same page."

"That's what you need, Travis. Get back to business," Ronnie said. "It's time to get focused. I'm glad you're not losing sight of the bigger picture."

"No, Ronnie, I haven't lost sight of the big picture," Travis said as he laid the diagram of the bank out on the dining room table. But he knew in his heart that Me'shelle was a part of that picture.

After going over the plan three times, all agreed that they were satisfied with the details. Ronnie announced that he was going home. Travis thought Jackie would follow suit and break out with Ronnie, but she had other plans.

"So, how are you?" she asked Travis.

"I'm fine, Jackie. Really," he said and sat down next to her. "And thanks for not riding me tonight."

Jackie smiled and laughed a little. "I thought one of us ridin' you was enough."

"You know, you and I never really did get to finish our conversation."

"What? About me loving you?"

"Yeah, Jackie. About that."

"Like I said, I'm cool. That's just something that I have to deal with."

"No, Jackie. When you dropped it on me, it became something we both have to deal with."

"Yeah, you're right. It was kinda fucked up for me to drop my little bit of baggage on you."

"Hey, that's what friends are for. But I don't get it. I mean, I love you, Jackie, but like a friend. I love you the way I love Ronnie. You know what I'm sayin'?"

"I love you like that, too, but there's something more, that's all. Like I said, you've always been my man. It didn't matter what I was doin' or what you were doin', or what we done with each other."

At the mention of their past sexual involvement, Travis said, "I was wondering if that was it."

"I don't know, Travis. I'm still trying to sort all this out in my mind. You know, at the time I thought I was just caught up in the moment."

"Me too.

"What was her name anyway?"

"Which one?" Travis asked.

"The first one."

"Oh shit. What was her name? She was your friend. You should remember her name."

"I know. Ain't that terrible? Too much weed making my memory bad," Jackie said. "It was my sophomore year at Rutgers and you had come down for the weekend."

"To go to some party with you. I remember. What was her name?" He paused, then it came to him. "Sharee French."

"That's her. She was mad as hell with me after that. She was so into me it wasn't even funny. I was glad to get rid of her, 'cause after that she started trippin'," Jackie recalled.

"I guess so. We were supposed to be sharing her, not the two of you sharing me."

Jackie smiled.

"I was shocked when you got on top of me and started ridin'. I know Sharee was. What happened that day?"

"I don't know, Travis. I guess I just wanted to. I wanted to feel you inside me. And every time after that, I'd always want to feel you inside me. You're the only man I ever had."

"You and I have shared so many women," Travis said. Then it hit him. "Wait a minute. Didn't you and Ronnie, before me and you?"

"Not exactly."

"What does that mean, Jackie?"

"Well, we did and we didn't."

"What does that mean?"

"You have to promise not to tell Ronnie I told you."

"I ain't gonna say nothin'. What happened?"

"Promise you won't laugh." Jackie paused. "We never really did it. I mean, we kissed and he felt on me, but Ronnie came on me while he was trying to get it in me."

Travis started laughing.

"You said you wouldn't laugh."

"No, I said I wouldn't tell him you told me. That shit is funny, 'cause it never stopped him from bragging about it for years. And you let him do it. Didn't say shit."

"I won't do that, bust him down like that. Not in front of you, anyway. You were my first, Travis. The only man I've ever had inside me. Only man I've ever wanted inside me, and I guess I'm a little emotional about it, that's all."

"If that's how you felt, then how come the only time we've done it is with another woman? Never just you and me. Why is that?"

"That's the only time I felt like it. Look, Travis, the whole thing is still kind of confusing to me. But like I said, I'm cool with it."

"Well, as long as you're cool with it, I am too," he said. "We got a big day tomorrow, so I'm gonna go and get some sleep."

"Okay," Jackie said and stood up. She walked into Travis's bedroom and got a big shirt out of the dresser then began to get undressed.

Travis came into his room slowly, looking a bit confused to see Jackie standing there naked. "Don't look so worried, Travis. I just don't feel like driving home just to come back in the morning," she said. She put on the big shirt and got under the covers.

"Okay," Travis said. "But I sleep naked."

"What's your point? I've seen you naked before."

Travis got undressed and joined Jackie between the sheets. She snuggled up close to Travis and put her head on his chest. Travis put his arm around her. "This is gonna be my last job, Jackie."

"Because of her?"

"No, not because of her. I've had this on my mind for a long time. But I'd be lying if I said that she isn't a part of it. I never wanted to make a career out of this."

"Either did I, but what else we gonna do?"

"Come on, Jackie. You make it sound like none of us got skills."

"Like what?"

"Like what? What else can you do, is that what you're asking me?"

"Yeah, Travis, that's exactly what I'm asking you. What the hell else have we got to do?"

"For the last couple of months, you've been doin' all right modeling. What about that?"

"That's just pocket money, Travis."

"You're a chemist and a damn good one. That was all you've ever really wanted to be."

"You're right. That's what I wanted to be from when we were kids."

"Have you gotten so far away from it that you can't see it anymore? I hope not."

"No, I haven't."

"You can still get back into it. With the money you got, you could go back to school and get your masters or a PhD. Jackie, there is so much more that you–shit, all of us could be doing."

"I know what you're trying to say, Travis, and you're right. I guess what I'm asking is what else can we do to bring in the kind of money that we can doing our thing?"

Travis looked at Jackie without an answer for a second or two before he said, "Nothing. But that doesn't mean that we don't have any choices."

"All that is easy for you to say, Travis. You stuck with your plan and banked that money, bought property, shit like that. All my reserves are just about gone. I need this to make it," Jackie said, knowing that the reason she had drained her reserves was her gambling habit.

"No, Jackie, you don't. You can make it another way. And you're right; I do have bank, so whatever you decide to do, I got your back. And you know this."

There was silence in the room after that, and it wasn't long before Travis drifted off to sleep. For Jackie, it wasn't that easy. She knew that as long as she kept gambling, she would have to keep robbing.

When Ronnie arrived at Travis's house the following morning, he found them seated at the table eating breakfast and drinking coffee. "Hope y'all saved some food for me."

"Of course we did, Ronnie," Jackie said.

When it came time to leave for the job, they gathered their equipment and left the house. As they were about to get in the car, Travis saw Me'shelle's car coming down the street. "I'll be right back," he said then walked away.

"We don't have time for this now, Travis. We got to go," Ronnie yelled.

"I'll be right with you."

Me'shelle parked in front of the house and got out. She came around the car and stepped to Travis.

"Hello, Me'shelle."

"Hi."

"I'm a little surprised to see you."

"I think we need to talk, Travis. Don't you?"

"I know we need to," Travis said. He reached for Me'shelle's hand.

Ronnie honked the horn. "We gotta go, Travis," he yelled out the window.

"Where are you going?"

"We got some business to handle," Travis replied.

Me'shelle put her finger over his lips. "You don't have to say any more. Give me the keys to the house."

Travis reached into his pocket and handed her the keys.

"Go on and handle your business. I'll be here when you get back," Me'shelle said, kissing Travis on the cheek before turning away and walking toward the house.

Travis watched her until she closed the door, then he got in the car with Jackie and Ronnie. "Let's go do this."

Chapter Thirty-three

At approximately 10:25 a.m., a 2000 black Chrysler 300 pulled into the parking lot at the Citizens Bank. Travis, Jackie and Ronnie assumed a position where two sides of the building were visible, and proceeded to run though their operations checklist. Once that was complete, the plan went into operation. "Mr. White, surveillance position."

"Acknowledged, Mr. Blue," Jackie said and exited the vehicle. She walked around the building until she saw the security guard. She watched him until he entered the bank. "One uniformed security officer entering the structure via the north door."

"Acknowledged, Mr. White. Stand by."

"Acknowledged."

Ronnie took out a set of high-powered image stabilizing binoculars and looked in the bank. From their position in the car, he could see clearly inside. "This image is so sharp, Travis. None of that blurred, shaking shit you usually get."

"It has two direct drive motors, one each for horizontal and vertical control, so it eliminates the jittery images caused by normal hand tremors."

"Maintain operational silence," Jackie said and laughed.

"Acknowledged," both Travis and Ronnie said.

"Stand by," Ronnie said. "Subject is moving toward the door."

"Acknowledged," Travis said. "Assume ambush posture, Mr. Green."

MOB

Ronnie got out of the car and moved into position to intercept the security officer as he exited the bank. While Travis covered, Ronnie quickly disarmed the guard.

"Go!" Travis commanded, and the three entered the bank.

"Nobody move!" Travis yelled. Once he had everybody's attention, Ronnie moved to get the employees out of the offices. He took the key from the branch manager. Jackie moved everybody out from behind the counter. When everybody was in the middle of the room, face down on the floor, Travis called, "One minute."

Jackie went to each teller's position and cleaned out the drawers. Ronnie unlocked the cart and got the money. Jackie handed her bag to Ronnie and exited the building through the south entrance to prepare for their escape.

Jackie made it to the car and moved into position outside the south entrance. She looked out at the street and saw a police car coming toward the bank. "Mr. Blue, local police vehicle approaching from the south. Estimate entrance into parking lot in thirty seconds."

"Acknowledged. Maintain position and stand by. Mr. Green, exit north door and assume assault position one."

"Acknowledged." Ronnie came from behind the counter and handed the bags to Travis. He went out the door and took the pump from under his coat. Travis secured the bag full of money to his body and waited for Jackie to give the word.

Ronnie moved around the side of the building and took up a position at the corner, where he could see Jackie parked in the Chrysler.

"In position, Mr. Blue," Ronnie said.

"Acknowledged," Travis responded.

"Police in firing position, Mr. Blue. Begin your approach," Jackie said.

"Acknowledged," Travis said then moved carefully to the door.

With the police car in position, Ronnie opened fire with the pump before the cop could get out of the car. Jackie covered Travis's exit from the bank. Once Travis had placed the money in the car, he began firing at the police car. Ronnie dropped the pump and ran toward the car. Travis took aim and shot out the rear tires on the police car.

Once Ronnie was in the vehicle, Travis got in and Jackie took off. She drove about a block before she turned into another parking lot, drove to the back of the lot and parked. All three jumped out of the vehicle and ran into the woods.

They ran for a half-mile before they came to a clearing in the back of another parking lot. They quickly ditched the trench coats and jumpsuits. Jackie, who now had on a dress, came out of the woods first. She walked causally to the second vehicle, a 2005 Dodge Magnum. Once inside, she pulled around to pick up Travis and Ronnie.

The ride back to the city was quiet and uneventful. They maintained the speed limit for the most part. There was one scare, however. A police car fell in behind them and cruised for a half mile before going blue light.

"Oh shit! Here we go," Jackie said.

Weapons were drawn as all prepared for another gun battle with the police. Then the cop went around them to chase after somebody else.

"That was too close for my taste," Jackie admitted.

Since Travis's house was occupied by Me'shelle, Jackie drove to Ronnie's house so they could count up and divide the money.

"Ninety-six thousand four hundred and eighty-two dollars," Travis announced.

"That's all?" Ronnie asked. "After all that shit, all we gonna come away with is less than thirty grand a piece?"

"I knew that last job would spoil us," Jackie said.

"The grocery store job was much bigger than I expected. But every job ain't been like that," Travis explained.

"Well, they should be. We takin' a lot of risk for a little bit of money. Maybe we should only do grocery stores on Mondays," Ronnie said.

"Yeah right," Jackie said. "And be in jail by Tuesday. Cops may be stupid, but I think they could figure out that pattern."

"You know, on our first job we each came away with sixteen grand. We made almost double that today and you bitchin' about it," Travis said.

"All I'm sayin' is we should be lookin' at higher value targets to hit."

"This was a good hit today. It's the kind of money we always been making when we go out. Now the shit ain't enough for you? Well, if you can find a higher value target to hit, you let us know," Jackie said.

"Well, I heard rumors about this house in Westchester that has noting but safes full of diamonds all through the house."

"I heard those same rumors. I also heard that place is so mobbed up that it would be suicide for anyone who tried to rob it. Put that shit out of your mind, 'cause it ain't happenin'."

"I'm just sayin' if we ain't gonna come away with a certain amount of money, then maybe we shouldn't go out."

"I'll keep that in mind." Travis stood up. "You know, it was you who said that we had to run a job soon because you needed the dough. Now I gotta hear this shit. That's it for me, man. I'm out!" Travis said.

"What the fuck you mean, you out?"

"From here on out, if you wanna do this, fine. Do it by your damn self."

"You just gonna up and quit on us like that?"

"I told you before, when we got into this thing, I never planned on us still being at it two years later. I had a plan. A plan for what I was gonna do to set myself up so I could live comfortable for the rest of my life. It ain't my fault that you spent all your money."

"This is fucked up, Travis, that's all I know. You gonna roll out on us after making this little bit of money. Come on, Travis. Let's hit one more big money target, and after that we can go our separate ways."

"No, Ronnie, I'm done. No more. Do you hear me? No more! No more robbin', no more shootin', no more gettin' shot at. It's over! You can do what you want."

"That's what it is; you're scared. I was right about you, Travis. You lost your nerve," Ronnie said.

"You're right, Ronnie. Absolutely right. I have lost my nerve. I don't want to do this anymore. We've been lucky so far; we haven't killed anybody and none of us have gotten hurt. But that's it. We've been lucky, that's all. I'm not gonna wait around for our luck to run out."

"It's about that bitch, ain't it?"

"What you say?"

"You heard what I said. It's about that bitch."

"Ronnie, you and me go a long way back, and I know that you're mad, so I'm gonna let that go. But you can think whatever you want to about why, and if you want to put it all on Me'shelle, be my guest. But it doesn't change the facts one way or the other. I'm out."

"You're a fuckin' coward, Travis! That's what the fuck you are, a fuckin' coward. Let that woman run you. You gonna run out on your partners, your friends, Travis? You ain't shit. Whatever happened to our rules? We supposed to be choosin' money over bitches. M.O.B. my ass! Get the fuck out my house, you fuckin' coward!"

"Whatever, Ronnie. Take me home, Jackie."

Travis walked out of the house without another word. Jackie looked at Ronnie and shook her head.

"What?" Ronnie asked.

"Nothing, Ronnie. If you don't know, I can't make you see it," Jackie said and left the house.

Chapter Thirty-four

Jackie dropped Travis off at his house before she went home. "Aren't you going to see Freeze?" she asked.

"No. I'll page him tomorrow," Travis answered.

"Call me if you need anything,"

"Thanks, Jackie."

"Call me tomorrow, okay?"

"I will," Travis said and went inside. Me'shelle was asleep on the couch, so he entered quietly to avoid waking her. He sat in the chair across from her and watched her while she slept. Me'shelle looked so peaceful, so beautiful.

While he sat there, he replayed the argument he'd just had with Ronnie. His desire to get out and get out now had everything to do with Me'shelle. When he looked at her, Travis saw the future. It was a future that didn't involve planning robberies, timetables, guns, the police, or people like Freeze making thinly veiled threats with a nine in his lap.

When Travis was with Me'shelle, everything just seemed so right. But that happy life was built on a lie. It was a simple lie, but still it was the foundation of their relationship. Travis presented himself as an honest, hard-working man. Although what he did was work, it definitely wasn't honest. He understood Me'shelle's reaction to the revelation that he robbed for a living, but he had hope. The fact that she was lying on his couch sleeping so peacefully meant that maybe he still had a chance at a future with her.

Travis thought back to the night that he and Ronnie and Jackie made their rules. They were the rules they had lived by. *Rule one, M.O.B. Rule nine, Let no one come between us.* By choosing to get out now and trying to make a future with Me'shelle, Travis had done just that. He tried to justify it within himself by saying that Ronnie had made the choice to break up what they'd built, but he knew in his heart that this was his choice. It was one that he hoped wouldn't cost their friendship.

When Me'shelle finally woke up, she found Travis seated in front of her. Over the last few days, she'd had a lot to think about. Her brother and sister-in-law were dead, and although she blamed herself for not doing more to help, Me'shelle had slowly come to terms with it. She concluded that even if she had given him the money, it would only be a loan against time. What he was doing was bound to end the way it did unless Bruce himself chose another path. Now she had to choose.

It was like the last few days had changed her somehow. Like she had grown up. She was a woman who led a pretty normal, uneventful life. Now that life seemed so far away.

Me'shelle thought about her reaction to Travis's news that he was a robber. She got angry and kicked him out. *I never want to see you again.* But there she was now, on his couch. She refused to support her brother's drug habit, yet here she was on the couch of a man who admitted he robbed a grocery store. When the police questioned her about Travis, she had no problem protecting him.

Part of her wanted to blame it all on love, but she knew that wasn't enough. Was she in love with Travis?

Sure, but Me'shelle knew why she was there, and it had nothing to do with love. Love could wait. Travis knew people. He knew the kind of people who would know who did this to her brother. Now she was thinking about revenge.

"Hello," he said.

"Hello yourself," she said, wiping the sleep from her eyes. "How long have you been here?"

"About an hour."

"And you've just been sitting there?"

"Watching you. You're very pretty when you're sleeping."

Me'shelle smiled and sat up. "We need to talk."

"I know. How's Brandy?"

"She's doing better. Thank you for asking. She's talking again. Not much, but she talks to me. She's scared, Travis. Scared that the men who raped her and killed my brother will come after her."

"Did she talk to the police?"

"Yes, and she gave them a description of the men who did it, but you know as well as I do that a drug-related rape and murder isn't going to be real high on their list of things to do. Maybe if they stumble over them . . ." Me'shelle gave a disgusted laugh.

"I don't know. I hear that Kirk is a good cop, so you never know," Travis said, trying to sound optimistic.

"But somebody has to do something," Me'shelle countered. She looked directly at Travis. "Anyway, I don't wanna talk about that now. I came here because I think we need to talk about us."

"I know."

"Where do we start?" Me'shelle asked.

"What do you want to know?"

"I guess you could start from the beginning. How did you go from a programmer to a grocery store robber?"

Travis looked into Me'shelle's eyes and briefly considered some very important facts. A few days ago, Me'shelle had thrown him out of her apartment and said that she never wanted to see him again. She had been to the police and could very well have told them that he was responsible for the grocery store robbery and who knows what else. Now she was sitting in front of him asking for his story. "What did you tell the police about me?"

"I didn't tell them anything about you. I wouldn't even say your name. They tried to say that you were involved with Bruce, or that maybe it was something that you were involved in that got them killed. But I knew better. I couldn't tell them anything about you, Travis. I know this was all Bruce's doing and you had nothing to do with it."

"But I had to ask."

"I've been wondering these last few days how I feel about what you do for money."

"*Used to do* for money. Before you go any further, Me'shelle, I want you to know that I'm finished with that life. Today I ran my last job."

"What brought this on? And don't say it's because of me."

"Well, I'd be lying if I said it was all because of you, but I'd be lying if I said that you had nothing to do with it. Does that make sense?"

"In a way."

"I mean, it has everything and nothing to do with you. I'd been planning to get out long before I met you, but I didn't think I'd have enough money to retire on."

Me'shelle just looked at him.

"It's like this: when I got into this, it was because me, Ronnie and Jackie had all lost our jobs and we didn't see any other way."

"I remember, you said 'Sometimes real life leads you to make real hard choices that you normally wouldn't.' But why that, Travis? You're a smart man. There's a lot of things that you could have done.

"But I guess it's not fair for me to judge you for that. That job belongs to a higher power than me. I don't know what you were going through at the time to force you to make that choice.

"What I need to know from you now is what you plan to do in the future. I can't live like that; I won't live like that, wondering every time you go off with your friends to handle your business if you're coming home. I won't live in fear that every time the doorbell rings it could be the police coming to take you away. That someday you may decide that you don't have enough money and you have to do one more job. 'Cause that one job will always lead to the next."

"You want to know the truth, Me'shelle?"

"Yes."

"The truth is that I'm scared. Scared of the same things you just mentioned. Whether me or Jackie and Ronnie will get shot or killed, or when I'll make a mistake on a job and the police will come after me. I don't want to live like that."

"So, what do you want?"

"I want to live a normal life, and I'd like the chance to live that life with you. When I think about the life that we've had these last few months, I know that's where I wanna be. Worrying only about what restaurant we're going to eat at and whether you'll be on time."

Me'shelle laughed. "You make it sound like I'm always late."

"Well . . ."

Me'shelle took a playful swing at Travis. "Okay, let's say I believe you when you say that you're done. Have you told your friends yet?"

"Yes. I told them tonight that I was done."

"How did they take it?"

"Ronnie called me a fuckin' coward and told me to get the fuck out of his house."

"What about Jackie? What did she say?"

"She's scared that there's nothing else that she can do."

"What does she do? Before she became a gun moll, I mean."

"She's a chemist."

"That's right. You did mention that. She'll be all right. They both will, I'm sure."

"Yeah, I just hope it doesn't cost our friendship."

"Have you ever killed anybody?"

"I'm not sure I should be answering all these questions."

"Why not? You think I'm wearing a wire or something?" Me'shelle asked and smiled.

"I don't know. You could be," Travis said playfully.

Me'shelle looked at Travis and wondered about the kind of person you had to be to both plan and execute robberies. She was disturbed by it, but at the same time, and for reasons she couldn't really explain to herself, it excited her. Travis Burns was the kind of man who went after what he wanted. *Just like he went after me.* She looked into his eyes. *He wanted me, and he got me.*

"Maybe this will ease your fears about that," Me'shelle said and stood up. "This will prove to you that I'm not wearing a wire." Me'shelle began to undress, throwing Travis every piece of clothing as she took it off. He happily felt each piece to be sure it contained no electronic devices. Once she was naked, Me'shelle made several turns in front of him. Once Travis was satisfied the she wasn't wired, he carried her off to the bedroom.

The following morning, Travis woke up early. He left Me'shelle asleep in bed and left the house to page Freeze. "Meet me at Cynt's," Freeze told him. "No, on second thought, since I know you don't want to run up on Mystique, meet me at Doc's spot this afternoon around four."

Travis laughed, but he appreciated the gesture. "I'll be there." He had only been to Doc's once and wasn't really all that impressed. The dancers were ugly, and Jackie said that the dealers stacked the deck.

That afternoon, he told Me'shelle he had to go handle some business with Freeze. She was reluctant to let him go until he promised it had nothing to do with any more robberies.

When Travis arrived at Doc's, he was pleasantly surprised to see that Doc had upgraded the quality of the dancers. Gone were the women with stab wounds and bullet holes, replaced by a variety of Nubian princesses to satisfy any taste. He took a seat at a table in the back of the room and waited for Freeze to arrive. Since he was not a regular there like he was at Cynt's, dancers didn't flock to his table. It didn't matter to him. He was there to take care of his business with Freeze and get back to Me'shelle.

As he usually did, Freeze kept Travis waiting. He had been there for over an hour when a fairly large man approached the table. "Can I help you?" the man asked.

"No."

"I said can I help you?" the man repeated.

"No. I'm waiting for somebody."

"Who?"

"What?"

"Who you waitin' for?"

"Who I'm waitin' for don't concern you," Travis stated as the people around them began to move out of the way.

"Everything that goes on in here is my concern. Now, who you here waitin' for?" The man opened his jacket to be sure that Travis saw his gun.

"Okay. Unless you gonna shoot me now, you need to back the fuck up off me," Travis warned and stood up. "I told you I got business here. Important business."

"Is there a problem here, gentlemen?" Freeze asked as he walked up.

"No," Travis said and reclaimed his seat.

"This guy says he got business in here. Said he's waitin' on somebody. You want me to put him out?"

"No," Freeze said. "I got him."

"You don't want me to—"

"What are you, deaf? I said I got him!" Freeze yelled. The man left angry.

Once he was gone, Freeze sat down and Travis discreetly handed him the envelope. "Sorry about that. I should have told you that they're on edge here 'cause they got robbed a couple of weeks ago," Freeze apologized.

"Maybe you should have. I wasn't gonna say your name, so it was about to get ugly."

"You could handle him. He's a bitch," Freeze said. "So, how did it go?"

"Everything went smooth. Cops came, but we handled them."

"Any problems I need to know about?"

"No problems. Like I said, cops came on the scene, but we handled them."

"Cool," Freeze said and started to get up.

"There's something I need to ask you."

"What?"

"You ever heard of somebody that calls himself Chilly?"

"Yeah."

"You know where I can find him?"

"He hangs out at a place called Rocky's. Why?"

"Me'shelle told me that her brother used to do business with somebody named Chilly."

"What's her brother's name?"

"Bruce Lawrence."

"Yeah, I know him. And yeah, he was down with Chilly. I heard about what happened. Her brother owed Chilly money. Chilly sent some people around to collect, and things got out of hand. But I know Chilly didn't send them over there to rape women and little girls. That ain't his style, but Chilly will kill a muthafucka about his money."

"Then he knows who did it."

"Maybe you should stay out that man's business. Whether he had something to do with it or not, it ain't none of your business."

Travis looked at Freeze and thought about Me'shelle. "I understand."

Chapter Thirty-five

Later that evening, Travis parked his car across the street from The Spot and turned off the engine. In spite of Freeze's warning to stay out of Chilly's business, there he was. As he sat in his car, he wondered what he was going to say, wondered if he should take the advice that Freeze had given him, and wondered what the hell he was doing there. He thought about Me'shelle, and what he was doing there became clear.

Travis reached under the passenger seat, grabbed his gun and stepped out of the car. Since he was determined to do this, he briefly considered coming back with Ronnie, or Jackie and Ronnie. But there was no point in involving them in this. They would think it was stupid, and they would be right.

Travis walked inside and took a look around. It occurred to him that he had no idea what Chilly looked like, and just asking for him might not get him anywhere. From the stares that he was getting, Travis could tell that he didn't belong there. If that was the case, he knew somebody would approach him soon enough and ask him what he was doing there.

He stepped to the bar and ordered a drink. The bartender looked at him like he was crazy and walked away.

"Something I can get for you?" asked a voice from behind Travis. He turned around to find three men standing in back of him. One held a gun in his hand. The other two had theirs in their waistbands.

"I'm looking for Chilly," Travis said.

"Who?"

"I'm a friend of Bruce Lawrence and I'm looking for Chilly."

"No, you a stupid muthafucka with a death wish," the one with the gun said as he put it to Travis's head. "Search him."

Travis was relieved of his weapon and took a fist to the stomach. The blow caught him off guard and knocked the wind out of him, but it didn't really hurt. Travis was running on adrenaline now. The two men grabbed him by the arms, in case he thought about doing something about the punch.

"What you wanna see Chilly about?"

"I wanna talk to him."

"About what?"

"About Bruce."

"What about Bruce?"

"Are you Chilly?"

"No."

"Then it ain't your business," Travis said. He suddenly realized how foolish this was. The smart-ass answer cost Travis two more shots to the gut; he felt the butt of a gun hit his mouth.

That hurt.

While the beating continued, a crowd formed around them. One man forced his way through the crowd. "What the fuck is goin' on here?"

"This muthafucka says he wants to see Chilly, Rocky."

"Who is he and what he wanna see Chilly for?" Rocky asked.

"He said he's a friend of Bruce Lawrence."

"No shit. I didn't think Bruce had any friends," Rocky said and slapped Travis in the face.

"Who is this nigga?" someone asked behind Rocky.

Rocky turned around to find Chilly and Derrick standing behind him. "He says he's a friend of Bruce. Wants to talk to you."

Travis turned up his bloody face and saw Chilly standing before him. Chilly looked at Travis and shook his head. "You must be a friend of Bruce, 'cause you really are a stupid muthafucka. You walk up in here by yourself, wanna talk to me about another stupid muthafucka." Chilly looked at Rocky. "He don't wanna talk to me, he wanna die."

"Hold up, Rock. Chilly, let me talk to you for a second," Derrick said and stepped closer to Chilly. "I seen this nigga before."

"Where?"

"He's with Freeze."

"Freeze? You sure?"

"Yeah."

Chilly looked at Travis again. "You don't want nothing from me."

"I wanna know what happened to Bruce," Travis said and Rocky punched him in the face.

"Nobody asked you to talk."

"Whatever went on with Bruce ain't none of your business. Get him out of here," Chilly said and walked away.

Derrick followed behind Chilly. "Don't kill him. Just take him out back."

Travis was taken to the back door of the club and thrown out into the back alley. He picked himself up from the pile of trash he landed in and thought, *That didn't go well at all.*

As he walked away, he realized that it had gone the only way it could have. It was stupid for him to walk up in there in the first place. And coming alone was worse. *What were you expecting, a nice sit-down conversation?*

Back inside The Spot, Chilly sat down at a table and pulled out his cell phone to call Freeze.

"Yo."

"Freeze, this Chilly."

"What's up?"

"You send one of your people over here to ask me some shit about how I run my business?"

"No," Freeze answered, knowing he meant Travis. "I didn't send him. And you know better than to ask me some shit like that."

"He with you?"

"Yeah, he's with me, so I hope you respected that."

"He's still alive. But he got educated while he was here."

"I can respect that."

"Who is this nigga, anyway?"

"He's a friend of Bruce's sister."

Chilly laughed. "I'm beginning to understand this shit now. She's a bad bitch, and bad bitches make niggas do stupid shit."

Freeze laughed. "I told him to stay out of your business. But I should have told him that I would handle it."

"Handle what?"

"I heard that he owed you money and you sent someone to collect."

"What about that is any of your business?"

"It ain't. Whoever you sent raped his daughter."

"Freeze, word is bond, I didn't know anything about that. Raped little Brandy?" Chilly thought for a second. "Well, I guess by now she ain't no little girl."

"That's still some fucked up shit," Freeze said. "I know that ain't how you do business. I know you got more honor than that, and I assured Travis of that. But like you said, bad bitches make smart men do stupid shit. So, I apologize for his disrespect, but I do ask that you do something about that situation."

"You have my word," Chilly said as Derrick tapped him on the shoulder. Chilly looked up and noticed that Detectives Kirkland and Richards were standing in front of him. "I'll get with you later about that. The police are here," Chilly said and hung up the phone.

Chapter Thirty-six

"I didn't mean to rush you off the phone, Chilly," Detective Kirkland said.

"That's all right, Kirk. I always got time to talk to you," Chilly said.

"You mind if we sit down?" Kirkland asked as he sat down.

"Have a seat, Kirk. Can I get you a drink?"

"No," Detective Richards said. "We're on duty."

"Shit, I know plenty of cops that drink on duty. Y'all stick around, you might see one or two of them. But enough of this small talk. What y'all want?"

"What do you think, Chilly? I wanna talk to you." Kirkland dropped a picture on the table in front of Chilly. "You know this man?"

Chilly picked up the picture and looked at it carefully. "I know this guy. His name is . . . Let me think. What's his name?"

"Bruce Lawrence," Richards said.

"That's right, Bruce Lawrence. He used to work at the bank where my wife does business. If I'm not mistaken, he got fired from there years ago for stealing."

"I heard that he works for you, Chilly," Kirkland asserted.

"Doin' what?"

"The way I get it, Chilly, is that Lawrence worked for you and he owed you money," Kirkland said.

Detective Richards picked up the picture and left the table. He began walking around The Spot, showing the picture around.

"He was found dead in his home a few days ago. The house was torn up, like somebody was looking for something," Kirkland continued.

"So what are you saying, Kirk?"

"I haven't done anything but state the facts in the case. I'm definitely not sayin' that you had him killed. If I was sayin' that, you'd have cuffs on. I just wanna know what you know."

"Kirk, let's stop this shit. You know who I am and you know what I do. Yeah, I know Bruce, and I told you from where I know him. You know that bitch nigga didn't work for me. So, what we doing here?"

Kirkland laughed. "Okay, Chilly, let's cut the bullshit. I know the weasel didn't work for you. Couldn't. He just ain't the type. But he was murdered along with his wife. Killers raped his wife before they killed her, and they raped a sixteen-year-old girl.

"I know rape ain't your style, Chilly, so I don't believe you're involved. This Lawrence guy is more likely a user, so I'm thinking that maybe he owed one of your people. They went to collect, things got out of hand and shit happened. Like I said, I just wanna know what you know."

Chilly sat back and looked at Derrick then back to Kirkland. "I hear what you're sayin', Kirk."

"I don't think you do," Kirkland said, looking around the room to see where his partner was. "I don't give a fuck if you animals kill each other off by the thousands. Shit, you muthafuckas can all line up against that wall right now and I'll shoot you fucks myself. You're all scum, selling death to your own people. You all need to die a slow and painful death, just like the one you're dealin' to them. So fuck you, fuck all of you to hell. But when you animals start raping little girls, see, that's different. I want this guy, Chilly. Follow me now?"

"I think you made yourself clear, Kirk." Chilly leaned toward him. "And whether you believe it or not, I think a line has been crossed too."

"Good. I'm glad we understand each other." Kirkland stood up. "So understand this: if I don't get this guy, and I mean get him soon, shit is gonna get real ugly for you." Kirkland walked away, collected Detective Richards and left The Spot.

As soon as the detectives were out the door, Chilly turned to Derrick. "First that asshole, now Kirk. Where the fuck is Rocky?" Derrick got up right away and came back quickly with Rocky. "Rock, did you send somebody to collect from Bruce?"

"Yeah," Rocky said quietly.

"You're tryin' my fuckin' patience, Rock. Who the fuck did you send?"

"I sent Miller."

"Who?"

"Warren Miller. You know Warren. He's the one they call the ugliest nigger in the world."

Chilly laughed. "You sent that crazy-ass crackhead to collect my money?"

"He does good work."

"Where's the fuckin' money then?"

"I haven't heard from him, so I didn't think he got it," Rocky told Chilly.

"Well, that asshole y'all just carried out of here and fuckin' Kirk being in here up in my face about it says that he did. Did you know that muthafucka raped a sixteen-year-old girl?"

"I didn't know that."

MOB

"So, you find this nigga and bring me his head."

a story by roy glenn

Chapter Thirty-seven

After a ride that felt longer than it really was, Travis parked his car in front of his house. By now, his face was throbbing and every bone in his body hurt. He opened the car door slowly and gingerly stepped out. After a quick scan of the block for Me'shelle's car, Travis moved toward the house, holding his back and walking like Fred Sanford.

The house was in darkness when he entered. Having not seen her car, Travis assumed that Me'shelle had gone home. He made it to the bathroom and turned on the light. "Damn," Travis said out loud when he saw his face.

"Oh my God."

Travis turned quickly and saw that Me'shelle was standing behind him.

"What happened to you?"

"I went to see if I could find out what happened with your family. You're looking at the answers I got."

"You didn't go by yourself, did you?"

Travis nodded.

"Are you all right?"

"I'm okay, but every bone in my body hurts."

"And what is that smell?"

"After they kicked my ass, they threw me in a pile of garbage."

Me'shelle went to the bathtub and turned on the water. "Come on. You need to soak for a while," she said as she began to undress him. "I'm so sorry."

"It's not your fault. You didn't ask me to go there and get my ass kicked. I did that all by myself."

"I know, but you did it for me. And I did kind of hint at the fact that you knew people who probably knew who did it," Me'shelle said.

Once she had gotten Travis out of his clothes, she helped him into the tub. She left him there to soak while she put his dirty clothes in the washing machine and got an ice pack for his face. When she returned to the bathroom, Me'shelle knelt down next to the tub and put the ice pack gently on Travis's face. There was quite a bit of swelling around his left eye and jaw.

"Hold that," she said, handing the ice pack to him.

She never intended for this to happen. Me'shelle looked at his face and felt terrible. Never in her wildest dreams could she have imagined that Travis would get right up and go after Chilly, and definitely not by himself. *What if they had killed him?* That would mean another death that Me'shelle would have on her conscience.

"I'm sorry, Travis." She began to bathe him, but found that her clothes were getting too wet, so she stood up and took them off. She got into the tub and continued to wash away the smell of garbage from his body.

Now that he was feeling clean and somewhat refreshed, Travis stretched out across his bed to relax. Me'shelle lay down beside him, and before too long, they had drifted off to sleep. They had been asleep for about an hour when Travis heard the doorbell. He glanced at the clock next to the bed.

"Twelve forty-five. Who the fuck could this be?"

He got out of bed, put on his pants and got his gun. His movements woke Me'shelle. "Where are you going?"

"There's somebody at the door," Travis said.

"What's the gun for?"

"Security." He took off the safety and cocked it. "Stay here."

As Travis left the room to answer the door, Me'shelle thought, maybe for the first time in her life, that she needed a gun. She had never held a gun in her hand, much less fired one. *But suppose they come after me? Suppose it's them at the door? Suppose they shoot Travis at the door and then come after me? What then? Travis should have left me a gun.*

She got out of bed and got dressed, thinking that if she needed to run or fight somebody off it would be better to have clothes on. Once she was dressed, Me'shelle cracked the door so she could hear what was going on out there.

Travis looked out the peephole and saw a familiar but unexpected face at his door. He opened the door.

"What's up, Freeze?"

"What's up? You gonna invite me in or what?" Freeze asked.

"Come on in," Travis said as he let him into the house. "Have a seat."

"You alone?" Freeze asked.

"No. Me'shelle is in the back."

Freeze didn't bother to sit down. "What the fuck was you thinkin' rollin' up on Chilly like that?" he demanded to know.

"I don't know. I guess I wasn't thinkin'."

"Yes, you were. You were thinkin' like a bitch-ass sucker."

"It was a stupid thing to do."

"What did you think they were gonna do, pull out a chair for you, and y'all sit down like a bunch of fuckin' gentlemen and discuss the situation? Do you think they were gonna just say yeah, we raped the girl and we're gonna turn ourselves in to the police in the morning? Is that what you fuckin' thought, Travis?"

"No."

"You know the only reason you're alive?"

"What's that?"

"They knew you was with me. That's the only reason you ain't dead."

"I'm sorry."

"I get a fuckin' call from Chilly asking me if I sent you. I shoulda known better. I shoulda known you were goin' over there. Now look at you. Face all fucked up. Any broken bones?"

"I don't think so."

"Do you realize the position that puts me in?"

"You? What position does it put you in?"

"You're with me, Travis, which means you come under my protection. Chilly is old school, so he respects that, which is why he didn't kill you for tryin' to involve yourself in his business. But them niggas still beat the fuck outta you. I'm supposed to do something about it. I don't do something about this, niggas start thinkin' I'm gettin' soft and they can come at any one of my people. Do you understand what I'm sayin'? Niggas thinking I'm soft is bad for business."

"I wasn't thinkin' about all that."

"No, you weren't. Shit, Travis, I oughta shoot you myself."

At that point, Me'shelle had heard enough. She came out of the room.

"Is that why you're here? To kill me?"

They both looked up as Me'shelle came into the room.

"No. That's not why I'm here," Freeze said.

"I told you to stay in the room," Travis said to Me'shelle.

"She can stay. I don't give a fuck if she hears what I have to say. I came here to see how you were doin'. And I came to tell you again to stay out of it. Don't you go anywhere near Chilly or his people. Let Chilly handle his business. And stay away from the cops."

"What about my niece? They can't just rape her and murder my brother and get away with it."

Freeze looked at Me'shelle then turned his attention back to Travis. "Chilly is the type of man who knows that type of shit is bad for business. You let this shit go, Travis. You let Chilly handle his business and you go back to doin' what you do. I want your word that this is no longer your problem."

"You have my word," Travis told Freeze.

"Wait a minute," Me'shelle protested, but Freeze ignored her.

"I talked to Chilly, and he gave me his word that he would handle this, so you're out of it. Now it's my problem," Freeze said and stood up. "Shit like this never needs to happen again, Travis. You understand me?"

"I understand."

Freeze walked toward the door.

"That's it?" Me'shelle asked, but Freeze continued to ignore her.

Travis got up and followed Freeze to the door.

Freeze stopped. "Oh yeah. One more thing I gotta say."

"What's that?"

"Whatever I do is always business. Never personal, even if it seems that way. Remember that." Freeze continued toward the door. "And it will never have anything to do with you and me. Understand?"

"Understood," Travis said as he let Freeze out and closed the door behind him.

"Who the fuck does he think he is?"

Travis smiled. "Freeze thinks he's the only reason that we're both not dead." He put his arm around Me'shelle and led her back to the bedroom. "And you know what? He's right." He took off his pants and began to undress Me'shelle.

"Even so, he didn't have to ignore me like I wasn't even there. That was disrespectful."

"True. But it is what it is," Travis said as he got back in the bed.

Me'shelle followed Travis under the covers. "So, that's it, huh?"

"That's it."

"I should just believe that these people are going to make everything all right?"

"No, Me'shelle. Even if they kill the guys who did it, nothing will change the fact that your brother and his wife are dead, or that your niece is traumatized by what happened to her."

"Exactly, so it's not over for me."

"What are you gonna do?"

"I don't know. What can I do?"

Chapter Thirty-eight

It had been a week since Rocky put the word out on the street that he wanted Warren Miller. After all that time, no one had any information that turned out to be worth anything. It was always "You just missed him" or "He was here yesterday" or the always popular "I don't know what you're talkin' about." Miller and his partners knew they were hot, so they were laying low.

Although he quickly dismissed the idea, Rocky gave some thought to calling the police tip line and telling them that Miller was responsible for the rape and murder of the Lawrence family. That would solve part of his problem, but he knew it wouldn't satisfy Chilly. No, Rocky knew that he was the one who sent Miller out there, so he had to be the one to drag him in.

As Detective Kirkland promised, the police were making life miserable for Chilly. Needless to say, Chilly was not happy about the situation and was starting to lose patience with Rocky. So, once again Rocky found himself on the street, but this time his approach was different. Now he started to push a lot harder, leaning on the people he was sure knew something and just weren't saying because they were scared of what Miller would do to them. But it was Rocky they really had to fear. He would be their nightmare now.

Rocky also decided to change one other aspect of his approach. He took his focus off the head and concentrated on the body. Word had gotten back to Rocky that there were three people who usually did jobs with Miller. One was found dead on the scene, one was called Blue, and the other's name was Jordan Davis.

MOB

Rocky knew Davis, knew where he hung out, and most importantly, Rocky knew his girlfriend, Jeanna Mitchell, and knew her well.

Late that night, Rocky knocked on her door. "Who is it?" Jeanna yelled though the door.

"Its Rocky, Jeanna."

"Rocky?" She looked out the peephole. A flood of memories came rushing back to her. "What you want?"

"I wanted talk to you, Jeanna. You gonna open the door or what?"

Reluctantly, Jeanna unlocked the door and opened it. It had been three years since she'd seen Rocky, and over that time she had let herself go. She had lost a lot of weight, her face was thin, and her eyes seemed to bug out of her head. Hair that was once long and beautiful was now nappy and stuck to her head. "What you want, Rocky?"

"You gonna let me in, Jeanna, or do I gotta stand out here?"

"You can come in, but I still want to know what you want."

"Maybe I just wanted to see you," Rocky said as he plopped down on her couch.

"Shit," she said, still standing by the door. "I ain't seen your ass in years, Rocky, and you expect me to believe that you just dropped by 'cause you missed me? I don't think so."

"Come here, Jeanna. Let me look at you."

"Why?"

" 'Cause I wanna look at you."

She walked over to the couch and stood in front of Rocky. "Happy now?"

Rocky looked her up and down. “What happened to you, Jeanna?”

“What’s that supposed to mean? You sayin’ ’cause I lost some weight and my hair ain’t done that I ain’t fine no more?”

“Yeah. You used to be fine as hell. Now look at you.”

“Fuck you, Rocky. I get my hair done and put on some clothes, I’m still the baddest bitch you ever fucked.”

Rocky looked at Jeanna and smiled. “You were, but not now. That glass dick got you now. You ain’t nothin’ but a crack ho now.”

“I ain’t nobody’s ho, nigga. My man takes care of me, so fuck you.”

“Still got them pretty-ass dick-suckin’ lips, though. Probably takin’ good care of him too.” Rocky smiled and rubbed his crotch.

“What you want, Rocky?”

“I’m lookin’ for Jordan.”

“What you want with Jordan?”

“I wanna talk to him.”

“What about?”

“I got business with him.”

“What business you got with Jordan?”

“That ain’t no concern of yours. It’s better that you don’t know anyway, Jeanna. You know that. Now, do you know how to get in touch with him?

“No. He just comes by here.”

“How often? Every day? Once a week?”

“You know, he just come by sometimes. Like you used to just show up here when you felt like it.”

Rocky wrote down his number on a piece of paper on the table. “You call me when you see him, Jeanna. I’ll make it worth your while,” Rocky said and stood up.

"How much?"

"Five hundred."

"You gonna kill him?"

"No, Jeanna. I just need to talk to him."

"You promise you ain't gonna kill him?"

"Yeah, I promise. I ain't gonna kill him. You just need to call me when you see him."

Rocky started for the door.

"Rocky."

"What?"

"Let me have a couple dollars."

"You ain't earned it yet."

"Come on, now. You know you got it."

Rocky reached in his pocket, counted off five twenties and put the roll back in his pocket. "Here."

When Jeanna tried to grab the money, Rocky held it above his head. "What you gonna do to earn it?" Without another word, Jeanna dropped to her knees and began to undo Rocky's pants. He sat back down in the chair and Jeanna proceeded to earn the money.

It had been three days, and Rocky still hadn't heard from Jeanna, but he wasn't worried. After he left her, he made the same offer to the guys who hung out on the corner, so he knew Jordan still hadn't showed up at Jeanna's.

It certainly wasn't from a lack of effort to get him there on Jeanna's part. She called everyone she could think of and had been everywhere that she knew Jordan hung out, but nobody had seen him.

Since that night on her knees with Rocky, Jeanna developed a plan. She no longer cared if Rocky killed Jordan. In fact, she hoped he would. Jeanna planned to take the money, get herself cleaned up, and make a play to get back in Rocky's good graces. The money and perks were definitely better than what Jordan had to offer.

Late one night, Jeanna heard his key hit the door. She panicked when she realized that she had left Rocky's number lying on the coffee table. She started to reach for it, but it was too late. Jordan had come though the door.

"What's up, Jeanna?"

"Hey, Jordan," Jeanna said nervously.

"What's wrong with you?" Jordan asked as he sat down on the couch.

"Nothing's wrong."

"What's this?" He grabbed the paper off the table. "Who number is this?"

"It's Rocky's number."

"Rocky? The one you used to fuck?"

"Yeah," Jeanna said quietly. She was scared, very scared, but she was determined to make this work for her.

"What was he doin' here?"

"Lookin' for you."

"Me! The fuck that nigga want wit' me?"

"I don't know. He said for you to call him. Then he said I should call him when I see you."

"Did you call him?" Jordan asked.

"No. Did you see me run to the phone?" Jeanna asked sarcastically.

"Oh."

"So, you gonna call him?" Jeanna asked.

"What I'm gonna call that nigga for?"

" 'Cause he wanna talk to you. He said he got business with you."

"I ain't got no business with him," Jordan said, but in the back of his mind he knew what Rocky wanted. He knew that Rocky was the one who sent Miller to collect from Bruce Lawrence, and that Miller had kept the money they got before they killed him.

Now it was Jordan who was scared. He snatched the paper off the table, balled it up in his fist and threw it down on the floor.

"What's wrong with you?" Jeanna asked.

"Nothing!" Jordan spit out.

"Okay, okay. You don't have to bite my head off. You bring something for me?"

"Yeah." Jordan reached in his pocket and threw Jeanna a bag of white powder.

"Why don't you go in the bedroom? Relax, get undressed, make yourself comfortable while I cook this up. Okay?"

Jordan simply nodded his head and followed Jeanna into the room. At that point, her plan was simple. She would cook what he brought her, stash some for later, and smoke the rest. Then she would fuck him until he went to sleep. Once he was sleeping, she would call Rocky.

Chapter Thirty-nine

When Jordan woke up, Rocky and three of his boys were in the room with him. “That bitch,” Jordan said. “I knew she was no good. Jeanna! Jeanna! Where the fuck is she?”

“She was outta here as soon as I got here. From the looks of it, she’ll be gone for a while.” Rocky laughed.

“All that shit she broke outta here with,” one of his boys said.

“Damn,” Jordan said as he reached under the pillow.

“Lookin’ for this?” Rocky asked and held up Jordan’s gun. “She handed it to me on her way out the door.”

“That bitch!”

Everybody laughed, even Jordan. Still, he knew what a fucked up situation he was in, lying in bed, unarmed, butt naked with three killers around him.

“What you want with me, Rock?” Jordan asked.

“Warren Miller. Where is he?”

“I don’t know where Miller is,” Jordan lied. “Rock, I swear. I ain’t seen Miller in at least a week.”

“I heard that you was down with him.”

“Yeah, we do some work together.”

“You was with him when he went to collect from Bruce Lawrence.”

“I was there.”

“Where’s the fuckin’ money?”

“Miller didn’t bring you that money?” Jordan asked, knowing that he hadn’t.

“No, he didn’t. That was Chilly’s money, and I think you know that, and that’s why all of you are stayin’ on the low. But it’s cool, Jordan. All I want is Miller.”

"Don't kill me, Rock. I didn't know that was Chilly's money. I swear, Rock. I didn't know."

"Don't cry like a bitch now," Rocky's boy said, pointing a gun to Jordan's head. "It was probably you that raped the kid, wasn't it?"

"No, no, please. That wasn't me. It was Blue that raped that girl!" Jordan yelled.

"Where is he?"

"I don't know, Rock."

"Shoot him," Rocky said.

"No!"

Rocky's boy pulled the trigger, but nothing happened. "Damn, Rock, I forgot I didn't have one in the chamber." He laughed and cocked it before returning it to Jordan's head.

Rocky smiled. "Now, you were about to tell me where Blue is."

"Come on, Rock. I'm serious. I don't know where he is either," he lied again. He knew exactly where both Blue and Miller were, at least where they were a few hours earlier.

"I'm gonna give you a chance to save your ass and come out of it with some money in your pocket."

"What do you want me to do?"

"I told you, Jordan. Miller, I want him. You were supposed to get four grand from Lawrence. Well, you bring Miller to me and I'll give you five grand. And do it quick. There's somebody else lookin' for him."

"Who?"

"Guy named Travis Burns. He runs a robbing crew. He's fuckin' Lawrence's sister. You better get him to me before this guy kills him." Rocky stood up and threw the crumpled piece of paper at Jordan. "My number's on the paper, but you knew that."

Rocky and his boys left the room laughing, but they left Jordan thinking. If this Burns guy was a robber, then he could use him as bait to get Miller and Blue out in the open where Rocky could grab him. Jordan got up and got dressed.

Once he made his way to where Miller and Blue were staying, he laid it all out for them. He said that he talked to Rocky, but Rocky didn't know that they killed Bruce Lawrence and took the money. He told them Rocky had been looking for them to give them another job to do, this time in Philly. Then he told them about Travis. "I hear this guy Burns is lookin' for you 'cause he heard it was you that killed his brother."

"Who's his brother?"

"I don't know. Probably some dealer you killed."

"You know this guy?" Miller asked.

"I heard of him. I hear he runs a robbing crew," Jordan said, knowing what Miller's reaction would be.

"Robber, huh? Then he got money," Miller said and Jordan smiled. "We'll get him before he gets us. He's just another muthafucka to rob. You know where to find him?"

"I know where his woman lives," Jordan said.

"Is she fine?" Blue asked.

"As hell," Jordan replied.

"Then she gettin' fucked too." Blue laughed.

Chapter Forty

The last few weeks had been stressful to say the least for Me'shelle. She had taken a leave from work and spent her days taking care of Brandy practically around the clock. Most of the day they sat in Brandy's room talking or watching TV.

Having Me'shelle there with her seemed to make Brandy more comfortable, but it had begun taking its toll on Me'shelle. Feeling that Me'shelle needed a break, not to mention that she was getting on her nerves, Miranda strongly recommended the she get out of the house for the day. "I'm sure Brandy will make it through one night without you."

Since she was out of the house for the day, Me'shelle called Travis on her cell phone to see what he was doing. He told her that he had nothing planned and would love to see her, especially since it had been a while since they had been together.

"Maybe we could have dinner, see a movie or whatever," Me'shelle suggested.

"Maybe we could do both," Travis replied happily.

"I need to change if we're going out to dinner. Why don't I come and pick you up? You can ride with me to my apartment to get changed."

"I'll be ready when you get here," Travis said.

On the way to pick up Travis, Me'shelle thought about how much she missed spending time with him. She knew that she wanted him to be a part of her life, which meant there was something Me'shelle had to seriously consider.

She was adamant that she wanted Brandy to stay with her, but Brandy had been through a lot. She'd seen enough crime and experienced enough violence to last a lifetime. Was Travis the kind of person that Brandy needed to be around? All Me'shelle had from Travis was a kiss and a promise that he would end his life of crime and violence. *Promises get broken every day*. Suppose Travis was neither interested in nor ready for the responsibility of having not only a teen-aged girl, but a teen-aged girl with issues? She wondered what he would say when she told him. If he said he couldn't deal with it, would that affect their relationship? In her heart, she knew it would.

When Me'shelle arrived at the house to pick Travis up, she asked if she could use his phone. "My battery died while I was talking to Brandy."

"How's she feeling?"

"She's doing much better. At least I think so. She still doesn't like being alone. She gets headaches. She doesn't eat like she used to, so she's losing a lot of weight. I think the nightmares might not be happening as often, because she is sleeping better lately."

"Well, that's good to hear."

"This is the first night in a while that I haven't been there with her, so you can understand why I wanted to check on her." The doorbell rang. Travis looked at Me'shelle. "I'll use the one in the back," she said without asking.

Not expecting anybody, Travis reached for and cocked his pistol. He opened the door and was surprised to see Jackie.

"Hey, you," Jackie said as Travis stepped aside to let her in.

"How you doin', Jackie?" Travis asked.

"I'm good. I was on my way to pick up Ronnie, so I took a chance and drove by to see if you wanted to ride."

"Where's Ronnie?"

"Some young-minded trick he's fuckin' with took his truck, his clothes and his wallet and left him stranded at some motel in Yonkers."

"He say what her name was?"

"No. He just told me the story and said to come get him."

"I don't know what he sees in them drama queens," Travis said, hoping the young-minded trick wasn't Pauleen.

"You don't know?" Jackie asked.

"Know what?"

"Them drama queens is crazy. And everybody knows crazy women got the best pussy."

Travis glanced toward the bedroom and thought about Me'shelle. "Come on, now. Not all the good pussy women are crazy."

"I didn't say *all*, but you've had some fools with that bomb-ass pussy, and so have I."

"True that. But good pussy or not, I try to stay away from them nuts. Besides, I'm off the market anyway."

"She back there?" Jackie whispered and pointed toward the bedroom. Travis nodded. "My bad," she whispered. "So, do I get to meet the little woman?"

"She's on the phone. I guess she'll come out when she's done."

"If she's any kind of woman, she'll be out here as soon as she hangs up to see what woman her man is talking to."

Travis laughed, but he knew she was right. "So, how's Ronnie doin'? Every time I call him he's running out somewhere or he's right in the middle of something and never has time to talk."

"What else is new? That's how he's always been. But other than this latest shit, he's been doin' all right. Still fuckin' up his money on women and trying to be a day trader. The market is just too unstable to make that shit work for him."

"He's not dippin' into his reserve, is he?"

"No, but I know that between the market and his usual spend it like it's water lifestyle, he just about ran through the thirty grand from the last job."

"Damn," Travis said, thinking that he hadn't spent any of his share. The day after the job, he wired all his money to his bank in the Caymans. Veronica had sent him back confirmation that his money was deposited in his account. "How you doin' with your thing?"

"What? The gambling? I've been a good girl the last two weeks, but that's only because Freeze banned me from all the houses," Jackie lied. "I'm too scared to roll up on another game, and I'm too lazy to drive, and I refuse to fly to Atlantic City."

"Damn, Jackie."

"I know I'm off the chain with it, Travis, and I need to get some help. I'm thinkin' seriously about goin' to Gamblers Anonymous."

"If that's what you gotta do, then let's do it. I'll go with you."

"Ronnie says the only reason I think I got a problem is because I'm losing and my money is gettin' low. Says I wouldn't be talkin' all this problem shit if I was winning."

"He's probably right about that part, but you still need to get help if you think you got a problem."

"I know you probably don't want to hear this, but Ronnie's been talkin' about we need to hit someplace soon. Either with or without you." Jackie held up her hands. "Before you say it, I know you said that you're retired."

"Right. I'm out, especially after the way he acted after the last job."

"Shit, Travis, that was just Ronnie being Ronnie. You know that."

"Yeah well, I guess it's me then."

"Well, you are the one who changed up on us." Travis scowled at Jackie. "Just being real. You are in a brand new favor now."

"Am I that bad?"

"I never said you were bad. Just different."

There was silence in the room until Jackie said "Hello."

Travis turned around and stood up quickly as Me'shelle came into the room. "Jackie, this is Me'shelle."

"It's good to finally meet you," Jackie said, extending a polite hand.

"So, you're Jackie, Jackie, Jackie." Me'shelle smiled and accepted her hand. "Some days all Travis talked about was Jackie, Jackie, Jackie."

"You're not jealous, are you? Because I assure you, you have nothing to fear from me. In fact, Me'shelle, you and I are gonna get along just fine," Jackie said as she looked Me'shelle over.

"Are we?" Me'shelle asked cautiously. The look on Jackie's face was making her feel just a little uncomfortable.

"Yes, Me'shelle, we are," Jackie said and smiled at Travis. "Because all I want is for Travis to be happy, and he is happy with you. We were just sitting here talkin' 'bout how he's changed. And what's changed him is you. You've been good for him. So, I'm hoping that change rubs off on all of us." Jackie stood up. "So, come give me a hug so I can go."

Me'shelle and Jackie hugged. Jackie winked at Travis.

"I'm not running you off, am I?" Me'shelle asked.

"No. I just stopped by on my way to perform a mission of mercy."

"What?" Me'shelle asked.

"I gotta go pick up Ronnie, but if y'all are gonna be here for a while, I can pick up Ronnie and swing back through."

"We were getting ready to go by Me'shelle's apartment so she can change for dinner."

"Mind if me and Ronnie tag along? I know Ronnie is dying to meet you. "

"No, not at all," Me'shelle said. "I'm dying to meet Ronnie too. I'll be a while changing, Travis, so why don't you go with Jackie to pick up Ronnie? Then you can come by my house and pick me up."

"You sure?" Jackie said sweetly.

"Yes."

"Come on, Jackie. I'll walk you to the car and tell you where she lives," Travis said, ignoring Me'shelle's suggestion.

Chapter Forty-one

As planned, Jackie made it out to Yonkers and picked up Ronnie. While he put on the clothes she'd brought for him, Jackie couldn't wait to tell him that she had met Me'shelle, and that she was fine. "He wouldn't even ride out here with me."

"What part of that surprises you? Pussy-whipped nigga."

"Look who's talking," Jackie shot back. "You calling him pussy-whipped, but some bitch left you out here butt naked, with no truck and no money."

Ronnie laughed. "I guess she didn't appreciate me calling her a triflin', money-grubbin' bitch."

"I think that's enough to piss her off. You should be glad that all she did was leave you here asleep. She could have cut your dick off."

"Maybe," Ronnie said and thought about a few other things that a pissed off Pauleen could do to get him back.

Me'shelle and Travis drove over to her apartment to get ready for dinner. On the way over, Me'shelle told Travis that she thought Jackie was sweet. "But should I be afraid of her?"

"Even though Jackie is at best bisexual, I don't think that you have anything to worry about," Travis assured her.

While Travis waited in the living room and channel surfed, Me'shelle wandered around her bedroom, trying to decide what to wear. The doorbell rang.

"That's probably your friends," Me'shelle said as she went to answer the door. She stepped out of her apartment into the foyer and looked out the window. Outside were three men she'd never seen before. It was Miller, Jordan and Blue. When they began to bang on the door, Me'shelle ran to get Travis.

Travis came out to take a look. "They're armed," Travis said as he took out his gun. "Is there another way out of here?"

"Through the basement and out the back door."

"Come on." They ran down the steps into the basement just as Blue kicked in the door. As Me'shelle escaped out the back door, Travis settled himself, ready to shoot the first one who came down the steps.

Blue was the first to come running down, followed by Jordan. Miller went into Me'shelle's apartment and began to look around. In the basement, Travis took aim and fired, but he missed. Blue fired back wildly, and Travis ran out the back door.

Me'shelle ran through the yard and climbed over the fence to the street. Travis was right behind her. He made it over the fence just as Jordan and Blue came out the back door blasting. Me'shelle ran down the block but stopped to look back for Travis.

"Keep goin'!" Travis yelled, but she waited for him anyway. Jordan and Blue hopped the fence and began shooting. Travis and Me'shelle ducked behind a car and Travis shot back. When Jordan and Blue took cover, Travis and Me'shelle took off running.

"Where do those woods lead?" Travis asked as they ran.

"It comes out on the next block," Me'shelle answered, still running.

Inside Me'shelle's apartment, Miller was tearing up the place, looking for whatever he could find, getting angrier by the second because there was nothing of any real value in the entire apartment. Miller was just about to search the bedroom when he heard voices.

Jackie and Ronnie approached Me'shelle's apartment building and noticed the door had been forced open. The wood on the frame was splintered and the door was hanging off its hinges.

"Do you hear that?" Ronnie asked.

"Hear what?"

"Sounds like gunshots."

"What part of that surprises you?" Jackie asked as she stepped into the foyer.

As Jackie stepped inside, Miller came out of Me'shelle's apartment. He raised his gun and fired at Jackie.

"Gun!" Jackie yelled as she pushed Ronnie back out the door.

Miller fired a couple of shots through the window before running into the basement and out the back door. Once the shooting stopped, Jackie and Ronnie went to the car, armed themselves, and came back to the building. They went inside the open apartment and looked around for Travis. Not finding him there, they closed the apartment and went to the basement, moving carefully down the steps.

By the time they got down there, Miller was gone and the basement was empty. Ronnie went out the back door. He could hear gunfire coming from down the street. "Get the car, Jackie, and meet me around the block," he instructed then ran though the yard, jumped over the fence and moved cautiously in the direction of the shooting.

Ronnie stood at the edge of the woods and waited for Jackie to get there with the car. "I don't hear any more gunfire, but I'm pretty sure that they went in the woods," he told her when she arrived.

"These woods come out on the next block. I'll drive around and meet you on the other side."

"Okay," Ronnie agreed and headed into the woods.

Travis and Me'shelle made it through the woods and hid behind a car. Travis knew that he had to be almost out of bullets. He looked at Me'shelle. She was out of breath and she looked scared, but she was surprisingly calm under the circumstances. "You okay?"

Me'shelle nodded, but she was scared, very scared.

"Get under the car and stay there no matter what," he told her. Me'shelle quickly complied.

Jordan and Blue came out of the woods and looked around. "You go that way," Jordan said, then he and Blue went in different directions.

When Travis heard them, he raised up from behind the car and fired, but in the darkness he missed. Ronnie heard the shots and ran in that direction. Jordan started firing back at Travis, who quickly ducked behind the car again.

Travis cautiously came up from behind the car and fired twice, hitting Jordan with two shots in the chest. His now lifeless body fell to the ground. Travis looked at Jordan's dead body in the middle of the street. But now he had to wonder where the other assailant was.

When he heard Travis's shots, Blue turned around and saw Jordan hit the pavement. "Shit!" he hissed. But now he knew where Travis was. He moved slowly toward Travis's hiding place. A car was coming down the street fast. Its headlights momentarily distracted Blue.

Ronnie came to the edge of the woods and saw Blue moving in the shadows toward Travis. He shouted "Hey!" When Blue turned, Ronnie fired at him. Blue fired back.

The car kept coming down the street as the two men fired at each other. Ronnie started running toward Blue, still shooting. Blue shot back then turned toward the car and froze. The headlights were so bright they were almost blinding. Ronnie was now close enough to get a clear shot at him. He fired and hit Blue in the head.

Jackie slammed on her brakes to avoid hitting the two dead bodies in the street. She jumped out of the car with her gun drawn. "Everybody all right?" she yelled.

"There's one more. There were three of them," Travis shouted as he came from behind the car.

"That must have been the one that was searching the apartment. I don't think he came this way. He musta got away," Ronnie said as he approached Travis and Jackie.

"Who are these guys?" Jackie asked.

"I don't know. They just showed up at Me'shelle's door," Travis said as he went back to the car to help Me'shelle. She crawled out from under the car.

"We gotta get outta here before the cops come," Jackie said as she got back in the car.

"That might not be for another half an hour," Ronnie said.

Travis helped Me'shelle get to her feet. "Are you all right?" he asked as they rushed toward the car.

"I'm all right," Me'shelle answered in a quivering voice.

They got in the car. Jackie drove away quickly, leaving the two dead bodies in the street.

"Thanks for coming when y'all did. You saved our lives, 'cause I was damn sure out of bullets," Travis told them.

"Ain't that what friends do for friends?" Jackie said.

Chapter Forty-two

Once they were safely back at Travis's house, each began to speculate about who the gunmen were. Me'shelle, who had been silent during the ride back to the house, finally said, "I think that it was the same people who killed my brother and raped my niece."

Everybody stopped talking and looked at her. "You think so?" Travis asked.

"It could be, Travis," Ronnie said.

"You did go after them," Jackie added. "They could have known where Me'shelle lived and been waiting there for her to come back."

"Brandy did tell the police that there were four of them. And the detective said they found one dead at the house," Me'shelle said.

"I think you're right," Travis agreed and walked to the phone. He paged Freeze.

When Freeze called back, Travis told him what had happened.

"I haven't heard anything about it, but I'll see what I can find out. You all right?" Freeze asked.

"Yeah, we're all cool."

"Who's there with you?" Freeze asked.

"Me'shelle, Jackie and Ronnie." Travis wondered why he would want to know.

"Okay, you stay there. I'll get back to you when I know something." Freeze hung up the phone knowing what he was going to do next.

"Freeze said he'd call back," Travis informed the others.

"I need a drink," Jackie said as she went to the bar.

"I need a drink and a blunt," Ronnie said.

"It's in the usual place, Ronnie. You want a drink?" Travis asked Me'shelle.

"Maybe later. Right now I just need to lay down for a minute," she said and got up.

"Okay. I'll be back there in a little while. But leave the door open and yell if you need me."

"You drinkin', Travis?" Jackie asked.

"Shit, yeah. Hook me up."

"I got you one ready. Now, you go on and relax. I'll check on Me'shelle," Jackie said with a sly laugh.

"Yeah, I just bet you will."

"I'm only kidding. You don't have to worry. I promise not to seduce your woman," Jackie said. *At least not without you.*

* * * *

Warren Miller stayed in the area long enough to see Jordan and Blue taken away in body bags. With nowhere else to go, he went to The Spot to see Rocky about that job in Philly. Miller thought that the way things were going, Philly would be the best place for him for a while. He could lay low for a few months then come back to the city a brand new man.

As soon as he hit the door, the room got quiet. He knew then that coming there had been a bad idea. It was too late. As Miller turned to get out of there, he walked right into Derrick and two other very large thugs.

"Miller, where you been? Everybody's been looking for you." They grabbed his arms and led him into the back room. It wasn't long before Chilly entered.

"Where's the other two that was with you?" Chilly asked.

"Dead," Miller answered.

"Let him go," Chilly said. Once they released his arms, Chilly looked at Rocky and demanded, "Give me your gun."

Rocky handed his gun to Chilly, and without another word, Chilly emptied the clip into Miller's body. He handed the gun back to Rocky. "Get him outta here."

Chilly went back to Rocky's office and called Freeze. "I just wanted you to know that I took care of that matter we discussed."

"I knew you would," Freeze said and hung up the phone. He would call Travis with the news later.

* * * *

For the rest of the night, they smoked and drank and tried to put the evening's events behind them. After a while, Ronnie stood up and said that he needed some air. Travis got up too. "I'll go with you."

"I'm a big boy now, Travis. I'll be all right out there by myself. And besides, I'm takin' mister sixteen-shot glock with me."

Ronnie stood outside of the house and took deep breaths, trying to calm himself after their wild night. A truck moving slowly down the street with no lights caught his attention. He took out his gun and moved to get a better angle on it. As the truck got closer and stopped in front of the house, Ronnie recognized the vehicle. He put his gun away and began walking toward the truck.

As the window went down, Ronnie approached and said, "What's up, Freeze?" He looked inside and was surprised to see Pauleen in the back seat.

"Nothing personal," Freeze said calmly and raised his nine.

"Strictly business," Pauleen said and smiled at Freeze.

He shot Ronnie twice in the head and sped away.

Travis and Jackie heard the shots and jumped up. "Stay here!" he yelled at Me'shelle when she called out to him from the bedroom.

They grabbed their guns and ran outside, but it was too late. They got to the street in time to see a truck round the corner. Ronnie's body lay dead in street.

Jackie dropped to her knees and held Ronnie's head as she cried. Travis ran back inside. "Call an ambulance! Ronnie's been shot!" he yelled.

When the ambulance arrived, the paramedics pronounced Ronnie dead at the scene.

Chapter Forty-three

On the night before Ronnie's funeral, Me'shelle waited until Brandy had fallen asleep before leaving the room to call Travis. She asked him if she could come over. Naturally, Travis said yes. He hadn't seen Me'shelle since Ronnie's murder. In those three days, she had called once to see how he was doing, but the conversation was a short one.

"You had a lot going on, Travis. I just went through all that with my family. To be honest with you, I didn't feel up to it again," Me'shelle explained.

"You don't have to explain, Me'shelle. I understand completely," Travis asserted, but he really was disappointed that she hadn't called more often. After the way he treated her when she needed him, though, Travis felt like he had it coming. It hurt, but like most men, he tried not to show it. "I'll see you when you get here."

When Me'shelle arrived, she tried to get right to the reason for her visit that evening. "Wow, where do I start? You know, it's funny when you have something to say and you go over it and over it in your mind, and you know exactly what you wanna say, then when it comes time to say it, you just can't get it out."

"Just say what's on your mind, Me'shelle," Travis encouraged, but he was uncertain. Just like she felt the day he admitted he was a robber, he was afraid of what she might be about to say.

"Okay." Me'shelle took a deep breath. "You know that I've been though a lot these last few weeks, and I understand that you have too. My family has been through a lot and . . . What I'm trying to say is that I'm not going to the funeral with you tomorrow."

"I understa—"

"Please, Travis, let me finish. I came here to tell you that I can't see you anymore."

"What are you sayin'?"

"I came here to say goodbye," she answered.

"Why?"

"That night, lying under that car listening to the shooting, I thought I was going to die. And then to see the bodies drop when you killed them . . . I know that I never want to go through anything like that again."

"And you won't have to, Me'shelle. Nothing like that will ever happen again. I won't let anything happen to you."

"You can't say that. And even if you could, I still have Brandy to think about."

"What about her?"

"I've got to get her away from here. Far away from here, someplace where she'll feel safe. Where I'll feel safe," Me'shelle said softly. "That's the only way Brandy is going to have a chance at living a normal life. She deserves that after all she's been through."

"That's fine with me, Me'shelle. I want to get away from here too. Wherever you go, I want to go with you. Be with you," he insisted.

"I don't want you to come with me," she said without emotion.

"Why?"

"Travis, you represent—what am I saying? You *are* everything that I have to get her away from."

Travis sat quietly.

"You robbed a bank and a grocery store, and those are just the two that I know about. I heard on the news that there were shootouts with the police both times."

"That's true. But all that is over. I've given all that up."

"Gave it up for what? For me? For love?"

"Yes, Me'shelle. I love you."

"And I love you. But what happens when the money runs out? Do you rob another bank? Or what if the police come after you? Do you shoot it out with them? And what happens when somebody comes to kill you like they did Ronnie? Do you kill him too?"

Again Travis had no answer.

"Travis, you're violent man, surrounded by very violent people. I can't, I won't be any part of that. It's already cost my family too much."

"I promise you that it won't be like that."

"I know that you mean what you're saying, and sometimes I want so badly to believe in the perfect picture you paint. But I know that promises get broken. Even ones we really mean." Me'shelle stood up. "I'm gonna go now, before I get weak for you and change my mind."

Travis stood up and stepped in front of her. "Please don't go. Don't do this to us. I love you, Me'shelle."

She put her arms around Travis and kissed him on the cheek. "Goodbye, Travis."

Travis held her tightly in his arms. When he let her go and stepped aside, Me'shelle walked past him and out the door without looking back. She cried as she walked to her car. She knew she had done the right thing, but it still hurt.

Travis stood in the doorway and watched as Me'shelle got in her car and drove away. He felt numb all over, like somebody had just kicked his insides out. He walked back in the house slowly and sat on the couch. He stayed there for hours, thinking for maybe the first time about the cost of the choices that he had made.

The following morning, Jackie came to pick Travis up for the funeral. As soon as he was in the limo, Jackie asked where Me'shelle was.

"She doesn't want to see me again."

"Where have I heard that before?"

"I think she means it this time," Travis said as he stared out the window.

"Okay, she means it this time, huh? If she had meant it the last time, you wouldn't have gone over there fuckin' with them people, and maybe Ronnie would still be alive."

Travis looked at Jackie. "Maybe. Maybe not."

"Look, Travis, I'm sorry. I didn't mean for it to come out that way. I know that this whole thing hasn't been easy for you. And for her to drop that on you . . . "

"I'll be all right," Travis said. He went on to tell Jackie every word that Me'shelle said.

Since Me'shelle walked out of his door, Travis had replayed the conversation over and over, like a movie in his mind. Sometimes his arguments would change, as he thought of the things that he could have and maybe should have said to make her stay. But Me'shelle's response would always be the same. And in the end, she wo[illegible]ays stand up and walk away without looking

Jackie sat quietly and held his hand while Travis talked. He spoke about how wasted he felt. Jackie's mind began to drift. *This is Me'shelle's fault. If she had stayed away from Travis, this wouldn't be happening. She used Travis to get revenge for her family. Now that she got what she wanted, she's gone again.*

The thought made her mad as hell. *She'll get hers in time.*

Once the funeral was over, Travis and Jackie walked back to the limo. "How do you feel?" Jackie asked.

"I buried my best friend today," Travis said coldly, and then had to apologize. "I'm sorry, Jackie. I know he was your best friend too."

"It's okay, Travis. I understand."

The driver opened the door for Jackie. She was about to get in when Travis saw Freeze standing off to the side. Travis grabbed Jackie by the arm.

"What?" she asked.

Travis didn't answer. He just stared at Freeze. "You know what, Jackie?"

"Tell me, what?" Jackie said as she stared at the man standing next to Freeze.

"I think Freeze killed Ronnie."

"What makes you think that?"

"It's just a feeling, that's all."

"Come on, Travis. It got to be more than that."

"Did you know that Ronnie was fuckin' his girl?"

"No."

"Freeze always used to tell me that if Ronnie ever put their organization or him in jeopardy, he'd kill him. And it would be business. If anybody knew that Ronnie was fuckin' his girlfriend, it would make Freeze look weak. That's bad for business."

"Who's that man with Freeze?"

"That's the reason we ain't ever gonna talk about this again. That's Mike Black. Killin' Freeze would be a death sentence, and Black would be the executioner." Travis opened the limo door. "I'm out of this life, Jackie. I'm gonna try my best to put it all behind me," Travis said. Jackie continued to look at Freeze. "You coming?" Travis asked.

"Yeah, but give me a minute," Jackie said and walked away from the car.

"Where are you going?"

"To speak to Freeze."

"Jackie—"

"Don't worry, Travis. I'm not gonna do anything stupid like accuse a killer of murder. Just wait here. I won't be long."

Jackie made her way slowly toward Freeze, thinking about what Travis had just told her. Did he really kill Ronnie? She had looked into his eyes many times and knew that if Freeze said he would, then he would.

"Hello, Freeze," Jackie said, noticing that she seemed to catch him off guard.

"What's up, Jackie?" Freeze said as he turned to acknowledge her. "Mike Black, Jackie Washington."

"Nice to meet you, Ms. Washington," Mike said. "Sorry it has to be at a time like this."

"I'm sorry too. Next time we meet it won't be."

After making sure that there was no way Travis could see what she was doing, Jackie discreetly handed Freeze an envelope to cover her recent gambling debts. Just as discreetly, Freeze took the envelope and put it in his pocket.

"I just came to pay my respects. I was trying to catch up with Travis, but I haven't seen him," Freeze said.

"He's already gone to the limo."

"Tell him I'll catch up with him later. But tell him that the situation he involved himself in is handled."

"I'll be sure to let him know," Jackie said as she left them.

"Jackie!" Freeze called to her.

She stopped to turn toward him.

"See you tonight?"

Jackie paused for a second. "Yeah, I'll be there," she answered, hoping in her heart that she would find the strength not to go spend her evening gambling. Then she thought about Me'shelle. "Oh, and Freeze, there's a personal matter I know you can help me with," Jackie said then continued walking toward the limo.

"Mike Black." A voice came from behind the two men as they watched Jackie get in the limo.

"Detective Kirkland, what are you doing here?" Mike asked as he shook the detective's hand.

"I was just about to ask you the same question," Kirkland said. "Out of work stockbrokers usually aren't your style. Besides, I hear this one was kind of sloppy."

Freeze rolled his eyes.

"I'm just ridin' with Freeze."

"Really? How do you know the deceased?" Kirkland asked Freeze.

"Went to junior high school with him."

"No shit. I never knew you went to school." Kirkland laughed. "But that doesn't answer all my questions. We found three dead bodies, and one of the DNA samples matched the DNA of a rape suspect. I did some checking—you know, cop stuff—and coincidentally, the other three were killed on the same night as this poor fellow. Now, that seemed a little more than coincidental, so I came out to satisfy my curiosity. And who is the first person I run into? My old friend Mike Black and his fateful companion, Freeze. What do you make of that?"

Mike laughed. "Nothing, Kirk. Like I said, I'm just ridin' with Freeze."

"See you around, Black. You look good. Island life seems to agree with you," Kirkland said as he walked away.

Mike and Freeze watched the detective until he got in his car and drove away. "Let's go, Freeze," Mike said. "By the way, you heard anything from Nick?"

DRUG RELATED
a street saga by
roy glenn
APRIL 2005

MOB

Chapter One

"Okay, Nick, you're free to go," Detective Kirkland said.

I stood up and looked at my watch. For the last seven hours, I had been in the interrogation room with Wanda, answering all of the questions that Detectives Kirkland and Richards had to offer. Kirkland opened the door for Wanda and they walked out of the room together. I followed them.

"It's really not necessary for you to walk me out, detective," Wanda said then looked back at me.

"These halls are filled with dangerous criminals." Kirkland always did have a thing for Wanda, so he had to escort her out of the building.

Dealing with Kirkland was old hat to her. "I've played this game with Kirk before," Wanda said once we were out of the building, "so don't worry. I got this."

I wasn't worried. I'd known Wanda Moore since I was eleven. She was a good lawyer, and like she said, she'd played this game with Kirkland plenty of times during his attempts to make a case against Mike Black.

"Thanks for hanging in there with me," I said as I started to walk away. There were still too many unanswered questions, the most pressing of which was how I got to be the only suspect in four murders.

I needed to think, retrace my steps; do something, anything to get myself out of this. Or maybe I would just go straight to the airport and catch a plane to the Bahamas to become Black's new permanent houseguest.

"Not so fast, Nick." Wanda grabbed me by the arm. "You're coming with me. You need to tell me everything.

a story by roy glenn

Not those covert army, need to know, bullshit answers you just fed Kirk. The whole story."

I looked at Wanda and considered giving her some covert army, need to know, bullshit answer then hailing a cab. But I knew she was right.

Wanda led me to her car and we drove to her house in the old neighborhood. It had been ten years since I'd driven through these streets. A strange kind of chill came over me that started me thinking about the old days.

"Black know about this?"

"Of course he does. Who do you think put up your bail? You know anybody else with a million dollars? He wouldn't turn his back on you when you need him, even though you ran out on him when he needed you. First Jamaica, then you."

"Lighten up on me, Wanda. I've been draggin' around that burden for the last ten years."

"I'm sorry, Nick. I didn't mean to go there. I just—"

"It's okay, Wanda."

"What happened, Nick?"

"There must be something I missed."

"What is it?"

"I don't know."

"Start at the beginning, Nick. Don't leave anything out. Even if you didn't think it was important at the time."

"It started when Mrs. Gabrielle Childers sat down in front of me. No. That's not right. It really began two weeks before, when Uncle Felix called and said he had a job that required our talents. 'A simple job,' he called it, and it was."

Until about a year ago, I'd been part of a special operations unit. Things went wrong on our last assignment, and only three of the members of our unit got out alive—James "Jett" Bronson, Monika Wynn, and me. We were flown back to Fort Bragg, where we were promptly debriefed and processed out.

Uncle Felix approached us the day after. He recruited us to do jobs for him that required our skills. Jett's specialty was electronic surveillance, computers, and all that high-tech stuff. Monika's specialty was munitions. The girl really got a rush out of watching things blow up. Me, my specialty was weapons, commando tactics.

You know, the killer.

At Felix's request, I convinced Jett and Monika to come with me back to New York. Felix set us up in a front business as private investigators. To maintain our cover, we actually did some surveillance jobs—some insurance jobs, a few skip traces. Nothing major, but it paid. Besides, the real money was in doing those little jobs for Uncle Felix.

"Just acquire the target and deliver. A walk in the park," I explained to Wanda. "And it was. A simple surveillance to get his pattern down and decide when to snatch him. Jett installed a remote video system in his house. Once it was installed, the system used standard phone lines that provide transmission and monitoring in real time at 28.8 kbps."

"In English, Nick."

"Sorry, Wanda. It operates at high speed, so the transmission provides clear color images at up to fifteen frames per second over a single phone line."

"Thank you, Nick," Wanda said.

"I'll try to keep it simple."

Wanda let out a little laugh.

"What's so funny?"

"Nothing." She laughed again. "I just remember when you could hardly read."

"Yeah, well, things change."

"Go on, Nick."

"It went off just the way it was planned. We picked him up at his house, and then Monika blew it up so there wouldn't be any trace. Then we left him alone, as instructed, in a car on pier 17 off of Fulton Street. The next afternoon I went by the office to type up my report for Felix and get out of there. But I was tired, so I sat back in the chair and before I knew it, I was asleep.

“I had been asleep for at least an hour before I opened my eyes, and there she was, standing in the doorway."

Chapter Two

Thursday, July 9, 3:47 PM

"I'd like to hire a private investigator." Her voice was deep.

"That would be me. Come in. Please, have a seat."

In my dimly lit office, it took my eyes a minute to focus while I shook off my nod. She walked toward me. From my vantage point, I could make out only that she was very well dressed, tall and slender, but not skinny by any definition I'd ever heard. She had the type of legs that I'd probably enjoy watching when she walked out, but I couldn't tell much more about her.

"Tell me what I can do for you, miss."

"Mrs.," she said with attitude. "Mrs. Gabrielle Childers. And I'd like to hire you to find my brother."

I started to tell her that I didn't handle cases like that.

But I didn't.

With my eyes now focused, I could see her face. I wanted her to stay.

Mrs. Childers, huh?

The way she said it, with so much attitude about it, it did something to me. So I decided to have some fun with it. "How long has he been missing, *Mrs*. Childers?"

"As far as I know, about two weeks."

"Any possibility that he could have just gone out of town? Took a vacation and not told you?"

"It's possible, Mr. . . . "

"Simmons. Nick Simmons." I liked the sound of her voice. It was soothing. "Please, call me Nick."

"Okay, *Nick*. It's possible, but it's not like Jake to be gone like this. Neither me, nor my sister, Chésará, have heard from him. Jake is kind of . . . well, anal. You know, everything in its place, all about details."

"Have you gone to the police, *Mrs*. Childers?"

"No. I haven't gone to the police."

"Mind if I ask why?"

She looked at me for a while. She had pretty eyes, but they weren't soft. They were cold and distant. But there was something enchanting about the way she smiled. She shifted around in her chair and crossed her legs.

She dug around in her purse and pulled out a pack of cigarettes. "You mind if I smoke?" she asked, almost as an afterthought.

"Please, be my guest."

She lit up. "I think my husband might be involved."

"All the more reason to go to the police."

"I don't want to go to the police until I'm sure that he's involved. That's why I want to hire you to prove that he's involved in it."

"Are you afraid of your husband, Mrs. Childers?"

"Yes," she said quietly and looked away. Her fear came through loud and clear. "My husband is a very dangerous man, Mr. Simmons."

"Nick. Please, call me Nick. What's your husband's name?"

"Alvin Childers."

I stifled a laugh, thinking, *How dangerous could somebody named Alvin be?*

"What makes him so dangerous?"

"He's involved in drugs. If he even thought I was talking to you about him or his business, he'd—"

"Has he hurt you before?" I asked, and she dropped her head a little. I had taken notice of the dark circles under her eyes that her makeup didn't quite hide.

"I don't see what that has to do with anything." The fear in her voice quickly gave way to attitude. But it was that attitude that I liked about her.

"Look, Mrs. Childers, you want me to prove that your husband is involved in your brother's disappearance, and prove it to the police at that. You have to tell me everything, *Mrs*. Childers."

She took a deep breath. "All right. What do you want to know?"

"Answer my question."

"Yes, he's hurt me before."

"Once, twice, daily?"

"More than once, and let's leave it at that," she said quickly and defiantly.

"All right, Mrs. Childers. Tell me about Jake then. Where he lives, where he works, his girlfriends, who he hangs out with."

"He has an apartment on Bronxwood." She wrote down his address and handed it to me.

"You got a key?"

"No."

"Know of anybody who does?" I asked.

"Jake is too particular about his things for him to let a lot of people have a key."

"He have a girlfriend?"

"Lisa Ellison," Mrs. Childers replied. I could tell by the way she said it that she didn't like the girlfriend.

"What about her? She got a key?"

"I don't know."

"You know if she's heard from him?"

"I don't know."

"You ask her?"

"No."

"Why not?"

Mrs. Childers rolled her eyes. "I don't like her." At least she was real about it.

"What about friends? Anybody he hangs out with?"

"I don't know," she said quickly. Then she said, "He's got a friend, Rocky. He grew up down the block from us in Philly. Him and Jake hang sometimes, but not that often."

"Do you have a picture of Jake?"

Mrs. Childers reached in her purse and handed me a picture.

"Looks like the bomb party. What's the occasion?"

"Jake's last birthday. We never had birthday parties when we were kids, so we really make a big thing of them now."

"How old is he?"

"Jake's thirty."

"He the oldest?"

"Yes."

"Who's that in the picture with him?"

"That's our sister, Chésará."

"Him and Chésará close?"

"Yes." She sounded offended by the question. "All of us are very close."

"How old is your sister, Mrs. Childers?"

"Chéz is twenty-three." Mrs. Childers leaned forward and went cleavage on me. "Are you trying to find out how old I am . . . Nick?"

The way her voice dropped when she said my name, *Nick,* it overpowered any objection I still had about taking her case.

Since I was trying to find out how old she was, I asked. "How old are you?"

"I'm twenty-seven."

That sounded good too, but not as good as *Nick*.

"When was the last time you saw Jake?"

"About two weeks ago. He came by the house. He told me that Chilly had been looking for him."

"Chilly?"

"My husband."

"Go on. What did your husband want to see him about?"

"He wouldn't tell me. But Chilly wantin' to see Jake was unusual. Jake doesn't have much to do with Chilly."

"Is your brother involved with drugs too?"

"No. Jake is a chemist at Frontier Pharmaceuticals."

"Any reason to think that your brother is dead?"

"No!" Mrs. Childers said.

I wasn't sure what to read into the way she answered, but there was something about the look in her eyes that screamed that she wasn't telling me something. I knew then that this was a case that I didn't want to get involved in. But still, there was an innocence in her eyes that cried out for my help.

"All right, Mrs. Childers, I'll look into it. Give me a day or two and I'll get back to you."

"When you need to contact me, leave me a message on my voicemail and let me know when and where I can meet you. Or call my sister; she'll give me the message. I really don't want to come back here." Mrs. Childers reached in her purse again, this time to retrieve her checkbook. Without asking what my rates were, she wrote out a check and handed it to me. "I hope this will cover your fee, or at least get you started. Money isn't a problem, so if you need more—"

MOB

I looked at the check. "No, Mrs. Childers, I think ten thousand dollars is enough to get me started." She stood up and I escorted her to the door. As expected, I enjoyed watching her walk.

"One more question, Mrs. Childers. Why do you think that your husband is involved?"

"Just a feeling. But that *is* why I hired you."

I left my office thinking. Not about the case I had just taken on, but about Mrs. Gabrielle Childers. I found her to be a very attractive woman to say the least. I wondered how any man could do anything to hurt someone as beautiful as her, or any woman for that matter. She sat there with such confidence and poise, until she started talking about her husband. Whatever he had done to her had left her with a lasting impression.

Now I had a real missing persons case. We'd done a few skip traces, but this was different. My first thought was to tell Jett and Monika about it, but it made more sense to find out what and who I had gotten them involved with. Suppose Mrs. Childers was right? Suppose her husband was involved?

This could get hectic with a quickness.

Jett and Monika knew nothing about the dope game. They grew up in the burbs, came from nice, middle class families. But not me. I knew the game all too well. I had been a soldier for Vicious Black before joining the Army two weeks after André met his untimely demise.

I drove to Jake's apartment to have a look around. I put on my gloves, let myself in, and proceeded with my search. The place was immaculate. Everything in place, just as Mrs. Childers said it would be.

MOB

I ran my finger across the coffee table. Very little dust. I went into the kitchen and opened the refrigerator. The date on the milk bottle had expired ten days ago.

The bathroom was next. Sink and shower were bone dry. The toilet had that blue water in it, so I flushed it. It came back even bluer. I moved on to the bedroom. There was nothing out of place in the closet. Bed was made. It was a safe bet that no one had been there in at least a week.

I went back into the living room and turned on Jake's computer. Once Windows 2000 finally opened, I went into all the items on his desktop. I used an old DOS command to show hidden directories. Then I went into Explorer and ran a search on all documents modified in the last thirty days. There was a directory filled with word document files, and a directory with spreadsheet files. There was one file in each directory whose last modified date was eight days ago. I tried to open them, but they were both password protected. I turned the computer off and decided I would come back tomorrow with Jett. Then I felt somebody behind me.

"Ouch!"